FIREreads

— ☉ **#getbooklit** —

Your hub for the hottest young adult books!

Visit us online and sign up for our
newsletter at FIREreads.com

 @sourcebooksfire

sourcebooksfire

 firereads.tumblr.com

ABOUT THE AUTHOR

Marieke Nijkamp (she/they/any) is the #1 *New York Times* bestselling author of *This Is Where It Ends* and *Before I Let Go* and the writer of *The Oracle Code*. She has served as an executive member of We Need Diverse Books. She lives in the Netherlands. Visit her at mariekenijkamp.com.

"Entirely gripping and fast-paced."

—Lucy Christopher, award-winning author of *Stolen*

"A compelling story of terror, betrayal, and heroism… This brutal, emotionally charged novel will grip readers and leave them brokenhearted."

—*Kirkus Reviews*

"Love, loyalty, bravery, and loss meld into a chaotic, heart-wrenching mélange of issues that unite some and divide others. A highly diverse cast of characters, paired with vivid imagery and close attention to detail, set the stage for an engrossing, unrelenting tale."

—*Publishers Weekly*

"A gritty, emotional, and suspenseful read and although fictionalized, it reflects on a problematic and harrowing issue across the nation."

—BuzzFeed

"Marieke Nijkamp's brutal, powerful fictional account of a school shooting is important in its timeliness."

—Bustle.com

"A compelling, brutal story of an unfortunately all-too familiar situation: a school shooting. Nijkamp portrays the events thoughtfully, recounting fifty-four intense minutes of bravery, love, and loss."

—Book Riot

EVEN IF WE BREAK

MARIEKE NIJKAMP

sourcebooks
fire

Published by Sourcebooks Fire, an imprint of Sourcebooks
P.O. Box 4410, Naperville, Illinois 60567-4410
(630) 961-3900
sourcebooks.com

The Library of Congress has cataloged the hardcover edition as follows:

Names: Nijkamp, Marieke, author.
Title: Even if we break / Marieke Nijkamp.
Description: Naperville, IL : Sourcebooks Fire, [2020] | Audience: Ages
    14-18. | Audience: Grades 10-12. | Summary: Friends Finn, Liva, Maddy,
    Carter, and Ever begin a farewell round of the game they have played for
    three years, but each is hiding secrets and the game itself seems to
    turn against them.
Identifiers: LCCN 2020005284 | (hardcover)
Subjects: CYAC: Best friends--Fiction. | Friendship--Fiction. | Fantasy
    games--Fiction. | Secrets--Fiction. | Horror stories.
Classification: LCC PZ7.1.N55 Eve 2020 | DDC [Fic]--dc23
LC record available at https://lccn.loc.gov/2020005284

Printed and bound in Canada.
MBP 10 9 8 7 6 5 4 3 2 1

To the dragons who saved me

ONE
FINN

We're leaving the world behind.

The narrow mountain road creeps higher, and with every step, Flagstaff and our small suburb of Stardust disappear a little farther into the distance. With every step, we're more alone. It's just the five of us.

It's not a comfortable walk—the straps of my backpack dig into my shoulders, my binder is sweaty, and my crutches keep slipping on loose rocks—but it's a beautiful one. The muddy road first winds around a dark and ghostly lava field, then nestles between a whispering pine forest and steep cliffs.

If only I could relax enough to appreciate it. But I keep my eyes on the ground. It's safer that way—and less painful too.

"Are you okay?" Carter falls into step with me, the two of us lagging behind the other three. Carter's the only one lugging a suitcase up this mountain, and it makes his pace more irregular than mine. His face is almost as red as his shirt, and he's sweating. The sun won't let us forget that it's summer.

"Please tell me you wore sunscreen," I say.

He rolls his eyes. "Yes, Dad."

"You like me a whole lot more than you like your dad," I joke, and immediately realize how mean it sounded.

Carter flinches, then takes a deep breath and looks at me with something that's far too much like pity. And underneath is a gentleness I haven't seen in years, reminding me of the exuberant gamer he was our freshman year, before he became the son his parents wanted him to be. "I'm glad you're here, dude. It's been a while."

I don't know how to respond to that. I'm not sure *I'm* glad. A weariness has settled in my bones and my joints, and it refuses to come out. At least this is the last time we'll come together as a group.

Too much has changed. Some friendships aren't meant to last. We've outgrown one another. There is too much hurt and history between us.

But Ever wants us to try one last time, and for Ever, I'll do anything.

Even if it means pretending everything's okay and putting costumes and characters over the cracks between us.

Even if it'll break me.

Even if it'll break all of us.

I glance toward the front of the group, where Ever navigates the road. They're with Liva, and the sight of her perfectly styled hair and flawless smile makes me tense up. Pain stabs at my legs and radiates to the rest of my body. If Ever's why I'm here, Liva's why I wouldn't be.

Carter is unperturbed by my silence. "So, what do you think Ever prepared? I mean, we all know this game will be another murder mystery. Our characters are only good at solving murders. But this is our last weekend together. It must be something special. Do you think it'll be our boss fight? Take down the BBEG? They've been secretive for weeks."

Although so much of me doesn't want to be here, I can't help getting drawn back into our game, into the world of Gonfalon. I *missed* this. But I continue my silence, trying desperately not to care.

Carter keeps talking. "We have the perfect location for it. Have you heard the ghost stories about this mountain? Apparently they go back for decades. *Centuries.* Do you think Ever will weave some of that into our story? You know, for full immersion? It would definitely make this weekend memorable."

I can't help myself. "Ghost stories, huh?" This doesn't seem like a haunted place. The mountain is green and blossoming under the summer sun. The foliage still smells of rain and the aftereffects of a storm. Birds chirp, eagles call, and every part of it is so tranquil, it chafes. Only the road itself is imperfect, scarred by a year of minor quakes.

"Mass murderers. Disappearances. Strange music coming from the shadows. The last thing the murderer's victims heard before he killed them was a music box melody." He looks up at the mountain and grins. "People die on this mountain, Finn."

"You sound *way* too excited about that. Besides, if people died, how did anyone know the music box was the last thing they heard?"

"Wouldn't it be fun to play through the night and then meet actual ghosts?"

"...no?" This is exactly why Fatima, my therapist, says white people die in haunted houses. We have no nose for danger whatsoever.

"Where's your sense of adventure?"

I roll my eyes. "Where's your sense of self-preservation?"

"Aw, c'mon. You don't think anything would actually happen?"

Underneath my crutch, a small pebble skids off the path, and I take a second to reposition myself. "No, I don't think anyone *actually* believes in ghosts. Not even nerds like you who go to the library to dig up local haunts."

Carter smirks. He's your average pasty-white all-American boy, with sparkling blue eyes and curly blond hair. "I'll have you know, I will always take nerd as a compliment, and in this case, I *didn't* go to the library. Liva mentioned it the other day when we were—oh."

He must see how my face falls at those words, because his face falls too.

Carter has never tried to talk about what happened. Maddy sort of brought it up once, asking how I was doing, but she was deeply uncomfortable. Ever faced it head-on, but they approach everything that way. And even then, I couldn't tell them all of it.

This is why I don't want to be here. It's not just what happened between Liva and me. The group fell apart after I got into that fight. We'd barely gotten used to Zac leaving. We were picking up the pieces. And instead of heading back into the game, I led us straight to an awkward three-month hiatus that everyone's pretending didn't happen.

I can't help but think I don't belong here anymore. No matter how much I used to, once upon a time. No matter how much I'd give to belong once more.

"It's okay," I lie. "We're all together, and that's what matters, right?"

We have to try. Or at least pretend. After all, isn't that what the whole weekend is about? Pretending?

We're only here to fall apart again.

Carter tugs at a strand of his sand-colored hair. He doesn't meet my eye. "I'm sorry, dude."

Yeah. "Me too."

Maddy glances back, her lips set in a worried line, but Ever and Liva haven't heard us and forge on ahead. One day, Liva and I will have the conversation we need to have. But it won't be today, and I won't be the one to instigate it.

"I meant to ask—are you looking forward to college?" Just like that, Carter has changed the topic, and something has subtly shifted in his face. He's bottled his vulnerability, put his mask back on. We all have our secrets, of course. Carter's is that beneath it all, he actually used to be a decent person.

I nod.

"You're going east, right?" Carter's father taught him to be in control of conversations, to always have the last word. This version of Carter never quite knows how or when to shut up, and this conversation is just another reminder of everything that's changed between us. Once, we were close enough that he wouldn't have had to ask this.

"Mm-hmm." Drexel University. One of the best game development programs in the country, and the one that offered me an almost full-ride scholarship. Plus, it's about as far as I can possibly get.

I want to be safe, and here isn't safe anymore.

Carter huffs with the effort of dragging his ludicrous bag. Poor guy. He couldn't possibly have anticipated we'd have to abandon our cars on the private drive because of a blockage, but he looks ridiculous. "I'm headed in the opposite direction. USC. I can't wait to get out of here. This town—this state—is getting too small for me. I want something that challenges me."

"Somewhere you can prove yourself?" My tone is harsher than I intended. This version of Carter—a bragging blowhard—brings out the worst in me. I take my eyes off the path and glance up at him.

He shrugs. "Yeah, I want to prove myself. Something wrong with that? Having ambition isn't a bad thing, is it? I want something more. Something *better* than all of this."

"Can't argue with that."

The path winds sharply to the right, and I have to focus on where I place my crutches—and my feet. The pine trees to my right seem to climb farther up the mountainside, as though they're shying away from the steep drop on my left, and honestly, I can't blame them. But when I turn the corner, I curse.

The path is blocked by another barricade of boulders that reaches almost as high as we do. A tree has cracked and is leaning on the boulders.

"Frack. This wasn't here yesterday either," Ever says. "They must have slid down the slope during last night's storm. We'll have to climb over. Do you think you two can manage?" They turn and glance at Maddy and me. "We'll climb over first, so we can help you on the way down."

We're only an hour into the trip and already things are going sideways. I shouldn't have come.

But I tense my jaw. "I'll be fine."

Something like anger or disappointment flashes in Ever's eyes. Probably both. They hate it when I refuse to accept help.

"Do you need a hand?" Carter offers, already reaching out to me.

I shrink away from it. "No, thanks. It's better if I find my own way across." I can't trust any of them not to let me fall.

"Sure, your call." Carter falls into step with Maddy and offers her his assistance instead. She nods gratefully. She'd gone pale at the sight of the boulders. After this trek, her knee must not be in great shape either. The road, which leads up to a cabin nestled snugly in a grove on top of Lonely Peak, used to be clear, but bad weather, climate change, and an honest-to-eldritch-gods mudslide have recently put the last few miles out of commission. I'm sure Liva's family will pay to fix it at some point, but they haven't yet.

Ever and Liva make their way across first, holding onto the tree for balance. The boulders, all different sizes, don't seem to be particularly stable, and there's a small voice in the back of my mind— one that sounds remarkably like my therapist—telling me I should accept the offer for help.

After three years of PT and occupational therapy, five years of hospitals and arthritis specialists, I know exactly where my physical boundaries lie. I'm just incapable of admitting they exist.

And they keep closing in on me.

"Your mind is playing tricks on you," my friend Damien would tell me. "Asking for help isn't weakness. And limitations aren't a weakness either. They just are."

So what should I do with them, then? I'd ask him.

He'd ruffle my hair. "Accept them. And yourself. I know it's difficult. I know the rest of the world teaches us differently. But you're not lesser because you're different. You don't have to push yourself into an uncomfortable mold to be considered acceptable."

But instead of speaking up, I wait for Carter and Maddy to cross too. They make their way gingerly, but as the rocks shift beneath them, small pebbles are sent flying over the edge, down a steep cliff. I focus and listen, but I don't hear them fall. It's an endless drop and a harsh silence.

Then it's just me. I realize what a terrible decision it was to wait until last.

"Finn, are you sure?" Ever says from behind the rocks. "I'm worried about you."

That settles my resolve, and I take the first step, climbing on one of the smaller boulders. It shifts and moves under my weight, but up is relatively easy. It's going over that's the problem.

Without sure footing, all I can do is place my crutches first. One step. Then the next. From this boulder to one higher up, a rock that looks a little more steady. Another step.

I lean hard on my crutches, because it's the only way I can keep my balance, but that makes it hard to ignore how shaky they feel. How tangles of pain shoot up through my legs every time my feet slip, every time my ankles overextend.

I'm a fool.

On the other side, someone shouts something, but my world has narrowed down to these rocks now. Whatever they say, it's not louder than the blood pumping in my ears.

I reach the highest point. The fallen tree hangs over the rocks, allowing the narrowest of gaps.

I'm going to have to fold myself through it, like the others did, and somehow catch myself on the other side. I put one crutch through, then lean on the rocks and follow with my head and shoulders, ignoring the pain. I turn sideways, one knee first, so I have a way to brace myself. Then pull the next crutch and try not to launch myself down, continuing to ignore the pain. I find a good place to put the crutches and turn all the way through.

When I tug my foot free from the branches, I nearly lose my balance, but I manage to catch myself and stabilize.

Another step—

And I feel the crutches slip out from underneath me. I don't know if it's the rocks that shift or if it's my own lack of stability, but it's as though time slows down, and I can feel myself fall, oh so slow.

Then my knee buckles. My ankle twists. With the elbow cuffs around my crutches, I can't reach out to stop myself, because the impact would destroy my shoulders. I can only close my eyes and let myself—

Collide.

Strong arms come around me, bracing against my downward momentum. Then, other hands join the first person, holding us up and slowing us down to a stand. I hardly realize I'm not falling anymore, because the world is still twisting around me, and I may have messed up my hip again.

"Finn." Ever's voice comes harsh and angry like punches. "You fool of a Took. Ask for help when you need it."

Firmly on the ground, I open my eyes. There are manicured nails around my arms—with the symbol of Gonfalon, a stylized, golden *G*, delicately painted on each one. I nearly flinch. "Don't—" Out of all my friends leaping up to help me, why was it Liva who succeeded? Pain burns in my ankle, but my anger burns hotter.

Liva lets go off me and steps back. Ever is directly behind her, glaring at me. Carter, frowning. Maddy, pale with worry.

I'm reeling with fear and fury and hurt, and it's so much, so overwhelmingly much, I don't know how to deal with it but to sink down and sit and ground myself. Breathe until I get my equilibrium back and my hands don't tremble with rage anymore. Wait until the anger—at myself, at Liva, at this cursed mountain—withdraws into the usual shadows.

"I thought you were smarter than that." Ever hands me a bottle of water out of their backpack. Underneath their words are others: *I thought you were okay with this weekend.*

"I am." For them, I am. Or I thought I could be, at least.

As I catch my breath, I glance around at the group. We're a collection of individuals, all of us broken, all of us fragile. But the thing that scares me most isn't that I might break us apart further.

It's that I *want* to.

TWO
MADDY

Finn radiates pain. He's so tense, it hurts to look at him. I wonder if he realizes it. In my experience, most people—most neurotypical people—don't. Even if they'll talk about nonverbal language and how important it is, they don't realize how unconscious most reactions are and how much they're sharing. But I do. You teach yourself how to read body language when winning a game—or navigating life—depends on it.

With Finn, his tension is in the tight set of his jaw. The way his shoulders crawl up to his ears. The fingers that twist around his crutches so hard, they've gone almost as white as his hair. The shadows around his eyes. Right now, he's the type of person I'd stay away from if I met them on the street, because whatever's beneath the pain feels dangerous.

I taught myself to be as fluent as possible in nonverbal languages because it's the only way to understand what people *aren't* saying, to carve out your space and claim it. It's the only way I can feel like I know what's going on.

It's the only way to lie convincingly too.

Yes, I'm doing better since the accident, thanks for asking.

Or:

Oh, I'm absolutely *looking forward to college after my senior year. It's going to take some adjusting since I can't count on a lacrosse scholarship, but I'll figure it out. Now that I know how easy it is to lose something you care about, I plan to work even harder to succeed at whatever comes next. Life is short, you know? You have to make the most of it.*

Casual smile. Subtle nod. Relaxed posture. Make sure to turn toward the person I'm talking with, maybe mirror their posture. (Mirroring is a bit more complicated than literally copying someone's body language, but it does put people at ease.)

Maybe I should teach Finn some of the tricks. Because Ever's nostrils are flaring, and they obviously don't believe Finn's okay.

Finn hands the bottle back to Ever and scrambles to his feet. "Let's keep moving, Ev."

"*Fine.*" They pack up and stalk toward me to offer me a hand. "C'mon, only a little bit farther."

I steel myself before I allow them to pull me up. I don't like it when people touch me. I don't like it when I'm observing a conversation and it suddenly turns to me. And I don't like the sharp stab of pain when I rest my weight on my leg again.

"We're a bit of a mess, aren't we?" I mutter. We all fall into formation as we keep moving down the path—Liva and Carter leading the way, Ever and me in the middle, and Finn behind us, quietly stewing.

Once we've settled into a rhythm again, the pain in my knee goes from stabbing to nagging.

"No more than we should've expected, I guess," Ever says. They're putting up a facade. Both Liva and Ever put a lot of work in this getaway, in different ways. "I just want this weekend to be good, you know? I want everything to go exactly right."

"Once we've found our way back into the game, it'll be better," I say. "I don't think this weekend will fix everything, but it'll be good to spend time together."

We've been playing this role-playing game together for three years now. We've overcome and adapted to Zac bowing out. We managed—sort of—without Finn. Returning to it now will be as natural as getting back on a bike. I hope.

Ever draws the straps of their backpack tighter and straightens their T-shirt. They're nervous. "You know, Liva and Finn are going to have to talk sooner rather than later."

"I know." I bite my lip and glance at Liva's proud posture as she's leading the way. "That'd be good." They wouldn't even have to mend things forever—just for this weekend.

None of us know what happened with Liva when Finn got beaten up. She was there, but wasn't part of it—she wouldn't be part of it. But she hasn't found a way to talk about it with any of us, even me. And none of us have figured out a way to talk about it with Finn. We just know that ever since that day, there is bad blood between them, and it's threatening to push all of us apart.

We used to meet up every week, but since February, we're happy if we make it once a month. And Finn hardly showed up for any of the games.

I reach up to curl my hair around my fingers before I realize the long black locks are gone. Cut off in a fit of *wanting,* and *needing,* and *different.* No more "Maddy, the injured lacrosse player," no more "Maddy, who got trapped in a burning car," no more "Did you know Maddy is actually *special*?" No more pain. No more uncomfortable layers and masks that I never wanted to begin with.

The corner of Ever's mouth pulls up. "I like the hair."

"Thanks." *I hate it.*

And I'm not the only one. When Liva showed up at my house yesterday without warning—while I was trying to make cookies for the weekend—she very nearly strangled me.

"If you told me you planned to get a haircut, I could've changed your costume," she snapped. "You should look like an inquisitor. You need to do the magisterium proud."

I didn't get a haircut per se. It wasn't a particularly well-planned decision. It just *happened*. It *just* happened. With scissors and hair clippers in front of a bathroom mirror, in a haze.

I felt a flash of something like satisfaction at her obvious disappointment, even if I'd shared that disappointment only hours before.

Liva shook her head. "I like things to be pretty. I want *us* to look pretty. It's the last time we'll be together like this."

The few words fell heavy between us and remained there. She sat at the kitchen table and took out her sewing kit, every movement measured and careful, like mine once were. "You used to understand how much this means to me."

The words were soft enough that I wasn't sure I was meant to hear them. Her shoulders dropped, and she kept her eyes on her designs, while my cat leaped on the table and curled up on one of the pieces of fabric.

It was true. Once upon a time, I would've consulted Liva before making any changes to my appearance. After all, Liva practically pops up when you do a Google search for the societal standard of "beauty" as I'd always been taught: long, wavy blond hair, pale blue eyes, translucent white skin, cheekbones sharp enough to cut. Liva won WyvernCon's costume contest three years in a row. She was born to be a famous costume designer or a set designer. And she shines when she's creating. Once upon a time, I would've gone to her first because I loved looking beautiful too.

But that was Maddy-before-the-accident.

Maddy-after-the-accident was about to mess up her fourth batch of cookies.

I kept trying. Less chocolate, more nutmeg, more cinnamon,

octagonal-shaped, like a twenty-sided die. But none of the cookies darkened to a crisp gold. The kitchen started to smell more and more acrid, leaving me increasingly out of sorts. I had only ever been able to approximate Nan's recipe, but whatever secret ingredient she used eluded me. *It's* patience, *my lamb,* she'd tell me. Or trust. Or love. Or something else both intangible and immeasurable that left me feeling antsy and on edge.

I reached my arms behind my head and popped my elbows, and tendrils of pain tickled down my arms. Not bad enough to hurt, just there enough to remind me of my body, my *here.*

Right after the accident, the physical pain was the worst. My knee felt like it was four times the normal size, and my leg could barely bear weight. But it didn't stop there. It gnawed at me from the inside out, as if my knee had melted to the bone in the fire and continued to burn, even when there was no fire in sight. With every passing day, it left me more ragged and uncertain, until I didn't just struggle to understand the world around me—I struggled to understand myself.

"An opera cape," Liva said after a long silence. "I'll change your cloak into an opera cape. You know, with one of those high collars? It's far better than a hood. It'll bring out your eyes and your pixie cut." She'd already laid out the design of my cloak across the countertop, a pencil at the ready. "I may have to change the shoulders a bit so you won't look like a 1950s Dracula, but you don't mind that, do you? I'll keep the length because I know you like it."

I turned away from her and tried to rescue the cookies that had managed to blacken despite my careful watch. "Sure, do what you think is best."

"What is best?" The kitchen door slammed against the wall and a five-foot-ten-inch perfect storm blustered into the kitchen. Sav. All smiles and muscles and long black hair. She had a ball clamped under one arm and was furiously texting a friend with her free hand. As of next season, she'd be the new defender of Stardust High School's lacrosse team. After I tore my ligaments, she took over my place in the team and in my other friend group—and kept it.

"Still training?" The words bit more than I'd intended.

She collected food from various cabinets. "Just finished up. I need to prepare for camp next weekend. Lacrosse season doesn't end because school's out. You remember, don't you? I only have a few weeks left to get in perfect shape to impress the girls from out of state."

Those words bit more than she probably intended too. Sav worried about my injury. She was with me every day when I was in hospital. And she couldn't help it that she had a neurotypical flair that I never possessed. But every jab felt like pain, regardless. Lacrosse was what had given me meaning, what had made every day a little bit brighter, and now it was gone.

"You're going to do your role-play thing again this weekend, right?" Before she slipped out again, cheese and vegetables and a container of hummus balanced on a plate, Sav glanced at Liva's work. "Cool. I can't wait to hear the stories. I hope it'll be great.

Also, Mad, if you try another batch of those cookies, save me some?" With a teasing grin in my direction, Sav pulled the door shut behind her, and her voice echoed in the hallway. "They smell delicious!"

Before the accident—BTA—I didn't know anger and pain could feel the same. I didn't think physical pain and emotional pain could simply be extensions of each other. Now, I could hardly separate the two. And I wanted to crash my fist into a kitchen cabinet or my knee into a chair. Find a more harmful way to stim. Either make the pain worse or make it go away.

Instead, I swayed back and forth and started batch of cookies number five, only to find the dough confused and the cookies burned again before I realized what had happened. I couldn't even remember putting them in the oven.

"Maddy?" Behind me, Liva was packing up her design. Smile tight. A frown across her brow. "I need to stop by Ever's, so I'll finish the cape at home."

"Maddy?"

I thought I'd answered her.

"*Maddy?*"

Ever's voice draws me back to the present. I blink and see them stare at me, shoulders hunched inward, head to the side.

I blink again and clear my voice. "Sorry, zoned out, I guess."

One of the reasons why I actually hate the haircut is because I can't hide behind my bangs anymore, so I can't glance at Ever and the rest of them to orient myself. I can only stare around me in wonder. We're nearing the grove where the cabin is. I feel like I missed the entire second half of the walk up. My knee *screams* at me, but even that didn't draw me from my haze.

My hands curl into fists inside my pockets, my fingers grazing what's inside.

I need to be careful of these moments. They're happening too often, and I feel like I'm losing myself.

Ever reaches out a hand to me, but right before touching my arm, they hesitate and keep a careful distance between us. "You know you can talk to us if you need to, right? You can talk to me."

What would I say? *I lost the place where I didn't have to think about who I need to be, a place where rules were clear and I excelled at them. I lost nearly everything I care about by simply trying to stay afloat, and this weekend, I'll lose the rest.* "Thanks."

"I'm just saying…when the others go off to college, we'll still be here. We won't have the game anymore, but we don't have to lose each other. You can talk to me. You can trust me." They stare away from me, toward the grove and the cabin, which is still nothing more than a large shadow amidst the trees.

Like with Finn, I don't think Ever realizes quite how obvious their body language is. In-game, their poker face is fantastic. Here, they're broadcasting their nerves. Their worries. And the fact that they're lying through their teeth right now.

I slowly unclench my hands and wrap my arms around my torso.

"I know, and I appreciate that. Let's get through this weekend first, see how everything goes."

They nod. Then a hesitant smile breaks through on their face. "You do have a murder to solve, after all."

I plaster a smile on my face too. Nod in the direction of the cabin. "So here's hoping we will. And that we'll survive the weekend in the process."

"I hope you mean *in-game*."

"Well, we do have a cabin in the woods. Isn't that asking for trouble?"

Ever hikes their backpack a bit higher up their shoulders. "Ah yes, the oh-so-idyllic, ultramodern cabin of the Konig family. Ghost stories aside, the only trouble we can get into is accidentally locking ourselves in or out. Liva allowed me to set up here yesterday, and it may be the most high-tech cabin I've ever seen. Stray bears couldn't make their way through those doors, they're all so well locked."

"Liva's dad is always worried about her safety." I hate those locks. Still, the smile comes easier this time. Ever's right. The cabin is a modern fairy-tale sort of place, and over the years, Liva and her parents kept refurbishing and modernizing it. BTA, and *despite* all the ghost stories, Liva and I spent countless nights here. She told me she'd keep me safe from the ghosts.

Now, I need to survive the weekend on my own terms.

I never did bring the cookies.

THREE
LIVA

From the outside, my cabin looks like any other in these mountains. Endless logs and a small, well-crafted porch with a door that leads to the large living room spanning pretty much the entire first floor, aside from the narrow kitchen at the back. A wooden staircase winds its way up to the second floor, where small guestrooms line the hallway, with a single decently sized bathroom at the back. It was built for simplicity, but my family added a sense of modernity.

But most of that is hidden away. It's not until you get close that you can see that the door, with cute wind chimes hanging in front of it, is reinforced and the windows are insulated. And inside, everything from the heating to the kitchen appliances runs on fully automated systems.

What can I say? Mom liked luxury when she still came up here, and while Dad despises unnecessary expenses—or emotional expenses—he always did everything for her. Now Mom spends most of her time in Miami, and the cabin is all mine. I take better care of it anyway—well, except for the road leading up here. I respect the history of this place. With a little help from the internet and Dad's credit card, I redesigned the large living room and kitchen after Mom left, bringing in all the original elements again, like the comfortable couches around the electric fireplace and the thick rugs.

I reorganized the five bedrooms, giving them all their own subtle themes. Forest lodge. Seaside mystery. Haunted mansion. Lava flow. And my room, of course. I stayed here long weekends with Maddy— and with Zac back when he wasn't an arrogant ass yet and we were still dating. By the end of it, he knew this place as well as I do. (Although as far as Dad was concerned, *those* weekends were spent with Maddy too.)

Being here feels like coming home. And I love inviting others to the cabin and allowing them to appreciate the luxury too. If only because it's interesting to see how they react to it.

I go to unlock the door, and Maddy eyes it with suspicion. We visited right after Dad had everything installed, and the wires tripped, locking us in for almost an entire day before help could come. It was

Zac, of all people, who got my SOS first and who managed to hack through the door.

He'd smirked once he got us out. "You should know better than not to have an exit strategy, Liv. Before you know it, you'll get caught in someone else's game."

Now, once the door opens, Maddy breezes through, barely glancing at the living room before making her way upstairs. She's always had the same storm-blue room. Even if *Maddy's* changed since the car accident, that hasn't.

Carter comes up next to me outside the front door.

"This place is beautiful," he breathes.

I feel a flash of satisfaction. "Thank you."

When he looks at me, he looks almost hungry. He's not in love with this cabin; he's in lust. "I can't believe you don't spend every weekend here."

I shrug. "I've considered it, but I do have to put in my assistant hours at the company. You know how it goes."

Carter kicks his suitcase. "Yeah, I know."

I smile thinly. Parents and expectations. We both have to deal with them.

"C'mon," I say. "Let's go see what Ever did with the living room."

Inside is like a whole different world, as if we crossed the threshold and truly entered Gonfalon, city of mages. Ever took the normal aesthetics of the cabin and expanded on them.

As a creator myself, I appreciate that. They have an eye for detail.

It's everywhere: in the signs that hang over the doors, indicating they're still locked; the chalk markings on the floor; the locks strewn across the table. They took a wooden staff and a wooden sword and mounted them on a plaque above the fireplace. It frankly looks a lot better than the deer head that usually hangs there, the one accessory that Dad never let me get rid of, because he shot it himself and he wanted it to be a reminder of the fragility of life or something like that.

Small mechanics and wind-up toys clutter the windowsills. The chairs are draped in covers I made years ago: mossy green with the seal of the Gonfalon city council cross-stitched along the edges. It's the same seal I've included in all of our costumes: a parchment scroll with a stylized, golden *G*, the same kind I have drawn on my nails. The *G* signifies we all belong together, at least for a few more days.

It can't last. I know that. I *know* that. It's a miracle it lasted so long. But that doesn't mean I'm ready to give it up yet. This group of friends has taught me so much about myself, about who I am and where I fit in.

Dad would tell me attachment is a weakness, but they made me stronger.

And until I have to let go, we're together, like we were when it started.

Finn leans his crutches against a chair. "*Wow*, Ever."

"You like it?" Ever whispers.

I turn to them. "Yer a wizard, Ev."

Finn nods in agreement, and I see the sparkle that used to always be in his stormy-blue eyes. His hesitant smile is bright enough to light up the room, even if the rest of him is still cautious and uncomfortable around me. I can't help but feel a disconnect too. Before Maddy, Finn was my best friend, but I didn't have access to the cabin yet. Seeing him here feels like two worlds colliding, and it leaves me unsettled.

Next to Finn, Ever's trepidation makes them look small as they stare at me. "I hope you don't mind my messing with the décor this much."

"Of course not." Even after three years of playing together, I don't know how to make them feel more at ease about my family's money. I know the differences between our situations are stark, but that's hardly my fault. I share what I have whenever I can—isn't that enough? A familiar sense of impatience gnaws at me. "I told you to make yourself at home here."

My words have hit their mark, and Ever flinches at the frost in my tone. Then they square their shoulders and plaster on a smile. They know as well as I do that I can't help that we live in different worlds. "Can you believe it's been three years?"

"No." Well… "Yes."

We were young and naïve when we started playing together. I was nervous when I walked into the school theater on our first day, and I *never* had anything to be nervous about in school…except, perhaps, making the best decisions for my social status. Joining a role-playing group wasn't necessarily one of those decisions, but there were reasons I did it.

The joy of playing.

The people. *Family.*

Finn. We were still close. When he extended the invite to me, how could I say no?

He looked so different then. All angles and anxiety. He was the quiet middle school kid who might be a math genius, might be a programming mogul one day. In the years since, he's come into his own. All of us have.

Maybe that's part of what makes it so hard to keep the group together; when we were just starting, the lines were easier. The conversations less uncomfortable.

Ever designed our Gonfalon adventures and pulled the group together. They created a world where they were powerful, while living in a town that would do everything to drain that power.

That day in the theater, they welcomed us with a story and a flourish. I was hooked from the moment they started describing Gonfalon. "It's the biggest city on this side of the Scarlet Sea, where ships from all the seafaring nations dock, so merchants can sell their wares. Where education and medicine are respected and thrive. Where the council works hard every day to make the city safer, more prosperous, and able to withstand any disaster or war.

"They call it the city of mages, and many think there is magic itself in the air. It's a safe haven for magic users who were shunned or turned away from their homes, which means Gonfalon is rich with cultures and stories from all across the continent. Still, the city is far from perfect. The crime rate is low, but not nonexistent. Powerful factions strive to gain influence, and the underbelly of Gonfalon is rife with corruption. The council does all it can to keep the peace, but despite their dedication, it's proven impossible to keep the city safe entirely. And that's where you come in. You're the inquisitors of the council, sent out when there are crimes and mysteries to be solved."

They leveled us all with a stare and a smile. "Your journey always starts with a murder."

There were six of us, then. Carter, who got dragged into the game by Maddy, whose younger sister happened to be good friends with Ever's sister. Something like that, anyway. I didn't know Maddy yet, but I knew *of* Maddy. A bit different, and an athletic star on the rise. We became friends through the game, despite her being a freshman to my sophomore.

Me. Finn. Ever.

And Zac. Because Zac did everything I did, and I did everything Zac did. We should've been too young to be the "it" couple of Stardust High, but somehow we were. He was a rich kid, like me, with generations of oil money in his family, like the insurance money in mine. He wasn't athletic enough to be a jock, but he more than made up for that with his parties. Pool parties. Dance parties. That time his family rented the whole Stardust Diner for his birthday and he invited our entire grade. He loved being the center of attention, and his generosity made up for most of his other flaws.

Everyone wanted him, and I had him, at least for a while. Zac and my presence meant no one could look down on our game, even if the food chain at our small high school still structured the world according to ancient tradition: athletic students, rich students, straight white students, everyone else.

The six of us spent every Friday afternoon together, and we fell deeper and deeper into the secrets of Gonfalon. We'd pause in the hallways at school to discuss theories. We met up in the diner. We lived in two worlds at once.

Zac never quite fit, though. The game didn't include as many battles as he wanted. He had to share the spotlight. Ever and Finn didn't take kindly to his biting humor, calling him out on his not-so-politically-correct remarks, even when the rest of us shrugged it off. He became increasingly possessive.

We inevitably broke up at the beginning of our senior year, just after last summer. He didn't take it gracefully.

"Are you saying you'd rather spent time with those losers than with me?" he'd demanded, though *he* was the one who'd spent the summer doing community service because he'd drunkenly totaled his mother's car, and he'd already been suspended for a week when he got caught cheating on a test, the real sign of a loser.

"They're not losers, they're my friends," I told him.

He snarled and slammed his hand into the locker behind me. "You don't have friends. You have pet projects."

"I don't know what you mean."

"You don't belong there."

"I do, and we're good together. They're talented, all of them. They're creative. They're *interesting*." Even though my heart was racing, I reached out and patted his cheek. "You're the one who doesn't belong, Z."

He shook his head in disgust. "You're truly your father's daughter. One of these days, you'll find out that life can't be organized to your preferences, and the choices you make come with consequences. When that happens, don't come crying to me, because I will enjoy every minute of it."

He was wrong, of course. In the game and out, we were far better off without him, though it took several months to adjust to the new normal. I didn't even consider inviting him here. I did rub it in his face that we'd be reuniting this weekend and celebrating three years of the game.

When Ever suggested bringing in another player after Zac left, I cut them off before they'd finished speaking. I knew what they meant—they correctly pointed out our group was Wonder Bread white, and they knew some people who might be a good fit if they felt comfortable at the table—but we'd finally gotten the balance right. Why fix what wasn't broken?

It was perfect at the start, and it will be perfect again.

One last time. I repeat that to myself as I part with Finn and Ever and head to my room upstairs. Subtle theme: storybook love. Everything in my room reminds me of the stories I built—posters from WyvernCon, a quilt made from costume pieces, and an old-fashioned storage trunk full of drawings, designs, and dreams (and one of Zac's shirts) that I dare not show anyone.

I unpack my heavy backpack and ignore the shadows that dance around me. I have nothing to worry about. It'll all work out the way it should.

I just have to make sure the group stays together, including Finn, who very nearly bowed out twice already. I can't help but admire that he showed up. Finn was there when it started. He should be here now, when it ends.

Because Zac was wrong: I can and will design life exactly to my preferences.

FOUR

CARTER

E veryone, listen up," Ever shouts down the hall, leaning out of their room. "If you haven't changed yet, do so now. I want to make the most of the time we have."

"Suit up!" Liva calls, following Ever's declaration.

In my room, aptly themed "haunted mansion," I deposit my suitcase on my bed and massage my arms, then begin to unpack. I know it's important to keep up appearances, but this was blatantly ridiculous. If my parents want to show off wealth, they could've bought me a fancy backpack too. But no, they said, traveling around with a backpack looks cheap and vulgar. I'm staying at the *Konigs'* cabin, aren't I? I shouldn't look out of place.

I wish I could've told them I was going to look out of place regardless. Liva's style is effortlessly elegant. No matter what I do, no matter how hard I work, no matter how much I try, I'm always going to look tacky in comparison. Even this room, done in subtle shades of black and gray, is decorated to understated perfection. If Liva wanted to hurt me, this would be the perfect way to do it—invite me to this cabin and remind me of everything her family has and mine doesn't.

She wouldn't care—*doesn't* care—about something as small as a suitcase. But try explaining that to my parents. It was hard enough explaining that I couldn't skip this weekend. They didn't want me to make a bad impression at work by taking vacation time. No matter that it's technically only an after-school job and I'm not supposed to work full-time. "You reap what you sow," as my mother is fond of saying. "Work hard, keep your head high, and you'll get what you deserve."

If those words were true, we'd have a cabin of our own, and the status to go with it. My parents work as hard as Liva's father. I work harder than she does. And it's not like we have it bad, at all. Not like Ever.

But we don't count in any way that matters. Liva's after-school job is as her father's assistant. I work in the same office, but all I'm tasked with is pushing papers.

Once I get to college, I'll find a way to change that, by any means necessary. A flicker of guilt pulses in my mind, but I push it down. I'll show them all.

"Don't you have any passions you want to pursue?" Ever asked me not too long ago.

I laughed at them. "Passions don't pay the rent, Ev."

They narrowed their eyes. "Humor me. What would you do if you had the choice? If you didn't do it for the money?" There was something else they didn't say, but they clamped their mouth shut.

I'd never truly considered that before. And maybe it was because we'd just solved another case in our game—the murder of a jeweler—but one answer immediately came to mind. I'd major in journalism. I'd still be an inquisitor, but I'd travel the real world. I'd go everywhere and uncover secrets and find truth and challenge the lies we tell one another.

I'd be brave.

Still. "Does it matter? I don't have that choice. And don't tell me you would do anything different in my shoes."

They smiled, and it cut straight through me. "You're right, I wouldn't. I'd take your job. I'd go to college and learn everything I could get my hands on. I'd make sure Elle would never have to worry about food and heat again. And I would eat fresh pears every day."

With that, they'd gotten to their feet, and I didn't know if I'd won the argument or lost it.

I kick my shoes under the bed. I take out the various pieces of my costume and dig up my coin-slash-dice purse from my suitcase. Inside are my trusted twenty-sided and thirty-sided dice, in various blues and purples, and a handful of Gonfalon coins, fake golds and silvers and coppers.

I toss it onto the bed and start to peel off my T-shirt, when a loud shattering echoes to my left. Not in here—the adjacent room. Like something—or someone?—crashed to the floor. I pull my shirt back on and dash out.

All the other bedroom doors are closed, and no one else seems to react to the sound, though I can't imagine I'm the only one who heard it. But the door next to mine is ajar.

I knock and push it farther open. "Hello? Anyone here?"

The door swings open. It's the bathroom, and it's empty.

Then, from the corner of my eye, I see movement.

A figure. Watching me.

My heart slams in my throat, and I swirl.

No one's there.

Just the door of the medicine cabinet. It's swaying above the sink. When it falls back in place, I laugh nervously. The person I thought I saw was just my own reflection in the mirrored door. But then the reflection fragments into a dozen smaller ones, like my face is cut to pieces, and I realize the mirror's been shattered. The only thing holding the shards together is the frame surrounding them.

I reach out to touch it, and the reflection of my finger fragments into half a dozen pieces too. Three pairs of eyes stare back at me.

"Bad luck to break a mirror."

I nearly jump out of my skin. Maddy leans around the door. She's already dressed and pulls an opera cape around herself. It's dark green, lush and rippling. Her brown eyes are focused on the mirror.

"I didn't—" My voice cracks and I clear my throat. "I didn't break it. I found it like this."

"Mm-hmm," she hums, as if she doesn't believe me. "Get dressed, Carter. You're late."

I want to argue that I *really* didn't do it, but she's right. I'll have to tell Liva about the mirror later.

I push past her and back into my room. Despite the summer warmth, the rooms are uncomfortably chilly, and I make short work of changing into my Gonfalon outfit. I strip down to the linen pants I wore on the way up—they double as fairly fantasy-looking—and pull a moss-green tunic over my head. It's long, reaching almost to my knees, and it's worn and faded a bit. But *lived in,* not *old.*

Liva made these tunics for us two years ago, for our annual WyvernCon trip. It was the first time we all dressed up, and as our own characters, no less. I told my parents we were going to a convention, but I didn't give any other details. I didn't change until I got to Maddy's house to pick her up, to avoid awkward questions. I didn't relish the idea of explaining any of this to my parents—and my mother would be certain the tunic was a dress, and then we'd get into an argument about *that.*

Next up, a leather cuirass that I bought at the following WyvernCon. It goes over my tunic like a breastplate. Although our summers get hot and there's no way I'll wear this for long, it's surprisingly comfortable. More importantly, it looks very cool.

Nothing wrong with keeping up appearances *and* caring about your appearance, right? Some days, they feel like two sides of the same coin anyway.

Now all I need is my cape. Liva made new overclothes for all of us for the occasion. She texted us the designs a week or so ago. Half capes for Ever and me. Hooded cloaks for Maddy and herself—though apparently that's changed, given Maddy's opera cape. And an overcoat for Finn, one that fits comfortably around his binder and won't get in the way of his crutches.

I purposefully didn't take a look inside the wardrobe until I'd finished the rest of the outfit, but as I go to reach for the door, it's already unlocked. I tug at it, and the door swings open, the cape hanging from a hanger.

I swallow a gasp. It's stunning. Liva has truly outdone herself.

The cape is made from glorious green fabric, shimmery and light to the touch. When I pull it on, it fits around my shoulders perfectly and falls gracefully over my arms.

I straighten, lift my chin, and stare at myself in the mirror. I look—I *feel*—like some kind of fantasy noble in this outfit.

One last detail left. I turn around and reach for my coin purse, only to find it isn't on the bed where I left it. With a frown, I scan the room and find it on the very edge of the nightstand. It looks different, heavier. Did I move it without thinking? I carefully reach for it and tug at the string to pull it closer.

When I do, the whole purse comes apart at the seams, and dice and dozens of Gonfalon coins scatter across the floor. Some bronze, some gold, but most of them tin—or rather, silver. They're the exact same coins as the ones we use in the game, except they're all still shiny. New and never used. Not mine.

They roll across the floor and dance around my feet. There's more here than my character ever had in-game. Hells, it would *break* the game; I could buy so much influence. Because while Gonfalon is sometimes a far better place to be than the real world, some rules are universal, and wealth will always equal worth.

I try to keep my breathing even. I've bought influence before, and no one ever noticed. They only ever appreciated my money.

But these coins... Why are they here? Who *put* them here?

A small piece of paper floats down to the ground, and I snatch it up before it gets there.

Six words and the chill from the room settles inside of me. My shoulders drop and my jaw tenses.

BREAK THE RULES. LOSE THE GAME.

I don't recognize the handwriting. I don't know if it's a threat or an observation.

I crumple the note and begin to pick up the coins, one by one. Copper. Gold. Silver. Each one goes back into my coin purse, tied together with pieces of string. By the time my fingers have passed across all the various pieces of metal, my heart rate has settled to a steady, cold drum.

Break the rules. Lose the game.

Someone knows what I've done. I'll have to do something about that.

FIVE

EVER

This was a mistake. I walk around the living room, making sure all the game clues are where they're supposed to be. The storyteller's robe clings to my shoulders. Normally, I feel more complete with it on, as if it's a magic layer of protection against the world. But right now, the fabric clings like a pair of hands, pulling me back from the precipice.

This was a terrible idea. Everyone is trying, more so than I expected in the first place, but this weekend can't live up to anyone's expectations, least of all mine. This game isn't home anymore.

I asked Liva about using the cabin and if her parents would

mind. "The cabin isn't an actual vacation spot for anyone but me," she said. "It's a status symbol. No one goes there."

The words took a moment to sink in. The idea that her family could have an extra home without caring about it was wild. I'm lucky to have a roof above my head and a place to sleep each night, but so many people struggle to find even that. And this cabin is just…here. Empty most of the time. That doesn't seem fair.

I didn't know what else to say, but I accepted the keys to the cabin. Because it has an open-plan living room that's twice the size of mine. Because it has all the potential to be a perfect getaway.

Because right now, our group is all patched up and duct taped together. Everyone is angry. Everyone has secrets. *I* have secrets. And I'm also somehow somewhere in the middle, unable to make it better. I can only give them a make-believe world to escape into.

While I wait for everyone to get ready and for the game to start, I stand in the middle of the still-quiet living room and whip out my phone. Before I think better of it, I scroll to my text thread with Damien. I still have my phone—we'll all put them away in the pantry soon—and I need a helpline.

> This was a mistake.

He replies instantly.

> Why?

Damien doesn't know the meaning of weekends—which is to say, his computer is always on, whether for his game development work or to chat with Finn and me. Our group chat started after Finn introduced us at WyvernCon, and Damien realized I have a passion for games too, be it TTRPGs instead of MMORPGs. We called the chat our *greater transformation* chat.

After Finn got beaten up, Damien and I started our own private thread, a place where we could share our worries without burdening Finn. And over the months, we kept chatting. The distance and sense of privacy meant I told Damien all the hidden parts of me, the secrets, the worries I shared with no one else—not even Finn. I'm not entirely sure he signed up for that, but as Damien says, "Every trans kid needs trans elders." And sure, he's only twenty-something, but, "We're family, after all. Perhaps not in blood but in other ways that count. So we link our arms and form shields. That's how we keep one another safe."

Because the group isn't what it used to be anymore. It's not like the last time you saw us.

I imagine it isn't, after what happened with Finn. Hatred is insidious. It doesn't attack once and then withdraw. Hatred is a parasite. It burrows. It gnaws at you. It tries to undermine the structures you have and leave voids

where your safeguards were.

He says it like it's no big deal. Like that's just the way things are.

I don't want it to be like that.

Of course not. No one ever does.

So what do I do about it?

You fill those voids with love.

The game?

Yes, for example. You and Finn both

love the game, and so does the rest of

your group. It can be a place of healing.

And trust.

Yeah. So. Remember when we talked

about how good role-playing games

are about trust? I don't think the group

trusts one another anymore either.

I hesitate, wanting to say, *I don't know if they can trust me.* But I don't.

> And I don't know how to fix that. I don't
> know how to fix them.

I don't know how to fix *Finn*. I can almost *hear* Damien sigh.

It isn't your job to fix them.

Of course it isn't. It's not my job to fix everything—but that doesn't stop me from trying to fix what I can.

> My friends are hurting. It's my
> job to protect them. It's my
> job to keep them safe.

No, your job is to love hard enough to
counterbalance the hatred. That's all.
And believe me, that's enough.

> I don't know if it is.

I don't know if I can.

Have you considered my offer?

An internship. A way out of this mess. An impossibility.

                              I don't know if it's for me.

He's quiet for the longest time.

What do you want to do, Ev?

Run away.

Hide.

Scream.

I want to *be angry*, because none of this is fair. This is the last time we're all going to be together, and I *know* Finn is hurting, physically and emotionally. I *know* Maddy feels lost, and Liva's parents have issues, and Carter has his sights set on a future far away from us.

I know everyone is struggling.

But so am I.

And they still have their whole lives spread out before them. They'll heal and mend. They'll find themselves again or build something new. I only have this weekend left. Mrs. Lee at Paper Hearts, the bookstore where I work, gave me the whole weekend off to "go and have fun," but I can only afford to take time off once a year. I need the money too much.

I want to get angry, but I don't. What's the point of it? It's the main thing Dad taught Elle and me. We don't do angry. We don't do despair. We don't burden others with our worries. We keep our heads down and work harder.

> I want to make this experience
> memorable. Make everything worth it,
> whatever it takes.

It's cost too much already to turn back now.

Ghost stories and all?

Ha. That teases a smile from me. I'd almost forgotten I'd told him about yesterday.

Liva gave me access to the cabin a day before everyone else. It was empty when I arrived, a thin layer of dust on the tables, and nothing but howling summer winds outside. Well, and a rat when I opened the kitchen cabinets, but I certainly didn't plan to tell her about that.

I let my duffel bag clatter to the ground and put down the large crate I lugged here from the driveway—I'd been able to pull up pretty close to the house because the two blockages hadn't affected the road yet. My shirt stuck to my back and rivulets of sweat ran down my face.

I pulled the two loose knives from my belt and dropped them on the rich, red couch. I juggled sabers and staffs. Locks and boxes. Everything I needed to make this elegant cabin into the perfect trap.

Of course, they were Styrofoam sabers and wooden staffs. Plastic locks and puzzle boxes. But to the untrained eye—which is to say, anyone who doesn't know anything about LARP or RPGs—it probably would've looked like I had an extremely sketchy hobby.

Setting up the cabin was like coming home. Not the physical cabin itself, which I hadn't been to before this weekend. Home was the scratching of a pencil on a page. The sound of dice rolling across a wooden table, and the shuffling of cards. The click of a lock when all the tumblers fell into place, the dull thud of foam swords colliding, and the joy of a solved puzzle.

Home was Gonfalon, the world I built for my friends, where everyone can figure out who they want to be and what they want to do in an ever-changing society, but where no one has to go hungry and no one has to be alone. And while the real world waited for no one, it occasionally paused. It granted us empty afternoons, without school, or my job at Paper Hearts, or the responsibility of watching my sister. Without worries, and with nothing but birdsong—or storm winds—outside.

It granted us this weekend to camp out in our imagination, one last time.

As I started unpacking the first boxes, the theme from *The Addams Family* blasted through the empty room. Noelle's ringtone.

I nearly scattered the hints I was holding and dashed for my coat pocket. I told her only to call if there was an emergency.

"What happened?"

"Ever? Do you know if Dad bought more macaroni pies?" She sounded distracted. She *always* sounds distracted. My sister walks through life with her eyes on the world around her, but her mind on philosophical conundrums. She's thirteen and reads Teresa of Ávila for pleasure. I would've laughed at her, but frankly, as Dad often told us, we both cope by solving puzzles. It's the way our minds work.

The thing is, though, it means she doesn't always realize what's going on in the world around her. And those were my macaroni pies. One of Finn's mothers made them for me. Ostensibly because she liked to explore her Scottish heritage and she needed someone to test her recipes, but honestly, she just wanted to feed me in a way that didn't hurt my pride. I knew it. She knew that I knew. But as long as we didn't talk about it, it was fine.

"Ever?" A hint of panic. "Are you there?"

I swallowed my disappointment, hot and overwhelming. Elle was going through another growth spurt. She needed the food more than I did, even if I'd saved them so I wouldn't have to eat a proper dinner later on. So she could have *that* full meal instead. "No, those were the last of them."

"Oh. Do you know—"

"Elle, I told you to only call me when there's an emergency. I only have today to prepare." It came out stronger and more exasperated than I'd intended, but I had taken an extra afternoon off for this. I'd saved up gas for this. I had "forgotten" meals for this.

"I know, but…" Her voice trailed off.

"But what?"

"Dad got called back into work for the afternoon and night shift, and I don't want to be alone."

So much for pausing the world. "Do you want me to come back?"

She hesitated briefly. "Yes? I mean, no. But yes."

I sat on the floor, right next to a cardboard strong box that Finn made, and pushed my nails into my leg. "Elle…"

"I'm not feeling well."

Not feeling well was Elle-speak for anxious. She hated being alone, and she was terrified of storms, which was a terrible thing during monsoon season. She tried to cope, but it was easier when Dad or I were around. We could stop her from scratching herself until she bled or biting her lip until it was raw. She needed therapy. We just couldn't afford it.

"I know how much this means to you," she continued, when I didn't immediately respond. "I do. I really do. But they said there's a storm coming in, and I just…I'm scared, Ever. At least come home before dark, okay?"

Returning before nightfall would cut my preparation time in half. Still…

"Okay," I said. "But if it gets to be too much, call me. If you need to talk, *call me*."

She stayed on the phone for a while, as I unpacked the boxes and found my rhythm. Until her breathing eased and I felt confident again. I still had to finish these preparations, hide the clues, map out skill checks.

After she hung up, the cabin was quiet. The birdsong felt more distant, and the creaking of the doors in the wind sounded like nails on a chalkboard. And I knew home was this too: laughter, company. Home was the opposite of loneliness.

I wasn't home in Gonfalon anymore. I had to pretend. For one more weekend. One last time.

Then end it.

As I unwrapped the last of the clockwork toys, the entire cabin grew quiet and even the curtains stopped moving. In the distance, the echoing notes of a music box started playing.

I froze. Liva had told me ghost stories about this place, and though I knew better than to believe those tales, the haunting, lilting melody made the hair on the back of my neck stand on end. Liva had said the sound of a music box was the last thing the victims of the mountain heard...

I grabbed a fake candelabra from the table and tried to figure out where the sound came from. "Hello?"

I took a few tentative steps toward the middle of the room and tried to pinpoint the source of the music. It remained distant and yet felt just out of reach. The chills that curled up my arms and neck felt like featherlight touches. "Is anyone there?"

A bright flash lit up the whole cabin, throwing shadows every-where. I yelped before thunder crackled through the sky, and I realized the flash was nothing more than a lightning strike.

But once the rumbling stopped, the melody was gone too. Disappeared, as suddenly as it came, leaving only silence and shadows.

Four sets of footsteps clatter down the stairs now, mirroring last night's storm. I glance around me as if the music box might still be here somewhere—and wipe my clammy hands on my shirt.

Ghost stories are for children, old man.

It's game time.

IT ALWAYS STARTS WITH MURDER. EVEN HERE.

There is a story that is told about Lonely Peak. A story about how the mountain got its name. A story that's been passed down as a warning: Once upon a time, this mountain was home to a serial killer. A solitary figure, a human poacher, who lived in a cabin far from the known world. No one knew exactly where he hid, but every so often, there were sightings. Traps and carved wooden figurines of animals. Trails of bloody prints and shadows. Threads of an old nursery song carried on the wind. And horror stories that were only told in whispers.

Travelers would go missing on the mountain. Hitchhikers and campers, who tracked the trails, never to be seen again. Locals, who would go for evening walks and never return. But when the sheriff's seventeen-year-old daughter went missing, the local police were finally forced to act on the rumors. They searched day and night, underneath the hot summer sun. But all they found was an abandoned cabin, a handprint, a music box, and a bloody, torn-off finger.

They tore down the cabin and excavated the grounds. They remained on the mountain for a whole month, desperately searching for traces of the man—or of the girl—but to no avail.

For some time after, Lonely Peak stayed quiet. Over time, nature reclaimed the site where the cabin had been. But on a starlit summer's eve, a young hiker reported hearing a girl sing in the distance. That night, an elderly man disappeared in the shadows of the cabin's former location.

In the years that followed, the mountain kept claiming people. But eventually, the story changed from murderer to nature—wildlife attacks and unprepared travelers. People started building cabins on Lonely Peak again. The cabins changed hands and were passed through families.

But in the dead of the night, by candlelight and shadows, the story of the serial killer is still told. The sound of a music box is still heard. And it is said all the cabins are haunted by the killed—or the killer.

The mountain is hungry. The night has teeth. And both demand to be paid their price in blood.

But that's not your story, tonight. Your story starts on a different peak, a thousand worlds away from here. Your story starts in a tower, where you've all gathered. You've known one another for years. You've grown up together. You claim to be friends, despite the secrets between you.

You are the Inquisitors. You were trained in the art of blood and magic, taught to seek out all crime that threatens the city and council of Gonfalon. You fight for justice—and freedom. For love of this place you've called home since you were born.

You are the council's most talented young investigators; you've solved mysteries that others would not dare to touch. So when one of the city's foremost councilwomen is found dead, you are the ones who are called.

This is what you know: five days ago, Councilwoman Joanna Yester didn't return to the city for a council meeting. Her body was discovered in this tower, in the center of an arcane circle, drained of all life. The tower was empty of all servants, cleaned of all tracks.

There were no further clues.

No one knows what happened. Some say the place is cursed. Some say it's the perfect murder.

And the council demands answers.

So you find yourself in Yester Tower. Where, despite their inventor's absence, Joanna's tinkerings still whirr. Where she warded herself and her experiments against intruders. It's up to you to solve her death. It's up to you to outsmart and dismantle the entrapments of her work room, her living quarters, and the tower—and quite possibly its curse or its secrets.

Welcome to the case of the lonely murder.

SIX

FINN

Ever has pulled on their robe and their role of game master, and there's intense quiet in the living room as they finish their introduction.

The story settles around us.

And I can't help but fall for it. The mood that Ever weaves teases me and pulls me in. It's magical, and despite everything that happened, despite all the walls I built around myself, I feel like I can be free here. Here, in this expensive cabin dressed up as a castle, with its rich window curtains and leather chairs, its weird dichotomy between classic furniture and high-tech systems.

Here, all our pain falls away and all that's left is murder. We're trained as inquisitors and healers and thieves. We've built a world and a life together.

I still wish *this* could last forever.

Ever glances in my direction, a smile and a challenge in their eyes. "Yester Tower is more than a simple tower. It's a winding castle full of rooms," they say, and it's almost as if they're talking just to me. "Joanna's personal quarters are still locked, and you have to find your way into her atelier as well. You may examine her body if you so wish, though no one knows what the arcane signs around her are. What do you do?"

I suck in a breath. Steady my voice. "We investigate."

With that, we're off. The living room is roughly divided in two sections. The couch and chairs in front of the electric fireplace are cordoned off with a green rope to form an out-of-game area. A safe space where we can convene and—quite literally—step out of character.

The other half of the room, where the dining table stands, is littered with clues. Ever's used red chalk to draw an arcane circle around the heavy oak dining table, while blankets give the appearance of a body on top. A quick glance tells me there are letters, clues, and puzzles hidden everywhere.

The area around the staircase and around the door to the porch are clean. In case we need an easy escape route.

Everyone snaps into action. Carter riffles through the papers, while Maddy examines the door to Councilwoman Yester's personal quarters, as currently played by the kitchen door ("Everything is warded!"). Liva crouches next to the arcane circle. We're a ragtag group of onetime friends and a ragtag group of adventurers, and we've all thrown ourselves headfirst into pretending this cabin is a castle. We pull on our characters like our costumes. In the world we built between us, everything is easier.

Even after everything, I'm not sure I'll find belonging like this anywhere else.

Ever observes from a distance and smiles. Underneath the hood of their supple green cloak, their thick, black hair is bound in an unruly ponytail, and there's a smudge of ink on their cheek. Shadows dance all across their face. They might as well be a member of the Unseelie Court, a storyteller to lure in unsuspecting travelers.

I take in every detail. The quirk of their mouth. The raised eyebrow. The way their right hand grasps the fabric of their cloak, the smallest hint that they're nervous. Their forest-green eyes settle on me.

"Finn?" Ever's voice is quiet. They normally only call us our characters' names when in-game. "Do you have a moment?"

I don't trust myself to answer, so I nod. I grab my crutches and make my way over to the other side of the room, near the door to the porch, somewhat out of earshot of the others. My ankle still hates me for that stunt on the boulders.

Ever bites their lip. Something of the game master persona slips, and there's just my best friend left. The person who, even if I'm not sure I can trust anyone else here, is the constellation in the night sky that keeps me steady. "I meant to say this before the game, but…let me know if there's anything you need this weekend, okay? I know the last couple of months have been hard, so just…let me know if there's anything. Physically. Emotionally. Anything."

Warmth crawls up my cheeks. "Yeah." I clear my throat. "Yeah. I…yeah. Cool. Thanks."

They take a step closer, and I take a step back, out of habit more than conviction. Ever's face shadows, but they take a step back too, back into GM mode. "I want you to feel safe here."

My breath catches. "Thanks. I appreciate that."

This is one of the reasons why I didn't want to come back to the game; we're one step outside of the real world. The normal rules don't apply. My walls don't hold up. Ever deconstructs me. And I'm helplessly, overwhelmingly, absolutely terrifyingly in love.

Again and again and again.

I do the only thing I can. I run headlong into danger. I pull a battered notebook out of my pocket, grab a pencil from the coffee table, and purposefully make my way over to Liva. Because there's only one way to play this and that's to play hard. "Do you see any sort of pattern?"

She tenses. *Freezes.*

It's all I need. I let my annoyance push away my vulnerability. Being angry is so much easier than getting hurt again.

"Not yet." Liva clears her throat and keeps her eyes on the makeshift corpse. "It's clearly an arcane circle, and some of these glyphs are traditional wardings and markings. There's blood magic here, and protection magic too." Broken circles and rune-like slash marks. I recognize them from the countless other murders we've solved.

But there are also glyphs that look like music notes, unlike anything I've seen before. And there's a small wooden carving of a raven. "How about those?"

"I don't know. Nothing I immediately recognize." She glances at Ever, who's been walking around the room. Not following me. Definitely not following me. "Right?"

Ever comes to stand beside us, resplendent in their green cloak, wearing a scheming smile and fully in game-master mode.

"Right. You don't know much about the nature of these glyphs," they say. "You've studied the arcane, of course. But this is different. Older, perhaps. Or more recent. Clearly magical in nature, but it's outside of your realm of knowledge. What it is exactly is up to you to discover."

Liva's eyes flick from Ever to me and back again. "Rogue magic?"

Also known as devouring magic, the type of magic that would destroy all others. "It seems likely. But if you want to know more, you have to spend skill points."

Liva frowns. "Not yet. Unless Finn wants to?"

"Nah, not yet." I keep my eyes on my paper. With my crutches leaning against my hip, I make a rough sketch of Joanna's body and her position with regards to the arcane markings, and wait for the heat of Ever's body to disappear. "What about the raven?"

"It's new. You've never seen anything like this before."

"Is there anything else of note we see?" I ask.

"Councilwoman Yester's body has lain here untouched since it was found. As you go through her clothes, you notice the body seems to be unharmed. There are no obvious wounds, whether by sword or rifle, and you see no scratch marks or any other traces of wounds," Ever says.

In other words, unless she was scared to death, this could only have been poison or magic, and my money is on the latter.

"What's her facial expression? Can we still see it?" Liva crouches near the "head" and gently pushes at the cloth with one perfectly manicured nail. It's almost as if she brushes a strand of hair out of a face. "Was she shocked, surprised, at ease?"

"Hard to tell," Ever says. "The state she's in now, her expression seems to have mostly disappeared."

Exactly.

"Any discolorations? Anything in particular about the color of her skin? Her lips? Her nails?"

While Ever shakes their head, I poke through the fabrics that make up the body. They're fleece. Simple square pieces in different blues and greens, with one moss-green piece signifying her cloak. As my hands follow the curves, I can almost imagine a real body lying underneath the cloth.

"As you go through Councilwoman Yester's clothes, you notice what fine quality the silk is. The stitching is exquisite. Her braided girdle, with a copper model of the council's seal, lies limply to the side. She wears a simple golden necklace with a tiny cogwheel at the center."

"Her pockets?" I ask.

They lean over me, and my breath hitches. "Her pockets are empty. It appears there are no clues to be found here."

Only when Ever moves to the other players, do I breathe again.

Liva glances up at me. "You know, you could tell them how you feel."

I tense my jaw. "Was there any particular reason why you think I'd value your opinion?"

It's cruel, I know that.

Liva flinches. "Finn…"

I shake my head. Anger is so much safer than feeling. "Don't pretend you care too much, Liva. We both know it's a reach."

Something like anger rushes over her face too. Hurt, but deeper than that. We used to be such good friends. It's evident still in the way she designed my overcoat. Not just in terms of the design— comfortable with or without binder, with enough movement not to impede my crutches—but in the style as well. Compared to my usual wardrobe of thrift-store goth, the bright red overcoat is by far the most colorful thing I own. But it's a bloody red, and it matches well with the crow skulls decorating my crutches, my pale skin, and my faded silver hair. There are leather straps on my back for my crutches.

A long, black leather belt wraps around my waist several times, complementing the look. It lets me be the chaotic queer disaster I missed so terribly. It stands out. She did that, because she knows me.

And I thought I knew her too.

I always considered the possibility I'd get beaten up one day. It's par for the course, isn't it? Stardust High can be misconstrued as fairly modern, and even fairly liberal—especially by Arizona standards. But that doesn't mean people like me—people like us—can fly under the radar. Most teachers and students are good about my name and pronouns, but I don't pass as a cis guy yet, no matter how much I want to. No matter how much I thought I did, the first time I wore a binder. (I realized soon enough there was far more to it, but those first couple of days, I'd *smile* every time I saw my reflection. I finally found clothes that fit, and I found pieces of myself. Mrs. Akashi at the thrift store started putting shirts and coats aside for me, once she realized how much joy it gave me to be able to present the way I felt.)

Still, Ever and I were two of the only openly trans kids at school. And we weren't just not cis enough, but also not wealthy enough—or abled enough. There were always a few people who thought it was edgy to taunt, and insult, and spit at us. Of course, by that same narrow-minded worldview, to those same people, we were at least white enough. We had Liva's friendship. We never bore the brunt of the bullying.

But I never really thought it would progress past slurs and pushing us around.

In a way, it didn't. They didn't start the fight. *I did.* That's the part only my therapist knows. I didn't mind that they spat at me and shoved into me as I walked across the football field on my way home. I'd learned to ignore that. I snapped and started the fight because they said something awful about Ever. Irrational gallantry, maybe? I never asked for *this* type of masculinity, but there it was.

There were only three of them—two cis guys and a girl, all of them seniors too—and I'd seen Liva walk up to the sports field. I knew I wouldn't be alone—

I *thought* I wouldn't be alone.

Of course, that makes it sound like a far more considered decision than it was; it was anger, mostly. And protectiveness. And being worn down by the pain of a subluxated shoulder.

I should have been smarter.

I shouldn't have trusted so foolishly.

I thought Liva was a friend. I thought she would have my back. That was the worst thing. When I think about that afternoon, I don't think about the people who took my punches and then beat me up. I know they are mean-spirited and shortsighted, and I don't want to give them the pleasure of having hurt me.

But I saw Liva from a distance. I saw her watch when they took my crutches and broke the cuffs off, which somehow hurt more than when they broke my wrist. I saw Liva stand there and stare. I saw her look away. She didn't do anything.

That was the moment everything shattered. The wounds have

healed, but the scars are still there. Perhaps it's good this is all ending. Perhaps it's good this'll be the last time we are together like this, figuring out clues, eating the dinner that Liva laid out, not noticing as the hours slip by. Friendships aren't meant to last forever, right?

Let me know if there's anything you need. Physically. Emotionally.

As the night passes, I keep coming back to that moment. I'll glance around the room and find Ever staring at me. The moment our eyes meet, they'll blush and turn away, arms wrapped tightly around their chest.

The game progresses around me, and outside, the sun has set. The shadows in the room have lengthened and the fireplace is burning low. Between the dark corners and the yellow light, it almost looks like a magician's tower. Next to Ever, Carter and Maddy are sitting around a puzzle box, trying to find more information. There are fragments of paper spread out on one of the tables. Carter's fingers are wrapped around a mug.

"...from the letters, it's clear that Councilwoman Yester had been in talks with the Leah Family, one of the ruling families of Gonfalon's underbelly. Not a family a council member would usually be in contact with. More than that, most of the evidence seems to have been carefully burned to ashes."

"We really need to open up this chest," Maddy says.

"Wait, wasn't the Leah Family behind that disappearance in the library?" Carter asks.

Liva walks toward them carrying a plate of cookies from the kitchen. "Oh yeah! That time when C almost lost his arm because he didn't pay attention to traps. That was fun!"

Carter scowls. "You have a weird concept of fun."

"Your arm got sucked into a stone wall. You should've *seen* yourself." She offers him the plate.

"Also," Maddy adds softly, "didn't you say you had everything under control?"

Ever can't suppress a smile, and Carter rolls his eyes. We've all come to learn Maddy's softest words pack the hardest punch.

"Hey, let's open this chest, shall we?"

I wander a little closer as Maddy picks up the puzzle box and sets to work trying to open it. It's a bit of a stereotype, getting the autistic girl to solve the puzzles, but she's also far better at figuring out the solutions than any of us are. More importantly, she likes it. She chose to be the puzzle solver. And she's intensely focused, as she shifts the puzzle box back and forth, twisting and turning it.

Her hands tremble. She has her tongue between her teeth and a frown creases her forehead.

Twist.

Click.

The moment the last piece of the box shifts into place and Maddy reaches to open the lid, the fireplace behind her *roars* to life.

A flash—like lightning.

A crash.

The flames jump from a light simmer, bright enough to add mood to the room, to licking tongues, bright orange and aggressive. Dancing against the glass as if they're trying to escape.

"*Hell no.*" Carter pushes back away from the flames—and his mug goes clattering to the ground. Ever yelps and jumps too.

I stare at the fire, mesmerized, my heart rate at least three times the normal speed. I want to step closer, and I want to back away, and between the two I'm frozen. "I—I don't think it's supposed to do that."

It's an electric fireplace, it should be under control. There's no way it should be able to burn so…violently.

"You *think*?" Ever's voice ranges three octaves in two words. "Someone should cut the power. Liva, find the fuse box!"

The flames grow higher, unreasonably so. They're crackling, or perhaps that's the electricity itself.

Carter backs farther away from the fireplace. "What if it explodes?"

It looks possible. The flames are beating against the glass now. The whole room has been turned a terrifying red in its glow, and it's already starting to become swelteringly hot in here.

"Maddy, get back here."

Liva stands over the overturned plate of broken cookies, scattered across the floor. They're mixed with shards of Carter's mug.

She blinks and blinks again. Her hands are trembling, and she's gone pale. Then she starts to laugh, and she shakes her head. "Screw you, ghosts." She crunches the cookies under her feet and makes for the hallway.

Over the roaring of the flames, we all hear a door open. A *click*.

A *yelp*. "Why are there *rats* in my cabin?"

Ever scrambles over to help, but I don't want to know.

Then...

The flames dissipate. The room goes dark. She's cut the power to the whole cabin, and the only thing left is the sparse moonlight filtering in through the windows.

In front of the empty fireplace, the puzzle box tumbles from Maddy's hands onto the floor. Her fingers cramp around air, as if she's still trying to hold on to the wooden pieces.

This is how easily we crumble.

SEVEN
MADDY

Their words sound like they're under water—or maybe I am. Something's churning inside of me, and I'm going to be sick.

"What happened there? Ever, was this your idea?"

"I appreciate atmosphere, but I'm not a fan of scaring people—or messing with electricity."

My skin is too tight, and I feel like I'm overflowing. Fire. *Flames.*

"Perhaps the fireplace malfunctioned."

"If that's the case, it had excellent timing."

I keep tapping my foot on the floor until my knee locks. If I were closer to the flames, I'd keep my hands too close to the fire until the heat scorched me and claimed me, and I would let it devour me. Instead, there's darkness, and I can't see or feel my edges. I need something to ground me, something to cling to. Am I supposed to react? How am I supposed to react? What is left of me?

"Maybe the cabin is haunted after all."

"Liva…"

I stare at the fireplace, but I can't seem to focus. I'm a million ants in a trench coat. I haven't picked up the puzzle box yet, and the roar of the fire and the crashing of Carter's mug echoes in my ears. If I was a lacrosse defender still, I would go running now, and I wouldn't stop until I ate the grass.

I like that image: eating grass.

"Did you do it? Did you rig the fireplace? Play into the ghost story?"

The world is twisting and turning, and tension crawls up from my knee. I hate ghost stories, and I hate people playing into ghost stories more. I hate the sound of things crashing, because I can feel it in my bones. I hate not being able to remember how to breathe. I hate everything. I hate them all.

"Maddy?"

The power comes back and a light flicks on. Finn's face filters into my vision. Furrowed eyebrows. Worry, perhaps. Impatience.

"Maddy, are you okay? Look at me."

I try to focus, but there's a disconnect between my body and my mind, like nothing about it fits anymore. I don't feel like I belong in this body, I don't know how to interact with this world. It feels like I'm observing through a veil, and I don't know how to move. Panic is a type of pain too.

In my periphery, Liva laughs, and there's an edge of scorn to it. "Why would I? I mean, I did tell Ever about the ghost story, so they could weave it into their introduction. You can't have such a cool setting and all these legends without at least doing something with it. But no, I didn't break the five-thousand-dollar fireplace for *atmosphere*, Carter."

"I'm sure Carter didn't mean anything by it. It is your cabin, after all."

Ever's words are met by silence. An intake of breath. "I know. I just don't like the suspicion. I'm not responsible for everything all of the time. And besides…" Liva's voice drops. "I don't believe in ghosts, but I also don't believe in angering them."

My hands claw and tremble at those words.

"Will you all *shut up*?" Finn's voice. Anger.

I flinch away from that too.

"Maddy. C'mon, focus on us." Ever's face appears next to Finn. They keep their voice level, gentle. Do they lean in? Tilt their head? So much nonverbal communication is tone of voice too, but Ever is in game mode now, and their tone is neutral and unreadable. They built feet-thick walls around themself. "Is it too much? Too loud?"

That sounds reasonable. It makes sense. I nod, but it's as if my body reacts a moment later, as if I'm not fully in control.

"May I touch you?" Ever reaches out a hand to me, and I stiffen.

"Okay." They withdraw their hand, but otherwise stay exactly where they are. "It was only a malfunction. I know it's uncomfortable and you're overwhelmed, but it was an accident, nothing more. Nothing will happen."

I hate that word. *Accident.*

It was an accident too when a truck crashed into my car and mangled my leg under the metal. It was an accident when the car caught fire—even the fire department said so. It was an accident, but I should consider myself lucky that I made it out alive.

I keep seeing the flames.

"Slow breaths, Maddy. In and out. That's it." Ever's voice is calm and low. I try to follow their counting, while my hands crawl to my knee, and my fingers dig deep into the skin.

I wish I could see. I want to understand. I hate being so overwhelmed.

In the background, Liva refuses to be silenced for long. "C'mon, I get being afraid of a ghost story. I remember the first time my father told me about the murders too; I didn't sleep in the cabin for almost a month, and when I did, I had to keep all the lights on. I checked for bloody prints and songs everywhere. But my point is, I was eight and I didn't know any better."

"Gods, Liva, some days you're absolutely insufferable, you know that?"

"So what, she's triggered? Is that it? It's only a *story.*"

There's so much scorn when Liva talks to Carter, and it's always mutual. The richest kid of Stardust High and the wannabe rich kid. From the very first moment, the two of them loved to hate each other, but while they fight hard, they also play hard. Or used to, anyway.

"Are you really that ignorant? Maddy is freaking out, and you peddle some nonsense about how she should suck it up? Triggers are reminders of trauma," Finn snaps, though the words make it sound as if he's repeating something someone told him. "If you've never been triggered, you should be thankful for that, because being forced back into the worst experiences of your life *isn't great*. Being stuck in fight-or-flight mode and not knowing if you can push your way through is absolutely terrifying. And maybe Maddy was overwhelmed by stimuli and nothing more, because that's also the way her brain works, but you could try being a friend instead of being touchy about it. It's not a good look."

In the silence that follows, I push my fingers deeper into my knee. The breathing doesn't ground me, but the pain centers me. It brings me back to my body. It reminds me I'm still here and *this* pain, at least, I can control.

As the pain clears my mind and overwhelms me in a more familiar way, I can see Liva stare at us, her cloak pulled tight around herself until it makes her look smaller. At Finn and Ever, crouched over me, and Carter with his back turned toward her. She narrows her eyes. "Fine. Whatever. It's still just a story, and you don't have to get upset about it." She sounds almost petulant. "And also, I *am* her friend."

Ever sighs. They rock to their feet and walk toward Liva, while I push myself up to a chair, leaning on my bad leg on purpose.

We're all such liars. Liva was my friend once. One of my closest. She and I and Zac spent endless afternoons together. They'd come to my games, and I'd been a foil for Liva's parents.

But something happened after the accident to push us apart. Maybe she decided to follow her father's footsteps. He doesn't have friends, believes that emotions are weakness. Or maybe we were never that close to begin with.

Maybe I happened. Maybe I've been pushing her away.

The others showed up, though. Finn and I grew closer after the accident. He came by the hospital. He went to PT with me. He let me ask him anything I wanted to know about pain and how to deal with it, although the answers weren't always what I wanted to hear. None of my doctors told me about how pain wears you down until you sometimes don't know where physical pain stops and mental pain begins. They didn't tell me about the anger and the fear and the helplessness. Finn told me and then, when I finally let him, held me while I let it all sink in.

I never asked him about painkillers, though. I swung by his medicine cabinet a few times, but I didn't want to take the stuff he *needed*. I only ever asked Carter to buy me new ones when my prescriptions ran out.

Because Carter was the only one who was allowed to take my hand and hold it without asking. Because I knew his body language better than my own. Because he was the other half of me, BTA and ATA. We were close and drifted apart. We foolishly tried to date once before we realized what a terrible idea that was. But no matter how much he and I changed individually, *we* didn't. He was like a brother to me, before I knew any of the others, and I knew he could keep secrets well.

Besides, he didn't seem to mind spending the money. He had enough of it.

Carter kneels in front of my chair now, right next to Finn, and brushes my fingers with his. "Do you need a moment, Mad?"

I lean toward him, twisting my knee on purpose. Finn never told me how reassuring physical pain can be. It sends a thrill through me. A restless trembling that leaves me breathless—a *hunger*. "I'm okay. I just…" I wave a hand. "What Finn said. Too many things happening all at once."

Carter's shoulders drop as he breathes out. Relief. Soft humor. "Good. I would hate to have to carry you down this mountain."

I softly punch his shoulder. "No chance."

"With all the strength you've amassed photocopying papers and running around with coffee orders?" Finn puts in.

Carter mock gasps. "Not all of us can hack their way into college, dude."

"It's called development."

"Fine. What *I* do is called an administrative apprenticeship."

"*Fine.*"

Finn's words snap, but there's a smile in his eyes when he looks at me.

I turn my hand so my fingers curl around Carter's. "I'm going to…throw some water on my face and maybe change into something a little more comfortable." It's far enough into the night that I could do with a hoodie instead of the opera cape. It's a decent excuse, though I don't need one after that trick my brain pulled.

Carter helps me to my feet, and when I stand, my leg seems to be on fire. Perhaps that's why my brain freaked out too. I had something for the pain around dinner, but that feels like hours ago. On days when I don't know where physical pain stops and mental pain begins, I need a solution to both.

The hallway is filled with shadows—when did it get so dark, anyway? I hold my fingers to the wall for a sense of security. No matter how clear I made it to Liva that I didn't want to hear her ghost stories, she always told me just enough before I could cut her off.

Some said murderers never leave Lonely Peak, that there's always one.

Some said the shadows are alive and like to play games.

Some said, in the darkness, you can feel the victims reach out for help.

Once in my room, I dive to my bag and riffle around in the locked compartment until I find my bottle of pills. I reach in and grab a few, maybe three or four. When my doctor prescribed them to me, she told me I shouldn't take more than three on a daily basis, but that was a long time ago.

As I swallow them down, the panic that's still at the edges of my mind crawls a bit closer again. Whispering at me that tonight, the pills won't help. Tonight, the pills won't be enough.

But as I chase it with water and breathe, the edges begin to dull and my head grows lighter. I can feel myself smile, unconsciously. My shoulders relax. My knee doesn't ache so much, and I feel calmer. More like myself.

I stare at the painting of a dark and stormy sea on the wall.

Everything around me dulls, and the restless trembling is replaced by a comfortable buzz. This is the only thing that keeps me standing.

Now that I'm not cowering away from the world anymore, I can see it far more clearly. The shadows are empty. The deep darkness is nothing more than storm clouds obscuring the moon, and the darkness makes the world softer. There's less *everything* all at once.

Except. When I place my cloak over a hanger on my door and pull a linen hoodie over my clothes, I am absolutely sure I see the cloak ripple. The arms reach up and toward me.

And I all but run back through the shadows to the living room, back to the game.

As your investigation brings you deeper into Yester Tower, you've narrowed your focus to Councilwoman Yester's atelier, where she worked on all her inventions. More information about her various contacts might be found there.

The deeper you circle into the castle, the more you notice wards around this place that disobey council guidelines, to say the least. Trigger plates near her cabinets that are not merely warded with familiar defenses, but complemented by unreadable chalk markings and lore words. The door lights up with a soft crimson glow.

You find three more carvings—a boar, some kind of catlike creature on six legs, and a hound. All the carvings are crude, and they all seem magical. With how they're placed throughout the tower, it's almost as if they're observing your every action. As if someone's playing a game with you.

The air around the tower smells pungent and sweet, of magic and decay.

In a world where the council has worked hard to eradicate even the faintest trace of rogue magic, seeing it on the doorstep of one of the council's finest is troubling. It's hard to believe one of your own would betray you.

So when you reach the door you think must be the atelier, you steel yourself against what you may find inside. That is, if you manage to get inside. The floor in front of the door is covered with crimson markings that simmer with power. There is an icy cool air coming from the room itself. You keep your distance, at first. You all know from experience—and some, well, more unfortunate investigations—that a simple door or a simple ward might be an insurmountable challenge. Some locks, you've come to learn, are not destined to be picked. Some locks you can break your teeth on—and your keys on. Some wards can burrow beneath your skin and bite. You hope this isn't one of those.

At the same time, you also know you are the council's best. You have no option.

You have to try.

EIGHT

LIVA

There's a tension in the air. I wonder if anyone else can feel it. When Ever describes music boxes inside the council-woman's tower, I can't help but imagine them here, like they were in all those stories, echoing in the distance.

"We should counterspell that ward," Maddy suggests. After the panic attack, or whatever it was, she has thrown herself into the game completely. Or rather, she has thrown herself headfirst into her character, and I understand that. When she's playing as Myrre, she doesn't have to be afraid or broken. The game allows us to try on different people.

A sense of discomfort has fallen over the group. Something no one can shake. It was the same after Zac left, except I thought we were past that now.

I grit my teeth. "Unless it's warded against sabotage. Remember that time in Kilspindle Fort?"

Next to me, Carter flinches. "Why do you have to bring that up?" Kilspindle Fort was one of our first quests together, a few weeks after we started our Rune and Lore club—then still known as the Gnomic Utterances Tabletop Society, after one of Ever's favorite books and because they didn't settle on a name for their system immediately.

In the quest, we were sent to the countryside to investigate the disappearance of two teen girls. We discovered the girls were part of a militant anti-magic group, part of an underground network that crawled its way through Gonfalon and its surrounding villages. The network hid their correspondence in a strongbox, half-buried underneath the roots of a tree. Carter spotted the strongbox first, but he never checked the weird collections of leaves and twigs around it. He simply tried to brush them away, and the next thing any of us knew, he was flying backwards, landing flat on his back. He barely survived.

I stare at him. "Because we're trying to learn from our mistakes."

"When have we ever?" he counters.

"There's a first time for everything."

"I can try to sneak in?" Maddy offers.

"Cor and I'll investigate first." On my other side, Finn grabs a piece of chocolate off a plate, though his hands are trembling. He's still not meeting my eyes. "Lente is…not wrong."

I'm very careful not to smile.

All our characters fall into their traditional roles. Corrin—that's Carter—and Feather—Finn—are our prime explorers and magic users. Maddy, as Myrre, is our thief, the very best at sneaking around and not being noticed. She used to team up well with Zac, who played our assassin. And my character, Lente, is the reluctant healer, here to protect anyone from harm.

We've all found our way around the fireplace again—though I've shut its power off permanently, and we make do with lamps and candles for mood instead—and all we have in front of us are snacks and dice. After an afternoon and an evening of figuring out the various traps of the castle, it's too dark now to try to unlock chests or solve puzzles. This last part is pure pen, paper, and dice role play. Outside of our circle of light, the world may as well have ceased to exist.

These have always been my favorite moments.

This, I will miss. If I were anyone else but Leonard Konig's daughter, I might have considered going into costume design as a career instead. But Father would never let me, and frankly, I don't want to. I want to be more. I want to be everything.

"I recognize value where I see it," Father said once, after I started working for him. "And you should too, if you're to take over this place one day. Recognize it and be on your guard against it. People like those friends of yours, they don't see the world the same way we do. They will claim a part of it, and if you don't work hard enough, they will claim *your* part of it."

I narrowed my eyes, recognizing a threat when I heard one. "I'll work harder, then."

Father nodded. "See that you do. You're by far the most talented person in this building, Liva. Don't waste that talent. Don't waste your birthright."

I smiled thinly. "Yes, sir."

I hated him, then. I hated him for pushing me harder than I thought I could be pushed, for seeing potential when I thought I'd dug to the bottom of it. But I loved him for it too. I loved that he believed my possibilities were endless.

Finn and Carter both use skill points and rolls to gather as much information as they can about the ward, only to find out what we already assumed. Devouring magic. Powerful and doubly warded.

"Three hells, what was the councilwoman hiding here?" Maddy grumbles.

She pushes forward a little to check for any other clues aside from the glyphs. Doors or trapdoors. Footprints. Anything.

In her haste, she trips, knocking into Finn and Carter.

She sends them off balance, breaking the spell Feather and Corrin are casting.

Disaster strikes.

Ever, the only one who has been walking around, crouches next to me, their voice low. "You see the signs light up to a bright red that extends from the glyphs. It follows a winding path through the sky. Then, the symbols flash."

They back away toward the table and roll a die, their eyes flicking between Finn and Carter. When the die comes to rest, they tense up and shake their head softly. Next to me, Finn breathes out hard, as though he already knows what's coming too.

And I smile. I know exactly what to do.

"When the spell is broken, the symbols flare. Feather, you are all but blinded. The others around you instinctively take a step back from the bright blue flash. But you stand directly in the path of the spell." Ever's voice fades. They swallow and reach for the three effect dice that are part of their game master's kit, the dice that they only use when shit is about to go down. "One moment, the rest of you see Feather standing there. Next, as you blink and struggle to regain your vision, there's only bright light and it flares ever higher—"

"Wait," I interrupt. I waited for an opportunity like this, to show exactly what I'm worth, and that it happens now, like this, is all the better. "I push Feather out of the way."

Finn snaps his head toward me. Ever raises their eyebrows. "Are you sure?"

Lente isn't a magic user or a fighter. She's weak compared to the others. But that's not the point, is it? Here, I can be a hero and a villain both, if I want to. After all, we're all complex and complicated. We are all the exceptions to our own rules.

I know Finn doesn't trust me to do right by him, but he's wrong. I'm no monster. I'm as loyal to my friends as they are to me, and I would help him through a rough spot any day. It's what I'm doing right now. I just don't care for getting dragged into fights that don't concern me. I don't play other people's games.

"I'm sure. I know what I'm doing."

Carter and Maddy only stare at me. Ever licks their lips. "Okay… okay."

I nod at them and purposefully ignore Finn's uncomfortable shifting next to me. "Don't worry. What are the chances it'll go wrong?"

They roll the dice. With three ten-sided dice, there's only a minuscule chance that all of them will roll a deathly effect.

There's a collective intake of breath when they do.

Oh.

Ever clears their throat. And again.

Everyone stares at me, and I go hot and cold all at once.

"Lente, you *feel* the light pass through you. You've never been at the receiving end of a flare like this. The light seems to burn through you, through your body, through your bones, through your thoughts. It's as if you've walked into a fire and it consumes you. It gnaws at your edges. It burns into who you thought you were. You scream. You struggle to keep standing—or maybe you've fallen already. You don't know what's left of the world around you, but you want to curl up and disappear inside yourself.

"Everything slows.

"You feel pain. With every breath and every movement. It's everywhere. It's everything. There's no escaping anymore.

"You hear screaming. It comes from all around.

"Then, nothing."

Silence.

Ever looks at the others. "The three of you, you see Lente fall. You see the ward go off, fiercer than anything you've encountered so far. And your compatriot, your healer—your friend—is devoured. Lente is gone."

Everything grinds to a halt. I have to try to remember how to breathe. Sure, character deaths have happened. But not on this level, not anymore. We're more powerful now, and we planned this whole weekend around the game. This...

This wasn't meant to happen.

"Wait..."

"You mean *gone* gone?"

"But..."

"She can't be."

"Isn't there anything we can do? Is there a body? Are there any signs of life?"

"She *can't* be."

I open my mouth and close it again.

Well. *Frack.*

It hurts. I didn't anticipate how much it would hurt. I knew it was going to happen in some way—I knew I had to say goodbye to Lente this weekend—but I never considered how much it would hurt.

"Liva…" Finn sounds shocked. "I… Sorry? Thank you?"

I wince. A small part of me wants to round on Finn. Tell him: *See, I do care. I proved that to you, how much more do you need?*

"There must be something we can do," Carter says. "Pull her body away from the ward. Go back to the council and find a way to revive her. It's been done before, right? There is magic powerful enough to save her."

Maddy stares at me, or perhaps she stares straight through me. Her cheeks are flushed. "I don't know if the council will let us. They're particular about life-and-death magic. But if you want to, we can try."

Do I want to? It's not up to me to decide. And now that the end is here, it feels eerie. I wasn't ready yet to say goodbye. I'm not ready yet to face that there's only the real world left now.

Maybe it's not too late to change my mind. It's not too late to find another way out.

Except, it is.

Giving up is not an option.

It never has been.

Both Lente and I believe the only way change comes is if you work hard for it. No matter if the people around me understand what we're doing or not. And I'll miss her.

The last time we all played together—with Finn there—we moved our way through the marketplace at the end of the day, without the clues we were looking for, when I felt a small hand reach for my pocket. Lente was far from the most dexterous—or even the most observant—character in our group, but through a combination of restlessness and luck of the dice, I caught the girl who tried to rob me.

In real life, I wouldn't have hesitated to do what must be done. Dad taught me from an early age about the value of fighting for what you're worth. And the idea of theft makes me sick to my stomach.

But in-game, I hesitated a second longer before turning the girl over to the city guard. Long enough for Finn—Feather—to step in, ask Corrin to hold the girl, walk me out of earshot and suggest we leave her be. He quietly argued the girl was skin and bone, she couldn't have been older than ten, and what she needed far more than to be chased by the guards was a good meal. Because for all Gonfalon's good sides, the city wasn't kind to everyone. "Not everyone can count on wholesome meals every day. Not everyone can count on comfortable beds. Not everyone has access to the council's healers. Shouldn't we serve all of the city? Those who can afford it *and* those who can't?"

I didn't think that was fair, and I told him. The magicians and merchants worked hard for their keep.

Feather smiled. "For me, what is fair is to give people equal opportunities and equal chances. The world benefits if we all flourish, but it suffers if even some of us suffer."

"So what would you like me to do, then?" I asked.

"Let her go. Give her a coin for some food. She needs it far more than you do."

As Liva, I never would have. It's not that I don't support charity—we are charitable at home. I know all too well some people are prone to bad luck, and some are vulnerable and must be protected. But I could not condone crime and living off the hard work of others.

As Lente…I still wasn't entirely convinced, but Finn was looking at me intently, and out of all of them he might've been the only one with a chance at all to convince me. It had been a rough day, and I wanted to go home. "Fine. Do what you must."

I walked back to the rest of the group and the girl, and nodded at the others. "Let her go." I took a coin from my purse and flung it at her before she could catch it, so it rolled on the cobblestones at her feet. The girl stared wide-eyed at it.

"Pick it up, then go."

She moved slowly, and of course, that was when Feather made his move. He pulled another handful of coins from *his* purse and pushed them into her hands, before picking up the one I tossed too. "If you need food and work, come to the council. The kitchens are always looking for staff, and I'll put in a good word for you if you want me to." Then he pulled a day's rations from his bag and passed those on too.

When the girl ran off, he turned to me. "Was that so difficult?"

There was something about the way the girl gobbled down part of the food immediately and saved the rest that could convince all sides of me that she needed it.

Lente understood what Feather did. She was always kinder than me—but weaker too.

I'd miss her. I'd miss her uncomplicated worldview.

Now, I glance away from my friends. "I need a moment to myself. I just...need..."

I need to get away from here, from everything I've lost.

NINE

EVER

Liva gets up and dusts her hands on her cloak. Without another word, she walks away. Away from the lights of the living room. Into the shadows and toward the rapidly darkening night.

"Liva."

She stops near the staircase but doesn't look back.

"Do you want company?"

She hesitates, then shakes her head. "No. Not yet."

"We'll figure out a solution," I say. "Revival. Another character."

This is not how it was supposed to happen. But throw in some terrible rolls and bad luck, and here we are. And now I have to decide how to go on.

"No…no, thank you." Liva wraps her arms around her chest. She's still turned toward the windows and the night outside. She's so tense and fragmented, like she's falling apart in the same way as the game. "It's fitting, I guess. Losing my character here, of all places. I don't want any of you to bring her back. Not now, not like this. Let it happen."

I close my eyes. The worst thing is, Liva told me just yesterday that she loved how I ran the game. That it was comfortable. Familiar. Even if she didn't know where my stories would go, she knew how I approached those stories. She felt safe here.

I failed her. I still feel that way about Zac too, though he quit the game of his own volition after he and Liva broke up. But I hated how much more comfortable—how much more at ease—I was without him there. It made me feel like a terrible friend.

So now I can't fail the others. Maddy has risen to her feet and leans against the mantle of the fireplace. Carter pushes the effect dice back and forth on the table.

When Liva has left the room, he sighs. "This is it, right? We knew this game would be the hardest one yet. One down…three to go."

Maddy immediately swings around and glowers at him. "What on earth is wrong with you, C? Why would you say something like that?" She shakes her head wildly, then she stomps out to the porch.

"Hey, not cool," Finn says softly.

Carter shrugs. "I'm just saying, it's the truth."

I pluck the dice from Carter's hands. "The idea is to end this on a positive note. Not to kill you all." Still, he has a point. Liva's character's death is a stark reminder of how everything can change from one moment to the next. It's a reminder of how this weekend will bring everything to a close.

Carter stands and moves into the kitchen, ignoring us. Finn and I exchange a look and then follow him through the door.

"The chances this would happen are infinitely small," Finn argues. "It was bad luck, nothing more."

"Sure. Maybe the dice are haunted too." Carter reaches for the cabinet that holds the drinking glasses. For all he tries to make light of the situation, his hands are trembling.

Finn seems about ready to ram his crutches into something. "Oh for the love of—"

"*Ouch!*" Carter pulls his hand back from the kitchen cabinet and stares at it like it bit him.

I rush over to him. "What happened?"

"The cabinet knob was red hot," he says, waving his hand around like that will cool it.

Tentatively, I reach out to touch the knob too, but it's a normal temperature. "Are you sure?"

Carter pushes his hand at me, and there's a clear red mark on his fingers.

"Maybe you shouldn't have tempted the ghost," Finn grumbles.

"Oh for the love of goblins…" Carter starts.

I breathe out hard. I can't deal with this arguing anymore. Damien was right; I can't fix everyone's problems. I still want to make this experience memorable. Just…perhaps not in this way.

"Right," I say. "We're taking a ten-minute break, because apparently everyone needs time to cool off. I expect everyone to get their heads back into the game when we reconvene."

With that, they head back into the living room, and I follow Maddy onto the porch. Maddy's already in the yard, zigzagging through the trees in the grove and darting away from the shadows, as if they might snap at her. She keeps the weight off her bad leg. She doesn't stop until she comes to a place at the trees' edge.

I move down to where she's stopped, and the whole world blinks into existence. The first stars are appearing in the dark night sky, the sliver of the moon rising into it. The mountains loom on the horizon, with the light pollution glow of the city filling the valley beneath us.

Wow.

"It used to be my favorite place," Maddy says. I didn't realize she'd noticed my presence; I must've gasped at the sight.

"Mind if I join you?"

"Nah." She sinks slowly to the ground, which is still covered in pine needles from last year's fall. She wraps her arms around her knees and rocks back and forth. "I needed a breather."

"We all do. But I think you found the border between Gonfalon and Flagstaff."

"Yeah." She doesn't sound like she necessarily appreciates it.

I kneel next to her and stare out at the mountains. "So, while Finn and Carter are fighting about ghosts… Who are you angry at?"

Maddy goes as prickly and untouchable as a hedgehog. "The dice. Carter, for being absolutely insufferable. And myself, most of all. I was so sloppy. I messed up there."

"You did." I could tell her she didn't, but what would be the point of that? If she had been paying attention, Liva's character would still be alive. "But it wasn't just you."

"Does that matter?"

"Did you do it on purpose?" I ask, point-blank.

Maddy sniffs. Her jaw sets. "Of course not. Doesn't mean I'm not responsible." She shakes her head violently. "I need to be better. Anger isn't going to stop me from feeling terrible."

I take a chance. Maddy appreciates directness. "Good."

She glances up at me, confused.

I half shrug and keep my voice level. "This is how we gain experience, both in this game and in life. We win some battles. We lose others. We learn and we keep going."

"I hate that life has gotten so complicated."

I smile. "I'm not sure it was ever uncomplicated."

Maddy shrugs. "I don't know. It was, at least, *less* complicated. It feels like everything is falling to pieces. And I don't know who I am without this game. I don't know where I can find other safe spaces that let me be myself."

She curls up. I can see her mouth work. I can see all the things she doesn't say yet or doesn't know how to say yet.

"It's hard, isn't it? Trusting others with the whole of you?"

She smiles bitterly and shakes her head. "It's so much easier to lie. You know that. You lie too."

"I…" *No, I don't,* I want to say. Out of habit. But Maddy's eerily observant. She once said she taught herself to be as fluent as possible in all the things people don't say, and it shows.

And she's right. "Yeah, I do."

"So what do you lie about?"

The question is so straightforward, I can't help but answer. "I lie about being okay."

She nods. "Yeah, me too."

I lie about the game too, though I can hardly tell her that. I lie about how much it means to me.

It's everything.

Most of us have enough to struggle with. The real world is bleak. But in Gonfalon, we can be ourselves without any limitations, fully the way we imagine ourselves. I worked hard to create a space that embraces joy and sorrow. Fear and courage. Everything that makes all of us real, and we encourage each other to explore it all. To talk about it all, no matter how scary. Here, everything is possible.

And that is the biggest lie of all.

I don't just want to make the game good for them; I want to stay here and never go back.

I reach out and place my hand over Maddy's. Carefully. Slow enough to give her time to withdraw. "I won't lie about this: You can trust me. As long as I can, as long as you need me, I'll be here."

She narrows her eyes and I wonder if she sees straight through me. She sniffs again. "Yeah."

It's the truth. I'm not going anywhere. Because even though I can imagine whole universes and make plans, reality always comes back to bite you. And some things are more important than following nebulous dreams. I'll make sure Elle has everything she needs, so one of us can succeed. She won't go hungry or be constantly tired. I'll make sure Dad doesn't have to worry about our ramshackle house. The bills will be paid on time, and he and I won't go hungry either.

And maybe when all of that is done, I'll figure out a way to build new worlds.

Until then...

"Let's go back to the rest of the group," I say. "We need to return to the game and figure out a way out of this mess."

I scramble to my feet and offer Maddy a hand. As she grabs it, loud, high-pitched laughter tears through the relative quiet. Maddy yelps. The sound comes from everywhere. It echoes off the mountain. It closes in and wanders off. It rises and falls, sharp enough to cut.

Then another voice joins in. Another. And another.

The cackling laughter morphs to howling as a pack of coyotes announces their hunt. Maddy mutters passionately, "I hate the outdoors."

"Same." I squeeze her hand, and we drag each other back to the cabin.

But the laughter and howling follow us—and on this haunted mountain, trapped in the shadows, I can't help but think it sounds like the screams of the dying.

LENTE'S DEATH CEMENTS THAT THIS PLACE IS FAR MORE DANGEROUS than you all anticipated. There are secrets here. There are traps that could easily kill you.

And as night falls at this lonely castle, far from the world, you cannot help but wonder what is next. Instead of finding answers, you've only found more questions: If Councilwoman Yester consorted with rogue mages, it makes no sense for them to have killed her. If not them, then who? If it was someone from the council, why would they have sent you there?

Over the last few years, you've always trusted the council implicitly. You never had cause to doubt them. Now there's a little voice in the back of your head that whispers you can't trust anyone's motivations. If Joanna Yester turned to the side of the lawless, anyone could have. Any one of you could have.

You're stuck here, in a lonely castle, and you're a prime target.

TEN

CARTER

We're back to playing the game, and the coins burn a hole in my purse like how the kitchen cabinet burned me. (And what *was* that? I don't believe in ghosts. I *can't* believe in ghosts. But something is *weird* about this cabin.) *Break the rules. Lose the game.* I keep thinking about what my character Corrin would do. He would carry the coins around for days, but ultimately hand them over to the magisterium. *I* would take them and happily spend them.

Because we jumped immediately into the investigation of Joanna's death, I haven't been able to turn them in yet. But if it's ever necessary to use them, I don't think I'd hesitate. Truth is, so far, I'm doing fine without the extra coins. I'm still standing, aren't I? That's more than can be said for some.

Seriously, I can't believe I outlasted Liva. Out of everyone.

I can't say I mind it.

Everyone is struggling. We're still standing at the same door— the kitchen door turned into the door for Joanna's atelier—and we haven't found our way in yet. Moments like these, I miss Zac's character Zilver. He would've charged ahead, consequences be damned. He would've laughed at our worries. We're too scared for that.

Maybe I should use the coins to help us. It wouldn't be the first time I helped myself to something I didn't earn. My stomach clenches—not with guilt, really, because I don't feel guilty about it. I may not have earned it, but I deserved it. My eyes dart to my friends around me. No, what I'm feeling is anxiety. Does one of them know?

It couldn't have been Liva who put the coins in my purse. If she knew what I did—what I'm *doing*—she would've gone straight to her father. She tolerates me well enough here and at school, but has resented me ever since I started working for their company. Like I'm trying to steal her job away from her. Like I ever *could*. I wish it were that easy. I wish she'd have to learn what it felt like not to have everything handed to you. No, she would've delighted in getting me fired.

Which leads me to Maddy. She knows. But she would hardly... what? Threaten to expose me? She's too dependent on me right now. If I didn't break the rules, we both would've lost ages ago. And I'd like to think I mean more to her. We play hard and we fight hard, but she's the only one I more or less trust.

I glance at Ever and Finn.

Ever catches my eye, and I clear my throat, heat rising to my cheeks. "We need to find a way into the door," I say, trying to concentrate on the task at hand. "If we can't dispel the wards, maybe we can find another way to break them. Destroy the markings, something like that."

"Do you want to give that a try? What would you like to do?" Ever asks.

I shrug. "Have we ever tried simply...brushing the glyphs away?"

"We haven't, because devouring wards can *kill*," Finn says. He seems to stare straight through me.

"I mean, sure. But."

"Do you want to try?" Maddy asks. She came back to the game with a distant look in her eyes, and seeing her like that is the only time I ever feel guilty.

I'm helping her—aren't I?

"I do," I say.

Finn smiles thinly. He certainly seems a lot more relaxed now that Liva is out of the room. Did *I* ever do anything to Finn to make him hate me like that? If so, I don't remember it, and I can't believe that's what's happening. I don't want to believe that's what's happening.

We're *friends.*

And Ever...Ever was here, all of yesterday. I know they know how to keep secrets.

"Are you certain?" they ask me, a calculating look in their eyes. It's the look we've all come to know as the *GM Look*. Are they this calculating outside of the game too? Did I just never realize? "How do you plan to do this?"

I breathe in deeply and try to keep my focus on the murder mystery. There's a question underlying their question. Am I ready for this decision to backfire spectacularly?

Normally, I would be. It's a game, after all, and there's something to be said for messing up with abandon. But we're one down already. And this weekend...

Here's the thing. I care about Corrin. He travels the world. He's dedicated his life to adventure and truth. He lives to right wrongs and bring to light injustices. And he may be nothing more than a character I made up, but I made him up from all the dreams *I* have. Corrin sees the world in shades of possibility.

Life in Gonfalon is simpler, more easygoing than the real world. Less...for lack of a better term, political? Corrin doesn't have to watch what he says, and not everyone seems so sensitive.

Of course I'm not certain.

I lick my lips and try to think, my mind racing through everything else I've seen in the game. "I run back up the stairs toward where we saw Joanna's unfinished shield. Since it seemed to be warded too, maybe I can use it to break one ward with the other."

I'm not entirely sure that's how shields are supposed to be used, but it's the only thing I can think of.

And Ever smiles slightly. Maybe I'm onto something.

"Do you tell any of the others what you're about to do?" they ask. "Or do you go by yourself?"

I may be running head-on into a trap, but I know what Corrin would do. The life of a curious fool longing for truth is a dangerous one. "I would bolt. I wouldn't tell any of the others."

Finn *hisses*. Maddy groans. And Ever's smile widens. "Good to know. If Carter and I could have the room, please. Just for a moment."

Oh cool. That bodes well. I sigh.

Finn gets to his feet, passing by me on the way out, and places a hand on my shoulder. "One down, huh? You jinxed it." It's meant in jest, I'm sure, but there's a shadow in his eyes.

Maddy goes next. "It was nice knowing you."

There's a twitch in my heart at those words.

They head in separate directions—Finn out onto the porch, and Maddy up to her room. Ever keeps their eyes on the notes in front of them, waiting until the others are well out of earshot before they say anything else. In that silence, the cabin closes in on me.

I hate being here. It's not just the coins burning a hole in my pocket, or the note that accompanied them, or the shadows that crawl in from the windows.

It's Liva. She made sure the cabin was well-stocked and supplied with delicious food. Even the assorted drinks on one of the tables—La Croix and Perrier, for crying out loud—seem like too much. And I don't know. It's clear she's rich. She doesn't have to flaunt it, right?

We all know.

And we all try to be like her, in one way or another. Money is value, my parents always remind me.

There's a twisted kind of satisfaction in Liva being the first to lose her character.

Gods, I wish Ever didn't have such a good poker face; I have no idea if what's happening is good or bad. But if I don't make it out of this scene, I can rest easy in the knowledge that I survived Liva.

It's petty. I know.

Once Maddy's footsteps have died down and the only sound in the cabin is our breathing and the wind creaking through the grove outside, Ever looks up. A hint of a smile on their face. They settle in right in front of me.

"You run up alone. Perhaps it's the memory of Lente's death that spurs you on, perhaps it's *knowing* you have a solution, right at your fingertips. But you move fearlessly through this tower with all its secrets and all its ghosts—"

A loud *crash* cuts them off, from somewhere close by.

My heart rate jumps.

Ever falters, then raises their voice. "Liva? Maddy? Finn? Everyone okay?"

The words are met with silence, and nothing more.

We listen—for either a call for help or the acknowledgment that everything's fine, nothing to worry about, but neither of those come.

"I'm sure if something were wrong, someone would've said something," I mutter.

"Or perhaps someone needs help and they can't ask for it." Ever stretches and comes to stand in front of me, their head still slightly cocked. I've seen them around their sister, and they look exactly like that now: equal parts protective, worried, and paranoid.

"I'm sure it's fine."

"I wish I could be sure too. Excuse me." Ever hesitates between the door and the staircase, and for a brief, irrational heartbeat, all I want to do is stop them, make them stay here with me. Play this game with me. This is *my* time, and I'm tired of it being interrupted.

"Ever…"

They don't respond, and a wave of anger washes over me. I clench my fists and try to swallow the annoyance, but it burns hot inside me. The moment Ever walks away from me, I get up and walk away too. I can't force the game to continue, but I can make my way to the kitchen to pretend I'm still in control. Even if all I do is stare at the cabinets and ignore the silence. I ignore the footsteps upstairs. I ignore the emptiness opening inside me.

It's always the same thing. Other things and other people are always more important than me.

And if people see me, it's never for who I am, but only for what I can do for them.

I reach for the coin purse and test its weight once more. Maybe neither the coins nor the note were a warning; maybe they were a hint. After all, following or breaking the rules aren't the only options. I can find my own way. I can simply stop playing.

Bend *the rules*. Win *the game*.

Truth is, to get what I deserve, I simply have to take it myself.

Some sounds can break through everything:

Silence.

Tension.

Night.

Imagination.

The idea that a pile of blankets can be a body. That cards can be real artifacts and puzzle boxes truly deadly. That dice are weapons.

Some sounds remind you this isn't a castle.

This is a cabin.

And a loud scream tears through the darkness, raw and filled with terror.

ELEVEN

FINN

A bat drops from the rafters and nearly tumbles onto my face before flying off into the night. I flip it off when it does. With no one to see me, and no one to judge, I can breathe. I could *break*. I want to be able to trust my friends. I want to go back to feeling safe amidst all of them, and I'm *trying*. But right now, I don't know if I can.

It used to be so effortless. We could simply let ourselves fall into another world and *thrive*.

If this game ends after this weekend, and I never see any of the others again, I wouldn't care.

Except about Ever.

When my brain calms, I get stuck on the memory of the touch of their hands, soft and careful, when they broke character for me.

Let me know if there's anything you need. Physically. Emotionally. I want you to feel safe here.

It hurts that they know me so well, that they care so deeply. It hurts in the best of ways.

I consider all the answers I didn't give. *I need* you, *physically. I need* you, *emotionally. I feel safe with you.*

Trouble is, that's exactly what scares me. I don't feel safe with many people. I have literally never asked anyone out on a date before. I don't have a clue how to go about it. I never did crushes before. I didn't feel comfortable enough in my own skin. I didn't know how much of a hang-up gender would be for other people—or disability, for that matter. If you're constantly told people like you don't have meaningful relationships, it's hard to believe you're allowed to try.

So a big part of me wants to stick to Damien's advice: *Try. Find your family and cling to it. Life is too short and too hard not to embrace every aspect of it.* It's part of why I ran, and it's most of why I came back. Because underneath all my fear, I want to make this the best game yet. Follow the clues and the signs. Play my heart out. And then hand it to Ever in a puzzle box.

Something crashes though the undergrowth, not far away from where I'm sitting, and my pulse pounds. It was just an animal, I think. I hope. Are there wolves or coyotes here? I pull my knees up to my chest and cradle my crutches closer, but it's dark enough now that I can't see beyond the small circle of light surrounding the porch.

"Hello?" I call out hesitantly.

Silence. Darkness.

I'm letting the ghost stories get to me. It was probably a squirrel or—

The door slams open. Ever. The bright light from inside filters out around them, making their shadow almost bleed into the darkness. It's too shaded for me to see their face; I can only hear their rapid breathing. "Finn, you have to come back in."

I scramble to my feet, my heart slamming in my chest.

"Something's wrong."

Carter appears behind them, holding one of the decorative fireplace pokers, his eyes wild, his cheeks flushed. When we all push into the cabin, Maddy is standing on the stairs, her face deathly white and her hands trembling.

She keeps glancing back over her shoulder, and her voice shakes as much as her body does. "Did you hear that? There was something—someone upstairs."

Carter dashes up to meet her. "Are you okay? How are you feeling?"

I'm still trying to catch up. "What happened?"

At the same time, next to me, Ever says, "We heard screaming. Are we all here? Where is Liva?"

Oh.

Everything snaps into focus. One of us is missing. "We have to find to Liva."

"We have to stay close together," Ever cautions.

They place a hand on mine. Carter reaches for Maddy. And the cabin feels cold and lonely. The only thing we can do is walk up the winding staircase and hope she's waiting for us at the top.

"Liva?"

Nothing.

Again, "Liva!"

Carter still holds hands with Maddy as we edge toward the bedrooms, his free hand continuing to grasp the poker.

Ever leans into me, a little. "Did you see her leave the cabin by any chance?"

I shake my head. "I didn't. I heard something moving in the brush, but it sounded like an animal." To be fair, I didn't hear anyone scream either. "I was a bit lost in thought."

They squeeze my hand.

Carter shouts again. "Liva!"

The door to Liva's room stands open. Something *moves* inside. We all pause, catch our breath, try not to meet one another's eyes, steel ourselves.

"Liva?" With one of my crutches, I push the door open farther. The room is empty, and the window is wide open. What I thought was movement was just the swaying of the curtains back and forth in the breeze. The night is dark and endless outside. "She isn't here."

"She can't have just…disappeared, right?" Maddy's voice is fragile.

Apparently that's exactly what happened.

The room itself looks well lived in. Liva carefully unpacked her bags, and it's clear she's stayed here many times before. Posters of WyvernCon and sewing patterns decorate the walls.

The bedspread is a quilt she made herself, constructed from pieces of all the costumes she made in our first two years of WyvernCon. There's part of the blood hunter outfit she created, and the very first magister cloak she tried. There's a square from the Spoiler outfit she made for me, a square from a Time Lord coat, and a slice of the space scavenger uniform Ever wore.

I trace my fingers over the quilt, an amalgamation of so much fandom. It's smooth to the touch.

I look around me, at the carefully folded robes, the pair of scissors on the bedside table, the coverless book with yellowed pages, lying on one of the pillows. And Ever, standing next to me. The quiet panic in their eyes. The way they seem to be shrinking in on themself.

A rush of anger courses through me. "This isn't funny." It's always Liva, hurting us. Every time. I repeat it louder, walking back out into the hallway. "Liva? C'mon, this isn't funny!"

I shouldn't worry about her, and yet I do. I hate her. She was one of my best friends once. I told her about my crush on Ever long before I told Damien. I *trusted* her. I hate her.

"Liva, please." Ever's voice trembles.

Our words are met with nothing but silence. The cabin is quiet. All we can hear is the wind through the trees outside, and the curtain, pushing in and out. A door rattles on its hinges, and Maddy starts to cry quietly.

"Maybe she needed some time for herself." Carter moves toward the window. "Or maybe the stories are true."

Then, metallic chimes.

A fragment of a melody, so soft it might as well be a memory.

The start of a song. A nursery tune, maybe.

It's uncomfortably reminiscent of the ghost stories that haunt this mountain, and it's terrifying until I realize it must be the wind chimes that hang on the porch, swaying in the wind. Only that. Nothing more.

"I see blood outside!" Carter rushes past me, down the stairs, and out the cabin.

"Carter, wait!" Maddy follows him, awkwardly, painfully, but determined.

"Finn?" I turn back around. Ever stands in the doorway to Liva's room. I didn't think it would be possible, but they've grown paler still. "Can you come in here, please?"

I follow them in, and they point at the windowsill. The breeze has blown the curtain back again, and now I can see a small wooden figurine sitting on the ledge.

A carving, like the wooden figurines from the ghost stories.

A coyote—very similar in style to the ones Ever themself used in their story, but not quite the same. It's cruder, the wood a different color.

Something pink and bloody lies next to it. At first glance, I think it's a piece of meat. But then I remember what Ever said when they introduced the story.

"It can't be…"

"What?"

All they found was an abandoned cabin, a handprint, a music box, and a bloody, torn-off finger.

Nausea rises into my throat, but I push it down.

Ever steps closer to me, and I flinch away. "I don't know what's going on here, Finn…"

"I don't know either. I don't want to know."

"Do you think someone took her for a ransom?"

I gingerly pick up the carving of the coyote and try my best to ignore the meaty shape lying next to it. The all-too-obvious fingernail caked in blood. Nail art with the Gonfalon symbol. "That's not how the story goes…"

If this is part of a game, I don't want anything to do with it.

But underneath the figurine lies a small note, splattered with gore. One word, written in blood.

LIAR.

TWELVE
MADDY

The worst plan in any situation is to split the party, every gamer knows that. But if there is blood outside, like Carter says, he shouldn't go alone. If the ghost stories are real, *no one* should be alone.

And I don't want to be alone either.

"Carter, wait!" My voice is barely audible, and Carter keeps rushing out. His shoulders are tense and he's shaking his head.

"Carter, wait, please!" I can't tell what he's feeling. I still feel his hand in mine and his comforting presence when we walked up the stairs. His whispered "sorry." But now he's running, and with every step he takes, it feels like the friend I've had since I was a kid is slipping further away.

Liva felt that familiar to me too, once upon a time. She was my unlikely best friend: the popular girl who didn't mind hanging out with the autistic kid. Popular and autistic shouldn't be diametrically opposed, but at Stardust High, they are. Being on the lacrosse team gave me some status, but Liva was my friend even before that. It took me months to accept it and stop questioning it.

I'm still trying to accept that it's gone. Our friendship.

She isn't.

She *can't* be.

She needs to be annoyed by my hair all through this weekend. She needs to be smug about her cabin. She needs to be unreadable, impossible, *here*.

But all I can think about is the blood Carter saw.

I nearly stumble over the last steps from the patio down to the yard as my knee locks and my body lurches forward. Carter's already disappeared into the dark.

Before I have a chance to panic, Carter is back, holding out a trembling hand. "C'mon, stay close."

I practically run to him. "Just don't move so fast, please?" I breathe the words into his chest, and he holds me too tight. Pain is radiating through me, and I'm worried—for Liva, for all of us. I have no way to focus the overwhelming chaos in my mind. I wish I could sit on these steps and stim and forget.

"Are you okay?"

There are layers to that question, but the answer to all of them is the same. "It hurts, C."

He pulls back, but at the same time, he reaches out to me and his fingers curl around my hand. He's steady and present, and though I can feel him shaking, he's what I need to keep moving.

Liva was like *that* too. And then the accident happened, and while I was recovering, Liva spent more and more time at her father's company. She had less time for the two of us. And when we hung out, I always needed an hour or so to get my friend back—because the girl who showed up was always the rich snob her parents wanted her to be.

And that hour kept getting longer. Eventually, she simply didn't come by anymore unless it was for a costume or something game-related. I tried to tell Liva about the pills once. I tried to tell her what the doctor prescribed wasn't enough. I hoped she might be able to help me, at least before Carter stepped in. She didn't seem to understand.

That night, my sister Sav said Liva and I both wanted the other to be someone different. I didn't know what she meant, but maybe I should've tried harder.

I know Liva has been going through stuff too, with the pressure she's had from her dad. If we find her—*when* we find her—I'm going to do my part to be a better friend. I hope she will too.

Carter and I stumble into the all-too-quiet yard, and Carter drags me toward a spot on the side of the cabin where Liva's room is. There is no path on this side of the cabin, only an overgrown clearing.

The only way I can think to stim is by balling my free hand into a fist and methodically pounding my hip. Something rhythmic. Something to keep me focused. I feel like I'm falling.

It feels like we've fallen into an upside-down world where none of the normal rules apply. Like I spent years studying a rule book to understand how the world works, and how people work, and how we can do magic between those two—and then we start the game with a completely different system.

I don't know how to deal with this.

I can't keep up. I'm scared, I think. I'm overwhelmed.

The world is so much and this pain stabs so deep.

Carter breathes hard, next to me. He squeezes my hand. He isn't necessarily calm, but he is calming me, at least. "I'm going to call for Liva again. Don't be scared."

"How can I not be?"

He winces, his expression falling somewhere between a grimace and a frown. He nods in acknowledgment.

Then he shouts, "Liva!"

We both listen for a reply.

His voice echoes against the cabin walls, bounces through the trees. And it's only met with silence. No birdsong, no coyotes, no rustling of the wind through the leaves.

Silence.

"*Liva!*"

Carter's voice sounds hollow.

I disentangle myself from him and kneel on the grass, raking my fingers through it. They come back wet.

In the faint glow of the cabin lights, I can see there's blood on the ground, and quite a lot of it. Dark, wet crimson stains on darker grass. Stickiness on my fingers.

My stomach twists.

"Here!" Carter kneels next to a blood spot and picks at something in the grass.

I squint. "What is it?"

"Looks to be some piece of cloth." Carter hesitates. "A swath of torn costume."

Oh.

I want to take a step back, but another piece of cloth catches my eye. Gold threading. Not a lot, but enough to make out Liva's handiwork—because I would recognize it anywhere.

I bite my lip and reach out, not *quite* touching it. "What is happening, C?"

Carter rocks to his feet. "I wish I knew. I really wish I did. But all I know is that we need to find Liva. She has to be here *somewhere*."

I'm still staring at the torn bit of costume. I saw her wear this only an hour or so ago, when she...when she... "She died in the game," I whisper.

"We don't know that she's dead," Carter responds harshly. "Maybe she's wounded. Maybe someone took her. Maybe she fell, and she tried to crawl away from the window."

But that seems like a ridiculous conclusion given the amount of blood and the torn clothes. The bedroom window isn't high up enough to kill, and if she were wounded, surely she would've called for help. She would've called out to us.

"Liva!" My voice shatters. I can feel it in my throat.

There's only a deep, desperate silence here.

Maybe it's because of that silence, but I'm convinced someone's watching us. I feel the eyes all around me.

I want to be invisible. I want to be anywhere but here, because I know, *I know*—this game, these friends may not have broken yet, but they will. Everything always breaks.

It's getting harder to breathe.

There are too many shadows between us and the city. Someone is watching us. Someone is waiting, prowling like an animal waiting to pounce on its prey. And we only have one another to stand between us and whatever is out there.

The night closes in on me, slowly, while Carter continues to look for clues. Presumably Ever and Finn are doing the same. They don't notice it. They don't see what's about to happen.

But I do. I felt the same way right before my injury and in the empty nights after. In the loneliness when my team stopped coming to visit and my friends didn't know how to talk to me. I was lost.

And we are lost now.

We're here, alone, and we have nowhere else to go. We don't have an escape route. We don't know what's waiting for us. We can't protect ourselves from whatever's out there with wooden rifles and foam daggers and make-believe skills.

"Are there any tracks down there?" Ever's voice, angled from the window, echoes through the yard.

I finally snatch the piece of cloth from the grass and push myself up, angling my body to keep the weight from my knee—and freeze.

Hanging out of the window, Ever is as pale as a ghost. But when I look up to them, that isn't what catches my eye.

Perhaps I should've seen it before. Perhaps Carter should've. We were so focused on the bloody grass, we didn't look up. Neither of us did.

Tunnel vision, perhaps—or fear.

There's a harsh intake of breath from Carter, a few feet behind me. Apparently when Ever called out, he looked up too.

The edge of the abyss roars around us.

The blood on the ground does leave a track. But it doesn't move away from the cabin. And it's not simple drops of blood either.

There are bloody handprints, some smudged, but most of them all too clear.

And they're crawling back up the wall—toward the window.

THIRTEEN
EVER

The handprints are leading up.

I stare at Maddy and Carter, pale and pointing, and then slowly look down the wall.

The handprints are leading up. Bloody handprints. Leading up.

I crumple the piece of paper Finn has given me. *Liar.*

Finn tugs at my sleeve. "Ev, we have to get out of here." I hardly recognize his voice. It's filled with hurt and fear and something else, rawer than anything I've ever heard.

"I…" I don't know what to say. Blood roars in my ears, and if our group is unraveling, then I'm unraveling too. This was a mistake. The words I texted Damien flash before my eyes: *My friends are hurting. It's my job to protect them. It's my job to keep them safe.*

Finn tugs harder. "We have to get the four of us together and *leave*."

Deep down, I understand that rationale. With the tracks leading into the cabin, the only sensible place to go is out. There really isn't a question about it. We should all convene on the porch on the other side of the building and go from there.

But.

"I'm responsible for her." I want to try to find her. *My* voice sounds weird to me too. Slower, and every word I speak feels new and strange. "Something has happened to Liva, and what if she doesn't get help in time because we ran down the mountain without so much as a second look back?"

"Ever," Finn says firmly. "If this had been an accident, Liva would still be here. What *wouldn't* be are bloody handprints. Or a note. Or a *finger*. Someone clearly has it out for her. I don't know if I believe in haunted cabins, but if it isn't that, then it's murder or kidnapping or something along those lines. She's richer than all of us put together. Her family could meet *any* ransom. But I'm not staying here to find out exactly what happened, and neither are you."

I nod. And I realize the something else in his voice is anger, as deep and as fresh as the first days after he got beaten up. He's so angry, he's trembling.

Just then, the power cuts.

All the lights in the cabin blink out of existence, and we're covered in a blanket of intense darkness. While my eyes struggle to adjust, panicked shouts filter in from outside. "What's going on there?"

"Finn? Ever?"

Finn moves his grasp from my sleeve to my elbow and pulls hard. "We're getting out. *Now.*"

I let him tug me into the hallway and down the stairs. But once we get to the bottom—and I'm not sure how we manage that without both of us breaking our legs—I pull back, because something tugs at the back of my mind. "Finn, wait."

"No."

One word, but it carries such finality. I want to punch him, and I want to reach for all the cracks and hold him together. He was my first best friend. Not just because he and I were the only two out trans kids at school for a while, not just because we flocked together for safety and community, but because he believed in me. And it kills me that he doesn't believe in us. "*Wait.*"

"No, we have to get out of here."

"We have to get our phones." I swallow hard and try to make my voice more audible. "We're going to grab our phones. That way, we'll have flashlights at hand. And maybe that way, we can still do something. And we should call the cops. And Liva's parents. Though I have no idea what to tell them."

I start pulling him, now. Toward the kitchen and the pantry where we kept our phones in their chest. Yet another one of the

WyvernCon treasures. Maybe we'll find other helpful stuff in the pantry too.

Quest items.

When I put the phones in there, I noticed the shelves were lined with tin cans and containers of food. But I also saw oil, matches, an AM-FM radio, a collection of batteries, and roughly two dozen rolls of paper towels. Enough to survive the zombie apocalypse.

We make our way to the kitchen, my arm outstretched to make sure I don't walk into anything—and trying my hardest not to imagine what it would feel like to walk into any*one*. But as we get inside and near the pantry, the pantry door creaks on its hinges.

I know, *I know* I didn't leave the door open.

"Finn…"

He shakes his head, hard. "We go in. We grab the phones. And then we run out. No dallying, no second guessing. We need our party together, and I'm done with this place."

I refuse to give in to hesitation. I nudge the door farther open and step in. The floorboards groan, echoing all around me, almost as if I stepped in and someone else stepped back. Or perhaps the floorboards on the landing creaked. I'm not entirely sure.

I don't want to scare Finn.

He leans in. "You don't happen to remember where you put the chest, do you?"

I stand on tiptoe, reaching for the shelves right next to the door. "Top shelf," I whisper. "Right here."

My hand smacks the empty shelf.

"Or not," he says.

I tilt my head. "It was, though. It was the only empty space left in the pantry."

All the shelves are packed with boxes and cans. I pat the shelves, trace the cans, but there is nothing out of the ordinary. The only notably empty space is the one I'm reaching for.

There is no chest with phones anywhere.

Dread settles into my stomach. For the first time, I think Finn may be right.

I reach deeper and curse. Something bites at my hand, and when I pull it back, I see thin shards of glass embedded in my palms and fingers. I brush at them, but they dig into my skin. "They're gone."

"They can't be."

"There's a lot happening that *can't be.* They're gone. They're not here, and someone replaced them with glass instead." My voice is loud and sharp, but I don't know how to rein it in. "I'm sorry, I didn't mean…"

Everything is slipping through my fingers, and the void that remains is slowly filled with panic. The tentacles of anxiety—the strongest of the eldritch gods—crawl up around my feet and legs.

"Do you have your phone on you still?" Finn asks, but I know he knows better. "Can you call one of us to see if we hear anything?"

"I put it in there for safekeeping too. I knew I was going to be distracted checking in with Elle, otherwise. And she told me to focus on the game."

I shake my head. The shock was easier because it didn't hurt so much. Now the ice-cold sense of dread and paranoia is taking over. Liva is gone. Gravely injured…or worse. The power is out. Our phones are gone. Someone had to have taken them. Someone's messing with the cabin, with us. And the four of us are stuck on a mountain, with nothing to protect us.

If this were a game, I couldn't have designed it better myself. But if this were a game, it would be twisted and disgusting.

"We're getting out," I say, louder than I intended. "I'm assuming the phones are gone because someone took them, and we already decided we're not going to wait to see who or why."

Finn and I, we're pushing and pulling each other out, and there is strength in being together. Holding on to each other is the only thing that keeps us upright.

"Do you think the ghost stories are real after all?" Finn whispers, as we navigate through the living room on feel and memory. Everything around us creaks and moans—and I keep wondering if there are other people here. The room is so infinitely big, I could be forgiven for thinking the walls could disappear and morph into night themselves.

It's colder than it was earlier tonight too. Although the temperature drops considerably during these summer nights, it's usually only chilly at worst. But right now, the cabin feels freezing.

Yes. No. I don't know.

I move around the table and toward the exit. "The story is generations old. The only thing that matters is getting out and calling for help."

"I know."

Finn says nothing more until we stand in front of the door to the porch, but when he reaches for the polished wood, I cover his hand with mine, and he breathes out sharply and leans into me. "I'm scared."

I know. "I am too."

We push the door open, and the outside is as dark as the inside, at first. At least until my eyes adjust, and the faint stars and a sliver of moon give us light enough to see shapes and specks of color.

The wind chimes dance in the breeze, their music eerie and unwelcome.

There's only one figure waiting for us.

"Maddy?"

She's leaning against one of the heavy beams, her knees pulled up to her chest and her shoulders trembling.

"Maddy, where's Carter?"

She doesn't reply.

The music from the chimes drifts away on the wind and disappears.

And then...

Silence.

YOU PREPARED FOR TRAPS. YOU PREPARED FOR ROGUE MAGES. You prepared for murderers, wishing to stop you. You knew the investigation would be dangerous. You were ready for that. But the castle itself has mobilized against you. What seemed to be safe, feels treacherous. What seemed to be treacherous, feels deadly.

Except, it's not a castle, it's a cabin. The large hearth in the main hall is nothing but a faulty fireplace that doesn't even provide a source of light. The heavy stones are logs, really. Not built to withstand the ages. It's quiet in here. It smells of peppers and pine and Mountain Dew.

It's not a castle, it's a cabin. Your daggers are made of foam. Your rifles made of wood. And you feel far less equipped to handle this.

FOURTEEN

FINN

M addy? Are you okay? Where's Carter?" I crouch in front of Maddy. She rocks back and forth so gently, it's almost as if she sways in the wind. There are stains all over her hands, and she keeps absently rubbing at them.

When she doesn't reply, or seem to register my presence, I repeat my questions with a hint of impatience. My hands are tingling. My stomach churns. "Are you okay? Where is Carter?"

I reach out my hand to her, and she flinches away from it. It's almost as if she's lost too, but unlike Liva, she's lost in her own fears. Her breathing is shallow like she's on the verge of another panic attack.

I twist my head back and forth to loosen up my neck.

"Maddy, talk to us," Ever chimes in, moving down next to me. "Breathe. Tell us where Carter is."

"He went back inside." Her voice croaks. She's still rubbing at her hands, and I realize the stains are blood. My breath catches.

"What? Why?" I blurt. Ever and I share a look.

Maddy shakes her head and then keeps doing it. We're all dancing on the precipice of panic, but she's near falling. "To help me? To stop the pain. To stop the world from crashing down on me. Liva's gone, and Carter's gone back in, and there is blood everywhere." She turns her head toward the patch of grass outside Liva's bedroom, and the world spins when I see how much blood there is.

This is not good. This is spectacularly not good.

"Carter went back *inside*?" I repeat.

Maddy nods and Ever groans. "We have to go back for him. We have to get him out."

She nods again, but it's clear the words mean very little to her.

"Ev…" I touch their arm and jerk my head back, indicating we should step away from Maddy. My jaw is tense, and I keep clenching and unclenching my fists.

Ever nods, but they keep their attention on Maddy for a moment longer. "Maddy. Try to focus on us. We need to find Carter, and we need you to be with us."

When she doesn't reply, Ever rocks to their feet and looks at me. "We have to snap her out of it. We can't leave her like this, and we can't *stay*."

"We have to do something," I say. "But..." I walk to the edge of the porch and lower my voice, so only Ever can hear what I'm saying. It's something I haven't wanted to voice aloud until now, but we need to discuss it. "I have to ask... Do you think maybe the call is coming from inside the house?"

Their eyes widen. "You mean you think one of us did something to Liva?"

I wince. They trust so easily. "I don't know? I feel like we shouldn't discount any possibilities."

"No." Ever shakes their head. "I don't want to entertain that thought. I *can't*."

"I don't want to either, but..."

"Like who? Carter?" They gesture around them with force, and I almost feel the rage and fear spilling over from their fingertips. "We were together the entire time. We only broke apart as a group when I wanted to do that scene with him."

"Maddy left several times." I glance past them, in the direction of Maddy, who is still trying to remove the bloodstains from her hands.

"Because she's *hurting*, Finn. Frankly, we all are. Life is complicated in different ways for all of us. That doesn't mean we go around killing one another."

"I'm not saying anyone did this. But people are capable of all kinds of things. And I can keep trusting people and getting hurt, or I can try to be more sensible about it." I scowl and look away from them, but despite my determination, the words taste like bile in my mouth. It's so much easier not to get attached to people, but I don't think I can live like that. I hated Liva and I wanted to hurt her. She was my friend, and she forgot about me. But I never wanted her to come to harm.

When I turn to walk back to Maddy, Ever's hand grabs my shoulder, and they pull me around and toward them. They wrap their arms around my shoulders. Slowly, I put my arms around their waist. We breathe in the same air. We can feel our heartbeats echo against each other.

Even if everything else feels wrong in the world, this, right here, feels right.

In a way, I hate that it does. I wish I could pretend it didn't. This—happiness—doesn't belong. Not here. Not now. But then, maybe here and now are all we have left.

Damien took me aside at WyvernCon this year and told me to, for the love of Talos, ask Ever out already. He said point-blank, "I see how you look at them. I see how they look at you. It's worth a try."

"What if they say no?" I asked him.

"Then you go on being friends. As long as you can respect each other's wishes, your friendship is strong enough to withstand that."

"What if they say yes?" is what I actually wanted to know.

"Then you still go on being friends, but you also try to make the relationship part work, whatever that means to you."

"How on earth do I do that?"

He laughed. "Ikram and I are still trying to figure that out, but

I'll let you know when I've completed the manual. Truth is, the most important parts are communication and trust. Figuring out what it means to be together, what you want and need from each other, what you're comfortable with. And kissing. The kissing is one of my favorite parts."

I blushed, and he laughed harder.

"But it's also investing in friendship. Because you can have the friendship without the relationship, but you can't have the relationship without the friendship."

"I wouldn't want to give up my friendship with Ever for anything," I admitted.

"That's good. I wouldn't want to give up my friendship with Ikram for anything either." Damien tapped his phone and pulled up a picture of him and his boyfriend in outrageous Regency costumes. They were both laughing so hard they were almost crying. "This world is a messed up and scary place. It's lonely to go through it on your own. So, you have to find your family. You have to find people who will stand by you and make you laugh until you cry, and who will hold you while you cry until you laugh again."

"Yeah." I bit my lip, trying to process his words. "Wait, you mean the world doesn't get less scary after high school?"

Damien put his phone in his pocket and rolled back to the front of the game stand. He'd once told me if my pain and joint instability got worse and it happened that I needed to use a wheelchair, we'd figure it out together. *Wheels are fracking excellent; they're freedom*, and he'd teach me how to make the most of them. "Hasn't happened yet. Of course, it's only been a couple of years, so maybe it takes some time."

"Well, that's a comforting thought."

Damien stared straight through me. "It does get easier, though. Not because the world is less cruel or life makes more sense. But because you start to realize everyone feels this way."

One of the other game devs at the booth, a pink-haired Moroccan woman in her late twenties, laughed. "He's right, you know. You think there are people who aren't constantly anxious? In this economy? No way. Anyone who tells you they aren't afraid is lying. But that's how you know you've found your people. When you can be scared together but also stronger together. And at some point, you discover if you're going to be afraid anyway, you may as well do the things that scare you."

"Thanks for your wisdom, Grandma Nour," Damien teased, and something about the way they interacted told me they'd had variations of this conversation countless of times.

Nour grinned. "You're welcome, young 'un."

Damien swirled back to me. "So ask them out."

"Cosigned," Nour added.

Now, in the dark, Ever holds me until the tension drops from my stance—and theirs as well—and I breathe out sharply.

We shouldn't stand here. We shouldn't make targets of ourselves.

"I know it's hard to trust anyone," they whisper into my shoulder.

I tremble. "Ever…"

"But pushing everyone away will only make you more vulnerable."

"You're one to talk," I mutter.

"I know."

"Would you lie to me?"

"We all lie on occasion." They grimace. "But not about anything worthwhile. And besides, that's not the point. We're not going to split the party again, because even if you don't know how to trust us yet, we have your back. We're in this together and we'll get out of this together. It seems someone put a lot of thought into terrifying us, but we can't let that get to us. Clear heads. We won't sit by and start a fight amongst ourselves."

"And then what? Walk down a mountain in the dead of night? We can't safely run away if there's anything outside waiting for us. I can't navigate those boulders in the dark." I can't help the edge of panic and impatience in my voice.

"Not on your own, but we can manage it together." They disentangle and take a step back, looking me in the eyes. "Come on, are we adventurers or not?"

I almost laugh derisively. "In a game."

"Do you trust me?"

This time, I don't hesitate. "Unconditionally."

"Then trust me with this. We go and find Carter. And then we go home."

FIFTEEN

CARTER

Going back was a ridiculous idea. I shouldn't be here. But Maddy was so upset, and it hurts me to see her hurt. I know she needs her pills, she needs something against the pain, she needs something to ease her nerves. She started talking about going back in, and I couldn't let her.

Of course, a tiny voice in the back of my mind wonders whether it's really a better idea to leave her on her own, outside, but the handprints led in too. She'll be safe outside.

She *will* be safe outside. Right?

Besides, this mountain can't be haunted for real. This doesn't happen to people like Liva. It doesn't happen to people like *me*. But it *mostly* doesn't happen to people like Liva.

As long as I keep telling myself that, a better explanation will show up. An explanation for Liva's disappearance. The blood. The fireplace.

The mountain is hungry. The night has teeth. And both demand to be paid their price in blood.

I *really* shouldn't have gone back in.

I push my hands into my pockets and find scattered coins there.

Break the rules.

I wish I still had some of the bravado from earlier. I kept thinking whoever put those coins there meant I'd lose the game we were all playing. Now I can't help but wonder: What if *this* is the game? What if Liva's disappearance is only the start of it, and we're all pawns in a ghost story, on a board we're not aware of? What if the coins weren't the warning, but the note?

Lose the game.

I pull my hands from my pockets and shrug my coat closer. The cabin creaks around me, and I run without caring what's in my way. I'd rather fall down than not try. Games aren't won by being too careful.

If I play by the rules, I'll lose too. I know that all too well.

It's why I started stealing from my work.

I didn't even want the job at first. When my father first brought up the idea of spending my afternoons and weekends there, right after sophomore year, I'd told him, "I'm not sure insurance is the career for me." I had other dreams. I wasn't sure what they were just yet, but wasn't that what college was for? Figuring yourself out?

He was adamant. My mom worked at Liva's dad's office and could get me a job. If I followed my parents' plan, I could save up before college and wouldn't drown in student debt. He told me the responsible thing for any man to do, especially in insecure times, is to secure that money early on. Anything less, according to him, would be lazy, careless, and stupid.

Ever wanted to punch him when I shared that remark with them.

I very nearly took them up on the offer.

But then I got my first paycheck. It was less than I expected, but it was still more money than my parents ever gave me. I could buy the clothes I wanted, the gifts my friends wanted. I could buy friendship itself. I barely felt out of place next to Liva—or Zac.

I grew used to it. I forgot about the idea of other dreams; they were childish anyway.

Instead, I started to pay attention and found ways to be better. I noticed I did the same work as fully salaried employees, but because I was "young" and "inexperienced" and "technically an intern," I got paid a pittance for it.

I hid when Liva walked around the floor to bring messages from her father, because everyone tensed up and she pretended not to know me. Or maybe she truly didn't see me.

I snooped around because it's easy to grow used to money and easier still to spend it all. Not the first year working there, but the second. After my parents told me I should try harder to make a good impression. After Liva breezed past me one too many times. After I graduated to another internship and still did the same work as regular employees and still wasn't paid enough for it.

I learned that playing by the rules only brings you so far, and the ones who made it furthest in the office were the ones who bent those rules to suit them.

I learned to do the same.

And no one ever noticed the books didn't add up.

It was what I had to do, I thought, if I ever wanted a life like Liva's or Zac's, with enough money to throw at problems and the ability to afford a second home. But the cabin doesn't look like a rich, welcoming place anymore. It keeps growing colder and darker.

Maybe I was wrong. Maybe this does happen to people like us. Or maybe it does happen to people like Liva.

I glance at Liva's room, which is still empty and filled with shadows.

I didn't wish this on her. Did I?

I definitely wouldn't wish it on myself, in any case. I have to keep my head down, grab Maddy's pills, and run back out.

I reach out to the handle and push her door open—and pause.

In the dim light of the hallway, something glimmers in front of the door next to Maddy's room—my door. I blink and stare, thinking at first it's a trick of my eyes or my brain, but when I stare, the shimmer is still there. And the door is ever so slightly cracked, allowing moonlight to filter out.

I take a careful step closer and reach down as far as I can. I don't want to kneel or crouch because it would leave me vulnerable. I don't want to be curious. But I am.

The wood is rough and splintered, and my fingers catch on it. Until my fingers touch the wet substance, and moonlight illuminates the ward in front of me.

Because it is a ward, exactly like the ones Ever has so often described in the game. Like the ones around the fake body we played with. Endless symbols, drawn in blood.

No. Nope. Absolutely not.

I want this twisted and messy game to be over. I want to go back to the time before. I want this not to be happening.

The moment I take a step back from the door, a shadow passes through the moonlight. Fleeting. Indistinct. A darkness in an already dark night. A bat or a curtain. A tree branch or a person.

Does it matter? Does it matter what's out there if we don't get out of here tonight?

A floorboard groans. I spin around, but nothing. I push my door open farther, to let more light filter in, but the light does nothing. Almost as though the shadows are too plentiful here to be turned away.

The wind outside sighs. The wardrobe creaks. Then another shadow, and one of the curtains tumbles down from near the window, scattering coins all over the floor. They're rolling toward me like they did when they fell out of my cloak, and it's like a nightmare.

Like being haunted by your worst decisions.

I've had enough. I'm done.

Maddy will have to do without her pills. We have to get out, now. *I* have to get out.

In my room, the mattress bounces. The bed springs squeak as if someone sat down.

And my feet remain frozen by panic and fear.

All I can see is my overly big suitcase, which is nothing more than a silent shadow. The coins on the floor are still rolling and spinning happily.

I'm convinced, I'm *convinced*, if I hold my breath I can still hear someone breathing.

Fingers pass through my hair.

My heart slams into my throat.

I take a step back, in the direction of the stairs, pushing myself close to the wall. I reach out to steady myself, and I turn to bolt.

"You're making things up again," I whisper to myself. "There's no one here."

"Wrong."

HERE'S WHAT NO ONE HAS TOLD YOU, WHAT NO ONE WILL TELL YOU. To you, this world is real. The game master weaves it around you. It's the greatest gift they can give you. They build the game. They are the game. They tweak and push and tease and draw out, to let every person who is a part of it have their challenge, to let every player shine. They create sorrow and joy and heartbreak.

But that world shivers and crumbles. Sometimes, when the game twists in unexpected ways, even the best game master can be caught off guard, and they keep the world together with well-placed words and imaginary duct tape. Sometimes, when you all lose focus, the rules fall by the wayside, and they're like tears in the fabric of that reality.

And some days, like today, the worst happens. And parts of the world crumble and break.

And the game master does too.

SIXTEEN

MADDY

M addy? C'mon, we need you to be here. For Carter. For us." Ever's soft voice helps me to get my breathing under control, but the restlessness inside me doesn't dissipate. My heart beats too loud in my ears. My hands are shaking, and my whole body has tensed to the point of pain and exhaustion. As if I've run a marathon—or as if I've run for my life. And I'm still in flight mode.

I need to understand. I just want to understand.

"Maddy." Ever keeps their voice low. Soothing. Like they're talking to a cat. "Listen to me. Focus on my voice. What do you see?"

Their hand, hovering above mine. There but not quite touching.

"What do you feel?"

The cold from the porch creep into my bones. The roughness of the wooden planks.

"What do you hear?"

The sound of crickets in the grove somewhere. The wind chimes. Finn and Ever, breathing and worrying.

"What do you smell?"

Pine. Night. My own sweat.

I start to laugh at that, without meaning to, but it's so blatantly absurd. The narrow tunnel in front of me widens, a little. Enough to see Ever sag in relief.

"Are you there?" they ask.

"Maybe." I bring my shoulders up to my ears. Clench my fists and try to slowly relax again. My throat hurts, as if I screamed for hours, but it may be a side effect from forgetting how to breathe. The world around us feels distant, as though there's a veil between us that I still need to push through. Or perhaps I can stay on this side.

I was doing so well. I hadn't had a panic attack in months, and this is my second time today. Maybe painkillers aren't a great coping mechanism, but I need the world to quieten again. The dark helps, but the fear and the anger and the worry and the pain are all too much. They push at me from the inside out.

I don't know how to deal with it, and I'm bursting at the seams.

Ever reaches out a hand to me and pulls me to my feet, Finn at their side. "We need to go find Carter," Finn says.

We do. He went back inside before I could stop him, though I can't remember the exact details. I was freaking out and pacing, and there was so much blood on my hands.

I just need the world to quiet. I rub my hands on my tunic and the dried blood feels uncomfortable and flaky.

Carter should've been back already.

"C'mon." Ever and Finn form a united front, impossibly determined to go back in.

I don't want to. I don't know what kind of shadows the cabin holds. I can't imagine I used to feel at home here.

But still. Of course I'll go in. Liva's already disappeared. I'm not about to lose Carter too. I'll go in, even if I really, really, really don't want to.

It's just one step, and then another.

Through the door. (I prop it open by putting one of the Styrofoam swords between the door and the frame. Just in case. I've hated that door since Liva and I got trapped in here that time, and I don't want that to happen again. I don't want to be here to begin with.)

Through the room, toward the staircase.

Breathe. The world around me is empty here.

We all stay within touching distance from one another, though none of us touch. Finn looks up at the stairs and yells Carter's name.

Then, nothing. No movement. No sound. No extra pair of footsteps. Just silence.

Silence.

More silence.

I ball my fists and pound my leg and the stabs of pain force me act. "Carter? Carter! Are you okay?"

No response.

Ever turns to us. "Stay put and stay close together."

Briefly, they reach out so their fingers touch Finn's. Then they square their shoulders, clench their jaw, and head into the dark hallway. I wish we would've stopped in the kitchen to grab a knife from one of the drawers. Something is wrong. Again. Everything is wrong. Constantly.

Something is waiting for us out in the darkness.

One step and then the next.

It's so cold in here. Maybe Carter found another way out, though I'm positive there's only the one door to the porch.

"I'm not sure it's a good idea to go farther in," I whisper.

"We can't leave Carter on his own," Finn says, though there's doubt in his voice too. And something else. Something I can't place.

Ever starts climbing. "We're not leaving him behind. We're not splitting the party again."

So we feel our way around because there's nothing else to do. All the doors upstairs are closed, and without a window to the outside, we have no light source.

It hits me again; all the doors upstairs are closed. Sickening unease unfurls in my stomach.

"Did you close Liva's door when you were in here?" I ask.

Ever clears their throat. "No. But maybe Carter did?"

I shake my head, though I doubt they can see it. "Let's stick close. Carter went to my room, so let's look there first."

"Do we all go in?" Finn asks. "Or do we need to keep watch while you look around the room?" He yelps quietly when Ever apparently punches him.

"If something happened to Carter, we're not sending you in alone," Ever says, and there's no arguing.

I *want* to protest. I want to tell them both to stay safe, because I don't know what to expect when I open the door. Because it's my fault Carter went back in in the first place. But they both face me with staunch determination, and I know they won't back down. It's a little easier to stand straight with the two of them at my back.

"Thank you."

Without further ado, I push the door to my room open. It creaks a little. It creates a dark, cloak-like shadow that passes over us and into the hallway.

Four candles burn in the room. They're small enough to belong to a birthday cake. They circle the bed, a good ten feet away from the door. But their combined light is so bright and unexpected, it disorients me.

They weren't here before. They don't belong.

"Carter?" My voice cracks. I lick my lips and sway back and forth on the balls of my feet.

Ever reaches out to squeeze my shoulder, and I nearly jump out of my skin.

"I'm sorry," they immediately apologize. "You looked so spooked. These weren't there before, right?"

I blink against the flickering flames. My eyes water. "No." I take a step closer to the candles and one of the floorboards creaks, gives a bit. From nearer the bed, it's obvious the candles are each stuck to a nail, to keep them steady. There are two others already snuffed out. They can't have been burning long; they're too small to last.

"Carter? Say something." My voice echoes.

My cloak doesn't hang on the wardrobe door anymore. It's spread out over the bed. I pick it up to see if it's covering anything. It's not. So I slide it on for warmth and protection.

That's when the music box starts chiming again. It's such a familiar melody. A lullaby that parents play for their children when they go to sleep. The kind of music box that grandparents keep as a souvenir from that time they went on a tour of Europe. Achingly familiar.

But it grows loud.

Louder.

Louder still.

Like someone has put a radio on blast, but all it plays are children's tunes. Wordless, melodic. Impossible to escape or ignore.

Then something crashes in the room next to mine—*Carter's* room—and the music abruptly dies on an off-key tone.

I run. Exactly like how I used to run, back when I still could. I push myself past Ever and Finn, and I *run* to get to Carter's room, to make sure he's there, he's okay, he's—

I slam into Carter's room. In it, I spot the broken music box before I see anything else. It's one of the small ones that Ever brought to the cabin to mimic the ones in the game, and it's been smashed to countless pieces against the door. It's impossible to enter the room without crunching the splinters of wood. I kick it all away as hard as I can and I try to orient myself.

There are candles here too. Also around the bed.

The covers of the bed are rumpled, and Carter's suitcase lies propped open against one of the walls. I still can't believe his parents made him drag a suitcase up a mountain, even if it doesn't necessarily *surprise* me.

"Carter? Come on, C, *answer me.*"

"Maddy, I don't think—" Ever stands in the doorway and their voice trails off. "I don't think—"

I turn to see what they're staring at. I follow their gaze.

Oh no. Oh no, no, no, no, no.

I take a step closer to the bed. It's not that it hasn't been made.

There's someone inside it.

I whimper and reach out to someone, anyone for support. Finn steps in and his shoulder bumps against mine.

In the darkness I can't see if the bed is moving. If someone's breathing.

"We'll have to pull back the covers," Finn says quietly, and all the fear and anger that laced his voice earlier is gone. There's just defeat, because we can all imagine what we'll find inside—nothing good.

I nod. "Together?"

"Yeah."

Ever walks around the bed and makes to uncover the bed from that side. They catch my eyes and nod. No point in delaying the inevitable, right? I nod too. Keep moving. Stop thinking. We pull the cover back and—

I scream.

Carter's body lies in the middle of the bed. His eyes are wide and empty. His mouth is set in a silent scream, and the mattress is red with blood. He's splayed out like Councilwoman Yester, like someone took a scene from our game and recreated it, arcane circle around him and all.

I'm going to be sick. On the other side of the bed, Ever has turned away too, and their body language is a chaos of horror. They sway. They keep themself standing only because they can lean on the bedside table.

And Finn keeps repeating the same word over and over again: "No. No. Nononononononono."

Unlike the victims in the game, Carter is real. He is our friend. He *was* our friend? He should still be here. He shouldn't have come inside. If only I'd been less of a mess, if only I'd kept my wits about me, if only…if only…if only.

On the other side of the bed, Ever sinks to the floor, and Finn immediately rushes to them, still muttering the same word.

I can't keep staring at Carter. I should close his eyes? But I don't want to reach out to him. I don't want my memory of him to be…this. I want to remember his gentle hands and the way he supported me. I don't want to touch him. For the first time in my life, I don't want to touch him.

I want to kill the person who did this. Who did this to him, and to the memory of our game. This weekend was supposed to honor it, and our friendship, and now...

Carter's left hand rests on his chest. Four of the fingers are curled around a small wooden carving of a rat, almost as though he's cradling it.

His ring finger is gone.

Unlike the victims in our game, the circle around Carter isn't drawn with magic. It's drawn with coins all around him. A piece of paper is quite literally pinned to his chest, sunk into his flesh, and I won't touch that either. I can't.

"What does it say?" Ever's voice sounds strangled. They have their arms wrapped tight around their chest.

It's only one word:

THIEF.

"Just like Liva—just like Liva's room." Finn produces a piece of paper in the same handwriting, the same bloodred words. *Liar.*

It takes everything I have not to scream again or toss all the coins from the mattress onto the floor.

"We have to get out." My voice sounds different, hollow, cold. It sounds like it doesn't belong to me. It feels like it doesn't belong to me. When no one moves immediately, I all but snarl at them, "Go. Now."

Someone—or some*thing*—is playing a twisted game with us. And they're inside this cabin. "We've got to run."

But a dull thud comes from living room down below.

And the all-too-clear sound of a lock.

SEVENTEEN

FINN

W e have to move." I reach out a hand to Ever and nearly tip
my crutch over.

Ever reacts almost instantly, grabbing it and steadying me
without hesitation. It's the simplest movement, and it's a low bar,
but outside of this group, most people don't meet it. Here, when
my crutches fall out of reach, everyone will immediately stoop
to pick them up. They grab whatever needs holding. They make
sure to walk alongside me in such a way that they don't kick my
crutches out from under me—and no one else gets the chance to
do so either.

We've changed and grown, and I've pushed them away, and they're still here.

We're all scared and frustrated, but they all still have my back.

Now, I feel emptier. As angry as I've been, I never would've wanted this for Carter and Liva.

———————

I pulled Liva into the game. And by extension, Zac.

Ever, Carter. And Maddy.

But our adventuring party started with the two of us. Ever and me, at lunch one day. Ever was a lowly freshman, and I a lowly sophomore, and we found each other because I sat in the cafeteria reading an RPG rule book, and they sat next to me. Zac passed us and scoffed, but I don't think Ever noticed it. They told me they had an idea for a role-playing game they wanted to test; I told them I wanted to be a game dev, and it was as simple as that.

Well, there was more to it, of course. They made me laugh. They stared straight through me with those piercing green eyes. They weren't awkward about my crutches. And they listened to me when I told them about my dreams for the future.

Even then, Ever was the type of person who listens so intently, they make you believe in yourself. And I wanted to believe in them.

The first time we met to play with the others, we all fell head over heels in friendship.

It was raining outside. It was a couple of weeks before winter break.

I hesitated in the doorway to the basement, where Ever was already setting up shop, but the others quickly followed. We stood around awkwardly. Two freshmen—Ever and Maddy—and four sophomores. Hands in pockets. Messing with our bags. In various stages of doubt and excitement. Not quite looking at one another, at least until Ever spoke up first.

"Welcome, adventurers." They smiled. "I always wanted to say that. Welcome to our Rune and Lore club, or as Finn wants to call it, the Gnomic Utterances Tabletop Society, a.k.a. NUTS. I'm thrilled you're all here, and I'm going to try my best not to mess this up too much. Over the next hour or so, we'll figure out how to play this game together and if you're all comfortable playing together. The system is loosely based on magic, mystery, and murder, and in my experience the best way to learn is to start playing." They motioned to the table that was set up along one of the walls. "Please, take a seat. Grab one of the dice and a character sheet, and I'll set the scene."

We all hesitated for a second longer, but there was something magnetic about the way Ever took charge. We all wanted to be here, after all. And what they said made sense; the only way to get started was to dive right in. In that way, it wasn't much different from any other game. Sure, there are rules to learn and techniques to master. But both of those things are pointless if you don't first have a feel for the ball.

Or the dice, in this case.

Ever perched on the edge of the table. "It always starts with murder." They started the story like they came to do every game. They had some note cards in their hand, but they mostly stared at us, as if they were weaving the story out of thin air.

"Welcome to Gonfalon. Welcome to the case of the deadly class."

And with that, we were off. Well, we stumbled our way through figuring out the system. The rules for magic and the rules for skill points. The rules for dice rolls and the rules for puzzles. We all started out with the same basic class, Ever explained, and we would diversify from there, letting the story guide us as we wanted to, instead of deciding everything up front. We started out as students, much like we were ourselves, though Stardust High would never ever consider classes in blood magic.

And we fell into our roles. I found myself near Maddy, who played a girl with a piracy background. I found myself figuring out Feather's heritage, and it was a wonderful experience of building a new persona and exploring parts of myself I was only partially comfortable with.

Ever checked in every so often to get a feel for the level of role play we all wanted. And before we could properly get into the case at hand, the hour and a half we had for the introduction were over, and we all had to go our separate ways. But none of us moved. We were all enthralled—or in the magisterium's words: bespelled—and we didn't want to go anywhere.

Our first WyvernCon was about three months after that first meeting, and we'd been playing together weekly for almost the entire time. You learn a lot about people when you solve murders together every week.

That is to say, we learned a lot about one another's characters.

WyvernCon was the first time the six of us took a road trip—and it was still the six of us then. Zac was there, throwing money at everything Ever couldn't afford, possibly only to piss them off. It was more complicated to be together and not only because of that. Inside our school theater, all we had to be was our characters. Sure, we brought our lives with us. Our bad days and our worries, our good days and our joys. But we met for the game, and everything else was secondary.

But WyvernCon was the first time we made a concentrated effort to hang out as friends too.

It was the first of many things.

The first time Liva made us costumes—and the first time she won the original design costume contest. Once she started designing, she started *smiling* again. She fell head over heels in love with creating, and underneath her carefully polished exterior, she was suddenly back to being the girl I'd been friends with.

The first time Ever and I met Damien (and the thousandth time I felt certain I was meant to be a game dev).

It was the first time I ever saw Ever lose their cool at anyone, when Zac laughed at an artist's zine in the artist alley—after which Zac all but ran out on us.

The first time we walked around the con until our legs were jelly, our wallets empty, our hearts full. It meant the rest of the group had to accustom themselves to my speed. Liva *also* spent money like she didn't even notice it, Carter tried to match her, and Ever spent nothing and tried not to let the others catch on.

One moment stood out brightest of all of the memories we made: when we met another gaming group—a party of four, GM'd by two girls, who led them through a cyberpunk dystopia—who sat next to us in an empty corner of the con floor, going through their loot.

Once we each realized the other group was a gaming group too, the introductions followed easily and bragging about our respective adventures was obviously the next step. They told us about hacking into a multinational company and going off-grid. We told them about going undercover in the magisterium and sniffing out spies.

I was tired and in pain, so I sat back against the wall and Ever sat next to me, and we watched it all unfold. Ever leaned into me a bit. "I've always thought this the test of a good game. Whether it withstands the stories told about it."

Liva and Carter were caught up in a heated argument with the healer of the other group. Maddy sat with one of the GMs, exchanging notes on the overlap between games and sports. And without thinking about it, I reached for Ever's hand. "It does."

Neither of us could stop smiling, not then nor on the long journey home.

We were a family. We should've been a family. But families look out for one another, and there was so much we didn't notice.

I shouldn't have come back here.

Maddy drags us onto the landing, where she holds up a hand, and *listens*. There's another dull thud. And another.

"Was that the door?" Ever asks.

She nods. "I think so."

"Do they lock at a set time?"

Maddy swallows hard. "Maybe? I don't know. I hate those locks."

Ever shakes their head. "It'd be too much of a coincidence too."

"Someone's *inside*." My voice trips and breaks, but for once, I don't mind the high tones.

We all take a step closer together. Huddle. Protect one another. But Ever shakes their head. "That doesn't make sense. It sounds like someone's pounding on the door, which they wouldn't do if they were inside, right?"

When they say that, Maddy moves forward as if she's been stung. "We have to get to the front door, now. I propped it open, just in case. I didn't like the idea that it could close behind us. Liva and I got locked in here once when her security system tripped up, and after the stuff with the fireplace, I didn't want to risk it."

"So that's a good thing, right?" Ever asks.

"It is, but the door will keep trying to close, and it will destroy the sword. So we have to get out before it does."

If the one door that leads outside closes—or if someone's between us and it—how do we get out?

I take the lead down the stairs as fast as I can manage. I'd honestly rather fall and break something than stay and get locked in. It's all a matter of priorities.

Then, the click of a lock—of multiple locks—once more.

Maddy pushes past me. "Those are the windows. Whoever tripped the fireplace must be doing this too. I don't know how. I don't particularly *care* to know how. But I'm not waiting here to figure out what else they've got up their sleeves."

Ever catches up with me, offering me a hand and a chance to lean on them.

I hesitate but stick to my crutches. Ever's the only one I would trust not to let me fall, but without being able to see much beyond our direct periphery, I'd rather trust my own instincts. "What do you think *Thief* means?" I ask them.

"What does *Liar* mean?" Ever counters. "I don't know if it's a message or a way to mess with us. I don't know if it matters."

I look past them at Maddy, who made it down the stairs and is now nothing more than a darker shadow against an abyss of shadows. The stairs seem to wind around her, making her into the eye of the storm. Still, she waits until we join her. She could run to get the door, but leaving our line of sight doesn't seem like a sensible idea anymore either. "Mad? Do you know?"

She winces and doesn't answer. "All I know is we need to get out. Come on."

EIGHTEEN

MADDY

Here's the thing. I never quite know if I'm responding the "right" way to anything happening around me. Should I be more scared? Should I be angrier? Should fear immobilize me? What happens around me and how my brain responds to it are two entirely different things, and I can't tell all the time how they're connecting.

But the grief is raw and angry and freezing cold.

Do I know what *Thief* means?

Does it matter?

Finn and Ever are whirlwinds of emotion right now. Intense,

overwhelming, and inescapable. I hate it. I don't have a healthy way to deal with them. I don't know how to. And with Ever and Finn as broken as I am, their feelings are all the more inescapable. I'm cold.

Focused. Breaking.

Carter would've been fine if he hadn't gone in to help me.

We're getting out, that's what we're doing. Everything else is secondary.

We have to stay close to one another.

I should've kept Carter close. I should've stopped him.

But somehow that makes it worse too.

We're all breaking, and I really want to dull the pain. All I want to do is to make it stop.

The pain from my knee sneaks its way up my leg and into my resolve. I've walked these stairs a few too many times today. I walked up a *mountain* today. I can hardly remember it.

And Finn's question keeps nagging at me.

"You know what the notes mean, don't you?" he says, persistent.

I bite my lip. "Not now, please."

"Is this something Carter did?"

"I don't know what's happening! We have to keep going. Now is not the time for this. If the door has closed, we'll be locked in."

The same pounding noise keeps coming from the direction of the door. It's weirdly visible, a dimly lit outline where a sliver of moonlight falls into the cabin. It's the next level stage of a video game, or the hints you get when you play in more accessible modes.

I beeline toward it—and immediately crash my knee into a chair that I could've sworn wasn't there when we walked in. The pain is sharp and angry. "*Frack.*" I can feel myself start to lose control of my breathing, and it's like I live on the edge of panic now—or the edge of anger.

There's a black hole inside my chest, and everything gets slowly pulled into it.

Carter's determination when he went back in to get my painkillers.

The first time Liva invited me here, and the blue room she decorated specially for me.

The laughter that somehow got lost between all of us.

Our joy. Our adventures. Feeling like we could save the world.

Everything tears at me, and I don't know how to respond to any of it anymore.

"Maddy? Are you okay?" Ever reaches out a hand to me, and I allow it. For a second. But instead of making me feel better, I want to take the chair and hurl it through the room. I want to take Ever and scream at them, not because of anything they did, but because of everything I did.

"I know it hurts," Ever says softly. "I wish I could fix it."

That's all I need to pull away again. They don't need to fix me. No one needs to fix anything. I need to find a way to dull the pain, but we have to keep moving. A little more careful now, because though the cabin isn't that big, it's a veritable obstacle course. Finn takes his crutches and holds them out in front of him, to make sure nothing else blocks our path.

The door keeps trying to close, as if someone rigged the automated locks. The Styrofoam sword between door and frame has been crushed to half its breadth, and if this goes on for much longer, there'll be nothing left of it.

The light from the outside becomes a little brighter, and the closer we come, the faster we move. I can all but hear the music change in the background. We're nearly out of here, and I don't know what's waiting for us outside, but it can't be worse than being stuck in a haunted cabin on a lonely mountain in the dead of the night.

If only it were that easy.

Finn is the first of us to reach the door. With his crutches, on even ground, he's faster than any of us. Now, he has to make do with being careful, but he leads the way, and I fall back because with every step, my knee is more insistent about reminding me it can't bear my weight. It's like a voice in the back of my mind, constantly telling me I can't stand straight, I'm not stable, I'm falling, I'm falling, I'm falling.

And somehow, Ever refuses to let me fall back alone, instead, matching me in stride.

But perhaps it's because we all have that singular focus—get to the door, get out of the cabin—that Finn doesn't see what's right in front of the door.

When the moonlight filters out and catches on Finn's crutches, they almost seem to gleam, especially on those spots where the color is scratched away and the metallic aluminum is visible.

But that's not the only thing that picks up the light.

Once he's reached the door, Finn stands in the middle of another arcane circle that *definitely* wasn't there when we all came back in. It's the same as the ones we used in game: a ward to protect buildings and doors from being entered.

It's the same as the one that killed Lente.

"*Finn!*" Ever and my voices mingle together. This is a warning. Whoever made it isn't done playing yet and knows our game inside out.

Finn turns his head toward us, but he's already moving to the door. It happens in slow motion. He drops one of his crutches to rest against his chest, the way he always does when he needs a free hand to hold or pick up something.

He reaches for the door *while* he turns and asks, "What's the matter?"

Ever manages to squeak out something that sounds like, "Stop!" and I'm silent altogether. It would've been too late anyway.

It occurs to me then that if someone went through all the effort to put furniture in our way and paint a magical ward around the door, they could've easily gotten rid of the fake sword that kept the door propped open. *Unless* they wanted us to reach for it.

Finn's hand touches the doorknob, and there's a flash. Something that sounds like the crackling of magic—or electricity.

He falls in slow motion too. Time slows as if, like Carter once described, the threads of time were prickly pear taffy pulled tight. Finn screams and flings away from the door, like some invisible force has picked him up and tossed him. He tilts backward. He loses his balance and stumbles and falls.

When he hits the floor with a crash, everything speeds up again.

Behind me, Ever yells or screams—and maybe I do the same because I hear an echo of voices. "Finn!"

Ever rushes toward him, and it's all I can do to hold them back. "Wait!"

Finn lies turned away from us, so tense his back arches and his legs crumple. He's pulled his arms close to his chest, and he moans.

"*What?*" Ever pulls themself away from me, but I cling to them.

"He was shocked, right? We have to make sure he's not touching any kind of electricity anymore. It would only make things worse." There's an irrational part of me that also wants to clear the magic ward before we step closer to Finn, though I know it can't have been *actual* magic.

Ever pulls me closer to Finn but seems to listen to what I say, because they check to see if Finn isn't touching the door anymore. It has to be the door. Surely you can't electrify a wall or the windows.

Once they're sure, they drop to their knees and cradle Finn close. "Finn, relax. It's okay, I've got you."

I reach for Finn's arm, the one he used to touch the doorknob, and it's still spasming slightly. A large fiery mark has appeared on his hand, like a burn mark. It's like what happened to Carter with the knob on the cabinet, but a thousand times worse. I try to get a sense of the wound, but he jerks away when I reach for it, leaving my hands empty.

"Finn." Ever's voice is more insistent. "Focus on me. Listen to me. We're going to help you. We're going to take care of you. Grab my hand and hold on tight, we're not going to let go of you."

Finn's frantic eyes focus on Ever, and with his good arm, he reaches for their hand. He squeezes so tight that it's clear Ever's uncomfortable, but it does calm him a little. "It hurts. Ever, what happened? It hurts. Oh gods, it hurts so much."

His breathing is labored, and he tries to get up, but Ever pushes him down again.

"Shhh, give it a moment."

Finn shakes his head and keeps shaking his head. "We were on our way out. We need to get out. We can't stay here and you can't stay here for me."

Ever's smile is as fake as the sword stopping the door. "We're all together. It's fine. We'll have one another's back and we'll figure out a way out as soon as you're on your feet."

"That seems dangerous." Finn apparently tries to smile, but it comes out crooked and almost like a frown. "This is not how *you* would build a dungeon, in any case."

Ever visibly, physically winces at that. "I wouldn't build a dungeon like this, ever."

"I know." Finn waves with his injured hand and bites back a string of curses. It's nothing more than mumbling.

I reach for the hand regardless and try to still him. The red looks rawer now, as though it's still burning.

"We have to find a way to cool him," I whisper.

At that, Ever turns to me and their eyes flash. Everything in their body screams worry and anger, almost mirroring Finn's own tension. I take a step back, because I don't know how else to deal with it.

They hiss, "I know you're trying to help, but it would be far more helpful if you could try some empathy and consideration. Finn is *hurt*, and not everything can be fixed."

I don't point out the obvious to them: that they suggested wanting to fix things not that long ago. That this is the smallest something that *can* be fixed, or at least made somewhat better. I don't point out how unnecessary and hurtful that empathy comment is, and they should know better than that, even if they're angry.

Ever sighs and rubs their hand over their face. It's all twisted up in frustration. "I'm sorry, that was not cool. I didn't mean—"

I push to my feet again. I wince at the pain. I keep my head down. I don't look at either Ever or Finn—although Ever immediately calls out to me—just at my own feet. I walk to where I know the kitchen is, without too many mishaps. I walk into another chair and nearly collide with a table. Something scratches underneath my feet, and I rebalance myself at the very last instant, before I twist my ankle on broken pieces of Styrofoam.

I keep walking. Because we should all stay together, but we also need to find a way to cool that burn and calm down Finn. We need a wet cloth or gauze, or at this point, a good, large knife. And the last time I checked, I'm still the only one who knows this cabin like the back of her hand.

I'll leave the door open between us.

It's not splitting the party if we stay on the same floor.

Right?

NINETEEN

FINN

I'm on fire.

The world twists and turns. It feels as though electricity is still coursing through me, like angry fireflies. I ache. Everything hurts. That's what I'm most aware of. The pain spreads from my hand and my arm through my entire body. I don't know how to move.

Living with an obnoxious, stubborn body means I learned how to fall. I learned how to break my fall. I learned how to fall and protect myself. I learned how to fall and keep breathing. I learned how to fall in such a way that I didn't break further.

But getting back up again is never easy.

Ever's hand is soft. It's an artist's hand.

I blink and try to pull the world into focus, to see them. My thoughts become clearer and clearer too.

"I'm going to try to help you up, okay?" Ever keeps their voice low, while they look at a point past me. "Maddy is grabbing something to cool your hand."

"That's a terrible idea," I whisper. It takes me two tries to get the words out right. I raise my voice. "Maddy?"

The answer comes from near the entrance to the kitchen, in another low whisper. "I'm here. I'm still here."

Ever winces. "C'mon." They get me into a half-sitting position. Three hells, the sudden movement hurts. Up is down and down is up, and I think I'm going to be sick.

I fall into them, and we both topple over. They hold me. Protect me. They help me to sit up, and there's a gleam of moisture in their eyes when I look at them.

"Are you okay?" they ask.

"I don't think so." I push myself up and crane my neck to see where Maddy's gone. "I'm not entirely sure what okay means right now."

The cold, darkened room holds no answers. My hands aren't trembling as much anymore, but I feel like I've done a few rounds with a dragon. Or been in a bar fight with an ogre.

I can deal with pain. I always have and always will. But that's familiar pain. It's the pain I can—to some degree—adapt to and understand. This is too much. Too overwhelming. What's almost as bad is that I'm bone tired. Tired enough that part of me wants to curl up and stay here, screw the consequences. It feels like my bones are made of titanium and my muscles have melted under the shock.

My burnt hand is still clawed and throbbing, and I cradle it close to me. I shouldn't have come here. I should've accepted that my role in this group was done, and left this weekend for what it was.

Ever scoops up my crutches from the floor and hands them to me. "I don't know what okay means either, but for what it's worth—and I don't know if it's worth anything—I'm glad you're here with me. I'd rather you weren't. I'd rather you were safe. But selfishly, I'm glad."

I don't know how to respond to that.

They stand in front of me, our hands touching when I take one of the crutches. They hold my crutch—and my hand—a beat longer, so tight they could bruise me. They look me over, probably to make sure I'm okay. They're close enough that I can feel their warm breath on my skin and the pounding of their heart through their fingertips.

Then, after what seems like an eternity and in the softest voice possible, they ask, "Do you think you were the next on the list?"

I open my mouth to answer when Maddy reappears at our side, juggling a wet cloth, a first aid kit, a box of matches, and a large bread knife. Her eyes are darting around the room. "I think we're all on the list. It doesn't matter who's next," she answers for me. "Give me your hand."

She slips the knife into the back waistband of her pants and pushes the first aid kit at Ever. Then, with trembling fingers, she starts to wind the cloth around my hand. It's cold to the point of freezing, and I shiver. It draws the pain from my palm and actually seems to stop the burning. It cools my head a little too.

"We should figure out bandages later, when we're out of here," Maddy whispers. "I'd rather not spend any more time here."

"We have to wait until Finn—"

"I agree, we have to get out." Ever's and my words overlap. "The question is: How?" I grasp my crutch a little tighter and stare at the door. It's still opening a smidge, and then closing again. Opening, closing. Desperate to be able to fall into the lock and secure the cabin. And it's almost as if everything crackles with electricity.

A real-life magic ward that we can't ward ourselves against.

"The windows, maybe?" Ever suggests.

Maddy has taken the first aid kit back and is rifling through it, as if she just needs something to occupy her. "The windows are reinforced. Pretty much everything in this cabin is. Liva"—her voice catches—"was afraid of bears. Or of the ghost stories. There is an override somewhere, if I'm not mistaken, but I don't know where." She finds a blister pack of pills and stares at it. It takes a moment or two before she speaks again. "We got stuck here once, two years ago. Didn't she tell you? Liva didn't want to wait until her father came up the mountain with one of their handymen to get us out of here—or maybe she didn't want to face him. So she called Zac, and he hacked the system to get us out."

I stare at Maddy, the words sending an uncomfortable tingle down my spine. Zac could hack the locking mechanism? Did he know we were here?

Ever sets their jaw. "What if we push something between the door? Like the sword, but firmer. Something that holds it open wide enough for us to dash through without touching the door or the frame."

I take another step toward the door, still keeping a respectful distance. There's a few inches between the door and the frame. "We could use my crutches," I suggest softly. "The rubber tips should be enough insulation against the electricity from the ward. I think."

Drawing in a sharp breath, I take a step forward and hold a crutch against the door. Ever gasps. Maddy drops the pack of pills. Underneath my crutch, I can almost feel the electricity crackle and reach out to me, like power building and waiting to snap. But—

Nothing.

I feel a little faint when I turn to Ev and Maddy. "I think that would work."

Ever reaches out and punches my good arm. "Why did you try that? What is wrong with you?"

I grimace. "I figured we have to get out one way or another, and I've never really been good with *not* pursuing terrible ideas."

That's a lie. It's only true in our game world. In this world, I've grown too careful. But it's easier to say this than to tell them the truth: if we don't do anything, we're trapped. Getting shocked again would've been a simple price to pay.

I incline my head toward the door. "It's heavy, though. We're going to need pressure on it to keep it open wide enough, and probably from both sides, once one of us has managed push through. It's going to take some coordinating to get all three of us through, one by one."

Ever still holds one of the crutches and looks at it speculatively. "I can do that. I can wedge it open from here, and once one of you slips through, you can be the counterbalance on the other side."

"Are you sure?"

"I'm not sure what the other options are. And this is worth a try, right?"

"You can do this."

"What do you want me to do?" Maddy has walked closer too, and she's closed the first aid kit again. With her free hand, she wipes at her cape, a repetitive motion that I'm not entirely sure she's aware of. The same flightiness is still in her eyes, and she keeps looking back at the pills. She looks small here. She's looked small since the accident, like she's lost, both in herself and the world.

I hesitate. "How are you feeling?"

She stares at me.

"How's the pain? How's your knee?"

I didn't know if she expected *that* to be the question, but after considering it, she nods. "It hurts, but I can still stand, even if I don't want to."

"Could you hold the door from the other side?" I hold up my

wrapped hand. "I'm not sure if I'm strong enough with one arm. I don't think I am."

Ever makes a choked sound, and Maddy's eyes flick toward them. "I think so. It's the best solution, right?" She licks her lips. "Do you want me to take your other crutch out? Are you okay to get out without it?"

Unless we try to open the door far enough to push chairs between it and then find an unsteady way to climb over—which doesn't sound like the best plan either—I don't see another option. We only need to get out. That's it. Three people through one door. It might be the classic RPG scenario, but it can't be that impossible, can it?

"I'll hold on to it for as long as I can, but yeah. You can catch me if I fall." I meant to say it in jest, to lighten the mood, because both Maddy and Ever look deeply worried. But I realize: I believe it. I haven't for a long time, but I trust that both Maddy and Ever will catch me when I stumble. "We'll do it together. It's the only way this is going to work."

"Okay," Maddy says. And then again, "Okay."

She and Ever share a look, and there's a story there that I don't know and can't read. But they both nod.

"*Okay.*"

At that, we all take our places. Maddy and I, right next to the door. Ever, directly opposite. Once we start pushing, we can't stop, because the Styrofoam sword will tumble out of the deadlock it's in now. Fortunately, the door swings open onto the porch, instead of into the living room, which would've made this infinitely harder. Now, all we have to do is keep the pressure on. Brace ourselves against the strength of the automated locking system—and run the first chance we get.

"Ready?" Ever asks.

I nod. "Are you?"

They set their jaw.

Maddy tenses. "What happens when we're outside, though?"

"We'll figure that out once we get there," I say. "One step at a time." I lean the crutch against her hand, so she can grab it when she sees an opportunity. Her fingers briefly touch mine as we both find the hand grip, and I make sure the crutch isn't held back by my elbow or my coat. It won't be easy to keep the door open from the outside, but at least from that point on, there'll be two of us trying. It won't just be Ever.

"Counting down," Ever says. "Three, two, one. *Let's go.*"

TWENTY

EVER

One step at a time? One *trap* at a time, more likely. There has to be something on the other side of this door too, because it's clear it isn't over yet. I'm not sure it'll ever be over. Even if we get out of here, we've lost parts of us.

Still. I take the crutch and place it against the door—and steel myself. But there's no electric shock, just the constant back-and-forth slamming of the door under my hold. I have to brace myself so I don't lose my balance.

I use the rubber tip of the crutch to find what seems to be the point with the most leverage—near the door handle—and push with all my might. I manage to make it three steps forward. The Styrofoam sword drops to the floor, mangled beyond recognition. But I can't move farther. It feels like the door is resisting the pressure, like one of those electric doors that jams when you try to push it.

"Do we need to help?" Finn asks.

No. I suck in air through my teeth. "You need to be ready to run."

With that, I yell and push.

I push because I need to get out. Maddy needs to get out. And *Finn* needs to get out. I wouldn't know what to do if any more of my friends got stuck here, and I certainly wouldn't know what to do if *he* did. So I push, because I hate that Finn can't trust us anymore and I want to prove to him—to all of us—that we're still good.

Because he has the world at his feet, and he deserves every bit of it. He deserves to be happy, because when he is, his smile lights up the universe. When he gets excited about something, he gets excited with his whole entire being. He bounces back and forth on the balls of his feet. He uses ridiculously wild gestures. He doesn't let anything stop him, and I want him to be happy like that again, I *need* him to be happy like that again, because it constantly feels like there's a fragment of my heart that's out of place when he isn't.

And I push because somewhere in the distance, Elle is waiting for me. I promised I'd be back for her two nights from now, to hear all about her weekend, all those wondrously bizarre treatises she read and the new girl on the block she wanted to hang out with. I promised to sit with her at night and tell her stories about our

Gonfalon adventures until long after she falls asleep, because she sleeps easier that way.

I push because I owe it to all of them.

And when I do, the door groans open farther. An inch. Another inch. A foot. And a half.

More moonlight filters through, giving all of us a clear path out.

"What if we push a chair against it? Something?"

I grit my teeth. "*Move.*"

"Okay." Maddy nods. She takes the crutch from Finn's hands and readies herself. At the same time, I breathe out, breathe in, and *brace*.

Maddy dives through the door, the crutch as a shield before her. Finn and I both hold our breath while she does, and she stumbles onto the porch, collapsing on hands and knees. Suddenly, I wonder if she won't get up. Or maybe she'll take the secrets she's so obviously carrying and bolt.

Some of that tension must show, because Finn takes his eyes from the door to frown at me. "A little bit longer, Ev. You've got this."

I nod, even while I can feel the door slip. "Maddy! Get up! I can't hold the door on my own much longer."

The words take an awful lot of effort, but Maddy scrambles to her feet and holds out the crutch. She takes up position next to the door, out of my line of sight, but I can see the tip of the crutch settle in right above mine—and then she pushes too. The crutch slips, and she nearly tumbles forward, but a moment later it's back in place. Trembly, wobbly, but there.

Relief shudders through me, from being proven wrong and from having some of the pressure taken off my hands.

Together, we can manage to keep the door steady longer, open it wider. Maddy is breathing heavily and Finn's eyes are wide. He's leaning hard against the wall.

"Are you ready?" I ask, between catching my breath and bracing myself again.

He stares at the door. Nods.

"Finn?"

"Yeah. Yeah, I'm good. I'm ready."

"Okay. *Go.*"

He dashes. His pace is uncertain, and he has his arms up to protect his head, but he makes it through unscathed.

Once he's out, I lose my grip on the crutch, and I'm the one to stumble. I would've been pushed back, the door slammed shut, if it hadn't been for Maddy holding it open from the outside.

She yelps. "Ever, what happened?"

"Nothing. My arms hate me."

"We need to get you out of there," Finn says.

"Hold the door as long as you can," Maddy adds, "and we'll push it from here. Just…hurry."

I nod, before I realize Maddy can't possibly see that from her vantage point, and in these shadows, probably neither can Finn. "Once more unto the breach." With that, I get ready to push myself out too.

But then, a voice echoes from another corner of the cabin. "Ever?" It's hard to tell whether it's coming from upstairs or somewhere around here. "Are you there?"

I freeze. *No.*

This can't be. This isn't happening. This can't *be happening.*

It's impossible. The voice is my sister's. It's *Elle.* But she can't be here. She shouldn't be here. I won't know what to do if she is.

"Ever, I'm scared."

Inch by excruciating inch, the crutch slips from my grasp at the sound of that voice. I'm frozen, and I don't know what to do but call back, "Elle? Where are you?"

No response.

"Ever? Did you say something?" Finn asks from outside. "Hold on, we're nearly there!"

"I don't want to be alone, Ever," Elle calls out.

I feel like I'm going to throw up as the realization hits me: I have to go back in.

"*Ever?*" Elle never screams, but the panic in her voice tears through me.

I gulp in fresh air and courage, and shout, "Hold the door open a bit longer. I need to check on—" Eldritch gods, I don't even know.

I let go of the crutch. It clatters on the wooden floor loudly, and I jump back from the noise. Outside, Maddy shouts. Finn swears.

Maddy still has her crutch wedged between herself and the door, but the constant pressure is too much for her.

The crutch slips. She screams and tries to push it forward, as a makeshift doorstop without the Styrofoam sword there, and I see it happen in slow motion.

She reaches forward, the tip moving toward me.

She overstretches, and the crutch neatly topples from her hands onto the porch.

She pushes herself between the door and the frame, to stop it herself. To save me.

Then she seems to rethink and jumps away at the last second, because that's the only right thing to do in this situation.

The door slams shut.

Finn apparently lunges for the fallen crutch because mere seconds later, he tries to smash it against the window next to the door, but it hardly seems to do anything. The sound of it is muffled now that there's a barrier between us.

I turn and walk back into the cabin, focused on the only thing that still matters.

"Elle!" She *can't* be here. She can't be. She's supposed to be at home, in bed already. Or reading one of her books until early morning, so she can spend the rest of the weekend walking around like a zombie.

"Ever? Are you there?"

I tilt my head and try to triangulate the sound. It seems to be coming from the far corner of the living room, amidst the darkest shadows of the cabin.

"Elle?"

Again, no response.

"Elle, hold on, I'm coming."

"Ever, I'm not feeling well. I'm scared."

"It's okay, I'm here," I answer. But the words tug at me, remind me of something. They wash over me like ice water.

I pause. The cabin is quiet except for the pounding of the crutch against the outside of the door, and Finn and Maddy's muffled shouting.

"I don't want to be alone, Ever."

I realize I've heard these words before.

"*Ever?*" The panic I heard the first time around is the exact same. Pitch perfect. My brain supplies a bit of the rest of the message: *They said there's a storm coming in, and I just…I'm scared, Ever. At least come home before dark, okay?*

Elle's voice has to be a recording. Specifically, a recording of the phone call we had only yesterday. And maybe it would be a relief that my baby sister isn't here, but it also means someone was there. Someone was close to her, close enough to pick up her voice. Close enough to have access to her.

I never truly believed in the idea of haunted houses—they make a great story, but I'm way too skeptical for that. Haunted houses don't leave notes. *Someone* got to my sister. Someone got to my *house*.

And whoever it was, they presumably still can.

I hate everything about this. I charge through the living room toward the sound, and I don't care if I bump into furniture. What's a few bruises now, anyway? I have to get to that recording.

"Ever? Are you there?"

"Ever, I'm not feeling well. I'm scared."

"I don't want to be alone, Ever."

"*Ever?*"

It takes me too long to find it. It comes from a music box sitting on a window frame. Not one of the ones I put there, but one remarkably similar. It's open. It's one of the ones that usually has a princess or a ballerina turning pirouettes, but here it's a carved cuckoo bird. Inside, there are endless notes and fragments of paper. And Elle's voice, looping. It's cut and pasted, but all of this was part of our phone call yesterday.

Who was there with her? Did she know she was being watched?

"Ever, I'm not feeling well. I'm scared."

"I don't want to be alone, Ever."

She *wasn't* alone, and that's the part that messes me up endlessly.

I slam the button and try to stop the recording, but instead, it morphs, slowing down and speeding up Elle's voice, drawing out her voice and compressing it. Ever? *Eeeeeeeeever?* Ever? *Ever?*

I take the music box, try to smother the microphone, and I throw it against the wall. Hard enough to shatter. I smash the pieces with the heel of my foot, until silence descends on the cabin once more.

And all that's left is a handful of notes in the same handwriting as the other two. Hardly visible, but I'm morbidly curious enough to carry them into the moonlight.

WORTHLESS, WORTHLESS, WORTHLESS.

Every one of us has a breaking point.

This is mine.

TWENTY-ONE

MADDY

I see the door close—just out of reach—every time I close my eyes. And every time I open them, I see Finn slam at the window next to it in desperation. I don't know how he keeps his balance like this. I can't imagine how much these movements are hurting him. But I also don't think he cares.

He looks at me once and the harsh lines and the intense combination of anger and utter despair cut through me. He's all angles and edges. And while I could interpret, it feels like I'm grasping at straws.

I keep doing this. I keep missing beats, and that seems to be the story of my life. Wrong moment, wrong time. Seconds, *heartbeats*, it makes all the difference, and I keep failing, again and again and again.

If I'd paid attention while driving, maybe I could've swerved to avoid the car who hit me.

If I'd paid attention when Carter went back in, I could've saved him.

If I'd paid attention when Ever let go of the door, I could've caught it.

If I'd been a bit more aware of the world around me, if I could *understand* the world around me, if I hadn't been such a failure, *if your brain just processed things the normal way, Maddy,* if, if, if, if, if.

Perhaps I simply shouldn't be here. Perhaps *I* should be the one inside. Either way, the air that felt refreshing just moments ago feels freezing now, and I'd like to disappear off the face of the earth, if I can.

Finn keeps slamming the crutch against the window. But like the door, it's locked and reinforced.

"It's some kind of safety glass," I remind him. "I'm not sure we can break through."

Finn turns and *snarls* at me. "I *know* that. You don't have to keep reminding me. Make yourself useful instead, because if we can't get Ever out, I don't know what I'll do." I don't know if he intended to say those last few words, because he's already resumed trying to break the glass.

I don't know what I can do, though. The other crutch is still inside. Ever is nowhere to be seen. What do I do? I have a bread knife and a box of matches, neither of which would do me any good. What are the other options? Pound at the windows with my hands? I'd break more easily than the glass.

Finn does too.

The rubber tip of his crutch skids off the window, and every time it does, he loses balance.

He breaks, one part at the time. First his hand slips from the crutch. Then his knee buckles. His shoulders dip. His breath is labored.

He pushes himself up again and again. There are small hairline fractures in the glass, and they seem to be enough to give him hope, but they don't grow beyond that. They don't widen.

It's just Finn. The glass. And the crutch that looks increasingly battered.

The second time his knee buckles, he drops and stays down. His shoulders are shaking.

Finn doesn't cry. I've never seen him cry. It's simply not a thing that happens. But right now, right there, he does. Quietly. He has his head down and turned away from me. He keeps himself as still as humanly possible.

But I can see the dark spots of his tears hitting the wooden planks.

There are still traces of blood too.

I stand awkwardly on the darkened porch, my hands outstretched, not knowing what comes next. I don't know what's expected from me, and it feels like my brain is constantly short-circuiting, like the door itself.

I failed him. I failed Carter. I failed them all.

I failed myself.

I *want* to know what I should do. I want to be able to do what people with normal brains expect of me. I want to cry. I want not to be frozen in terror.

I back away a step. Then another.

Then, before the rational part of my brain catches up to me and tells me what a foolish idea this is, I step off the porch and make my way toward the trees. Away from the spot where we found Liva's blood. Away from the room that holds Carter's body. Away from the cabin that tried to swallow us whole. Away from Finn, who turns and pushes himself to his feet when he realizes what I'm doing, furiously wiping at his eyes.

"Maddy! Stop!" His voice is hoarse, and I won't pretend not to hear it, but I can't listen.

Inside the grove, it'll be darker again. The world will disappear in shades of black and shadows, and maybe once it does, my head will quieten. Maybe the pain will stop. I can't, cannot, *won't* do this anymore.

"Maddy! Wait!"

I have to protect myself. I think I'll go mad if I don't, because everything inside me is shouting as hard as Finn is. The constant hum of failure and grief mixes with the heady buzz of fear and the sharp pain from my knee. Every time I close my eyes, I see all the images I'm trying to push away. The drops of blood on the porch. The look of betrayal on Finn's face. The empty nothingness in Carter's eyes. The pack of pills. Liva's proud smile when she showed us the cabin and when she showed it to me every time we visited. Her deft hands, creating.

I hear her scream. I hear Finn call out to Ever—and call out to me. I think I can maybe *still* hear him calling out to me. I hear Carter's voice, reassuring me, telling me that he will find my painkillers, that *everything will be okay, wait here, I'll be back as soon as I can. That's what friends are for, right? Don't worry, we'll sort it out.*

My feet crash through the grove. My cloak snags and tears on the branches, but I push through. I'm on my way to the lookout spot I showed Ever, and once I realize it, I come to a tumbling halt. I catch myself against one of the tree trunks, to slow my pace, and the suddenness causes my knee to twist and scream.

I scream too. My mouth closed, so I won't draw attention to myself. Until my throat hurts and I struggle to breathe.

The pain and sorrow only grow—and threaten to drown me.

I move on memory, away from the clearing but to another edge of the grove. Until I reach a point where the ground drops away. There seems to be a tear in the world, between a forest on the one hand, and a moonlit cliff on the other. I used to be afraid of heights, a lifetime ago.

I could simply step down; instead, I sit.

I lean against a tree and stare at the darkest stars and push my hands deep into the pockets of my coat. Then I hiss, pulling them out as if I, too, have been shocked.

The game isn't done yet. There is no escaping. And maybe there never will be.

Both of my pockets are filled with pills. I empty them out into the moonlit night and light up one of the matches to observe them more closely. They're exactly like the ones my doctor gave me. Exactly like the ones Carter buys for me. Blue. Round. Simple markings.

I find a small, folded note at the bottom of one of the pockets. It's folded in four, and on it, in the same handwriting as the other notes, though barely visible here, one word:

ADDICT.

It may as well have been an *Alice in Wonderland*-type note, because it's ever so clear what the subtext is here. Not just that I'm an addict—I am, aren't I? Or I could be. I never really thought of it in those terms.

But: *Eat me.*

It may be kinder than being stabbed to death or left to rot in a cabin. This is me. This is personal.

I am an addict, aren't I?

Huh.

I stare at the pills in my hands. There're enough of them that some slide from the stack and down the cliff. I tilt my hands a little. What a waste.

When my doctor prescribed me the painkillers for the first time, she gave me a firm talking to on how to use them safely. She told me she'd prescribed me the lowest effective dose and that I could only take them for a limited amount of time, only to deal with the most severe pain. I listened, nodded, and promised to follow the rules. I'd seen Finn with his painkillers; I knew how much they helped and how important it was to be responsible.

I intended to.

But it was so easy to take one. Take another.

She prescribed me enough pills for a week, which I later learned was more than the safety guidelines, especially because we didn't know yet what the lasting damage would be. But I took the pills for a couple of days and the remaining pain was minor enough that if I didn't look at the scars, I could almost pretend the accident didn't happen. I felt like I could *breathe* again. After that week, it was easy enough to convince her the pain hadn't decreased and could I please have a refill?

I started to realize that it wasn't just the pain. Once I took the pills, the world dulled. Everything wasn't quite so loud anymore, my thoughts weren't churning. I could spend whole hours just...doing nothing. I hated losing control at first, but the flip side was I didn't feel like I needed the control either.

I felt like I could fit in.

I felt like I belonged.

I could laugh with Carter whenever he came to visit. I didn't mind losing games to Sav. I didn't have to be constantly aware. The pills quieted the part of my brain that was constantly working, constantly interpreting, constantly adjusting—because if I didn't adjust, others rarely adjusted to me. I didn't have to think about what it meant to be me.

My doctor should have done something after the third refill, but perhaps she was busy or didn't realize what was happening, or perhaps she was one of those people—even medical professionals— who believe people with autism are innocent and incapable of lying. I guess all the terrible media had to work to my advantage once.

Besides, I was careful. After the first two weeks, I didn't just rely on the refills anymore. I found an old prescription bottle when I was plant-sitting at the neighbors' house. My dad still had some stored away from kidney stones, years ago. It's shocking how much people have stuffed away in their medicine cabinets that they're not aware of. And sure, I didn't know if the best-by dates affected anything—or if I built up tolerance—but it was easy enough to take that extra pill. And one more.

And one more.

Maybe the pain got worse. Maybe that's what happened.

Just one more.

I could grow to live with the pain, perhaps. In the back of my mind, I knew I didn't need them the way other people legitimately did.

But one more.

The pills I hold in my hand could last me for weeks. Or, at least a couple of them. That is, if I take them with me instead of taking them now, as is clearly the intended purpose.

Addict.

It would make life so much easier too, to just…stop. Stop the pain. Stop the fear. Stop the worries. Stop feeling alone. The pills are exactly as tempting as the person who put them there wanted them to be.

All I have to do is put my hands to my mouth.

I could.

Maybe I will.

I put my hands back into my pocket and pull away from the edge. I get to my feet and start walking in a direction, any direction, into the darkness.

I don't know yet.

TWENTY-TWO
EVER

Hey, Damien, remember when games were innocent?

We had that conversation this past WyvernCon, in part because I knew exactly what Damien would say and I needed to hear it.

He took a sip from his gigantic soda and shook his head. "First of all, what does innocent mean in this context? Neutral? Unassuming? Because if you think games ever were, I have shocking news for you. Every form of art or expression, including games, is by definition not neutral. Every world-building choice we make, whether it's including or excluding, focusing on one detail over the other, is a statement. Whether it's the puzzles we create, or what we describe as different or strange, it all matters."

In this deadly cabin, I can still see him smile at me. "If there was a neutral position, it would be as simple as including people like us in worlds—because we're clearly here in the real world, talking to one another—and somehow that's seen as the most political statement possible."

"Harmless, then," I countered.

"Harmless or not hurting? It's not a bad thing to occasionally hurt, whether it is heartache or joy or the pain that comes from discomfort. Hurt and happiness make us human, and if games can play a role in that, I can only applaud it. What brought this on?"

The same reason why I'm thinking about it now. I wanted to run a game that made my friends happy. Simply that, nothing more. Because I wanted to know that this dream I had, of designing games and building stories, actually mattered. Because I know stories have power.

"You're not really a ghost, are you?" I whisper now into the shadows. Elle's voice has dissipated and the music box has stopped playing. It's quiet. And cold, colder than it was when we were in Carter's room. And dark. The sound of my own voice is the only thing that keeps me from losing my mind completely. "It takes a whole lot of consideration to fix a cabin like a trap. It takes knowledge of our game to twist it into something so macabre."

Finn is still slamming his crutch against the window, though the sound is more intermittent now. He looks so small and broken. Behind him, where Maddy once stood, is only night.

He's alone. I have to get back to the door and find the other crutch, and try to get to him from the other side.

But I have a few more things to say to our ghost. "It's personal for you, isn't it? Why? Who are you? What have we done to you?"

I've wronged people, I'm sure. We all have. I'm not perfect, nor do I pretend to be. I try to do my best and take care of the people around me, but I can't take care of everyone and I have pushed people away to protect myself. "Was it one of us in particular? I know you think Liva is a liar, and Carter is a thief, but what does it mean? Care to elaborate?"

I don't need to know why they think I'm worthless. That one is obvious. Plenty of people do. Walk around with threadbare clothes and a DIY haircut for long enough, and people will have opinions. They look at my dad as if he doesn't treat us well, like he doesn't work long days to give us what he can. They look at my sister like she's a basket case for dreaming of going to college when she comes from a good-for-nothing family.

And me, well. My sins are clear in my presentation, aren't they? The thing is, I'm proud of who I am. I wouldn't change it for the world. But that doesn't mean the world doesn't try to change it for me.

The silence remains.

I remember Finn's suspicions and try again, a stab in the dark. "Zac?"

Nothing.

I failed Zac, I know. I held him to standards he couldn't—or didn't want to—meet. But the truth is, I wouldn't do anything differently. Asking someone to be a better person is a kindness, not a threat.

I reach in front of me while I walk, a little more careful this time. It feels as though the furniture has moved again while I had my back to it, but that's impossible. I bruise my knee against a chair, hit my elbow against a cabinet.

"Is this how Liva and Carter felt too? Did you give them time to consider your motive before they died?" The only way I can keep moving is if I make light of this situation.

I walk into Councilwoman Yester's "body" and the mess of blankets that have slid off the table and onto the floor. I try to kick out, and immediately my foot gets tangled in the fabric. It's heavy to move. Too heavy, almost.

As if there's a real body underneath my carefully placed bundle. If I kick loose too hard, it'll be uncovered.

Hands might reach out to grab me.

Empty eyes. A gaping mouth.

I scream my anger and my fear, and I *kick*.

The blankets fall loose on the floor, letting go of my feet. Fabric again, nothing more.

This is not how it was supposed to be. This is not how it was supposed to end.

Silence.

I realize the constant hammering sound has stopped, and when I look toward the window, it's empty. Finn is gone. *Finn is gone.*

No.

I dash toward it. He can't be gone. What happened?

Finn is my home. Outside of Elle and my dad, he's the closest thing I have to family. He understands me in ways they never could, even with all the secrets I've kept.

The cabin grows colder around me, and I don't know whether it's the actual temperature or my fear that chills me to the bone—and deeper.

I should've told Finn my secrets, both the ones that I was afraid of and the ones I was ashamed of. I should've held him more often.

I should've held Elle more often too. I should've protected her from the world whenever I could, and done a better job preparing her for life, even if it wasn't necessarily my job to do so. I could have. I should have.

I don't want to die with that regret in my heart. And I don't want Finn to be gone without having told him everything that haunts my heart and my head.

There's a magnificent crash.

I leap back, my heart hammering.

A hand grabs hold of the window frame. Then another. It's red and raw.

I take a step back—not that that'll do me any good while I'm trapped here.

Then Finn reappears. His light hair shines silver in the moonlight, as he pulls himself to his feet. A bruise forms on his head and his hands are trembling. If he goes any paler, he might become translucent—or phosphorescent.

I fell, he mouths.

Oh. I don't know what to say. Fear and relief surge through me with equal strength. Enough that when I try to draw breath, my voice catches and I tear up instead.

Finn is there, and his eyes are trained on me, and he presses his palm against the glass.

It's not warded then. Not electrified.

In my absurd relief, somehow that's what my brain snags on.

I kick a puzzle box out of the way. It breaks with a sharp crash, and I push closer to Finn. Until I'm close enough to also reach the window, to press my hand against it from this side and try to hold him.

It's not comforting to have him so near and not to be able to feel him, but it helps to be able to look into his eyes and know he's still standing, know he's still breathing, know he's still trying to get me out.

There's so much I want to tell him.

I move away from the window and look around for the crutch I'd dropped by the door. My brain runs wild. Every time I kick against something, I'm equal parts sure it's the crutch or a trap.

"We'll figure out a way out of here," I tell the darkness in my game-master voice. "I won't let you win. We've faced down the world before and didn't let it break us, and we won't let you break us either." My poker face is on. I may be lying, but at this point, does that matter?

It takes me the better part of an eternity before I stumble across a lone metallic something. When I accidentally kick it, it clatters.

I crouch down and reach for it, until I have a hold. The crutch is a bit battered from being tossed, the edges of the hand grips sharper than before, but I can make do.

I hold it up to Finn. "Okay if I smash it?" I shout.

He tilts his head, then nods. "*Please.*"

We set to work, hammering at the window with the crutches, like we're Snow White's dwarves or goblins in a mine. There's a methodical rhythm to it. Finn, then me. Finn, then me. I've never been more grateful for all those hours lugging boxes full of books around at the store, because while the work is hard, and I'm shivering, I can keep it up.

But the cabin grows colder and outside the shadows lengthen. In order to focus on breaking the window, I have to stop talking to the darkness. The silence and emptiness is yawning, threatening to swallow me whole. The smashing of the crutches doesn't change that.

It sounds like someone behind me is laughing.

A breath of air dances across my neck and sets my hair on end.

Ever, I'm not feeling well. I'm scared.

I don't want to be alone, Ever.

Worthless.

Worthless.

Worthless.

The crutch slips under my fingers. I have to keep my head in the game. It's only a cabin, there's nothing here. It's only a collection of logs and memories. That's all this place is and nothing more.

And it is said all the cabins are haunted by the killed—or the killers. The mountain is hungry. The night has teeth.

Raise the crutch, I tell myself. *Keep hitting the window.*

Keep the rhythm. Finn, me, Finn, me.

But no matter what we do, nothing changes.

Maybe I should stay here.

The worst we can do to the glass, it seems, is create some hairline fractures. I pull the crutch away and pound my fist at it, but it still feels as whole and unbreakable as it did when we started. Why won't it crack?

"Finn," I say, resigned, "it isn't going to work."

He doesn't hear me, or he pretends not to hear me. He keeps pulling himself upright, though his hands are trembling.

And I know: as long as we keep trying to get me out, he's a target.

"*Finn!*"

He shakes his head, hard. "I can't hear you, Ev."

"You can."

"No."

I take a wavering breath. "I'm going to stop."

"You can't stop me. Try to come out and *stop me*." There's a hint of panic to his voice.

I love him for being here and I hate him for it, because I need him to save himself. He shouldn't be here, not for me. "Finn, you have to leave. I don't know what's waiting for us in the woods, but you have to get down the mountain and *go home*." I pull my cloak a little closer around me. I cradle the crutch closer too.

Finn keeps shaking his head. "*No*."

I place my palm against the window, once more. And all the words I want to say, everything I want to tell him, coalesces in two words: "I'm sorry."

TWENTY-THREE
FINN

N^{o.} *No.*

This can't be happening. This can't be happening. Not to Carter. Not to Liva. Not to Ever.

Especially not to Ever. Never to Ever. I want all my friends to be safe. I don't know what I would do without them, but I don't know how to *breathe* without Ever.

The two of us celebrated my admission to Drexel together. I picked Ever up from Paper Hearts to go clothes shopping for WyvernCon. Liva was already working on our costumes, of course, but with a three-day con, we usually spent at least one day in regular clothes. In Ever's case that meant geeky hand-me-downs and modified basics. For me, it was a chic variant of thrift-store goth. I wanted some more weird, quirky black clothes for my wardrobe and was keeping an eye out for lace and velvets.

Mrs. Akashi, who owns the thrift store, always keeps the best pieces aside for me. She knows my tastes exactly and has a good eye for my figure; she finds me clothes that are flattering regardless of whether or not I'm wearing my binder. Mrs. Akashi knows that clothes are a form of radical expression and dressing in all black isn't scary, but creative. That I refuse to let the world push me into conforming, no matter how much being different occasionally hurts.

My goth style has never been just about the dark or the macabre or the makeup or the music I listen to. It is about discovering my taste and finding a piece of me. And it happens to have a small community built into it. Not so much at school, but definitely online and at cons.

That day, Ever convinced me to try on all the clothes Mrs. Akashi kept aside for me, even the ones I wasn't immediately sure about. Meanwhile, they made their way through the store like an adventuring party looting a dungeon. They picked out suits and dresses, racerback tops and the odd black-and-blue kilt. And every time I changed into a new outfit, they did so too. They took pictures of both of us to send to Damien, to show off my new looks before the con.

They didn't care one bit about how they looked. And I found them gorgeous no matter what they were wearing. I was quite partial to the last option, though: a suit jacket, a blue graphic top, and a kilt, with a bow tie to top it off. The look was far more extreme than anything they'd worn before, but it was made for them. They were positively radiant.

But when I offered to buy the outfit for them as an early birthday present, they made a weird expression, took the clothes off, and handed them back to Mrs. Akashi. "No, thank you. I appreciate it, but...no."

"This outfit was *made* for you."

"I don't think that's how thrift stores work, Finn."

"Ev—"

"*No.*" An unsteady breath. "No, thank you."

Mrs. Akashi tried to convince them too, but to no avail.

After the thrift store, I insisted on buying both of us disgustingly sweet cookie dough lattes, and they told me why they'd refused.

Ever stared down at their coffee. "When you said that, I realized you won't be in town anymore for my next birthday."

"I…" Right.

"Yeah." They stirred the drink listlessly.

"I didn't even think—"

"And you shouldn't have to." They picked up the cup, set it down again, and looked at me. Straight on. "I'm sorry. I'm *so proud* of you, and I don't want this to be about me. Let's celebrate you right now, okay?"

"You could come hang out?" I offer.

They shot me a crooked smile. "I'd love that, but we both know that's not going to happen. It's not only about the money. I can't abandon Elle."

Suddenly, briefly, I hated the prospect of college. I hated the idea of leaving and not being able to fix things for them or make life fairer.

I hated the idea of never properly being able to try *us*.

"You'll still be my best friend forever, right?" I asked, my stomach fluttering.

They reached out a hand and curled their fingers around mine. "Always."

"And it's only a year. You'll finish high school soon enough, and then you can come hang out. We'll take over the East Coast together. Both do internships for Damien, and you can get your game design degree, and I can develop everything you imagine." They wanted to focus more on the tabletop gaming side of things, and maybe try their hand at writing. I could only see endless opportunities to work together.

They couldn't meet my eye, but they attempted another smile. "You're my favorite person in the whole wide world. And I'm happy for you. I truly am. Don't think less of me for being selfish?"

I took a gigantic sip of my drink, because it was the only way to get rid of the sudden lump in my throat. "Never. And I will always try to be here for whatever you need. If not physically, then at least on here." I tapped my phone.

"For now."

I shook my head. "Forever."

Later that night, I told them the thing I love most about games is how everything is malleable, and every story seems to have a happy ending. The idea of a neatly wrapped-up third act, a perfect bow on things, was always comforting. And for life to not be like that felt like a betrayal, even if we should perhaps know better.

It's a betrayal. Especially now.

I never ever told them how I feel. I told Liva, over stolen drinks, once. I told Damien.

But I never told Ever.

And I *refuse* to have missed my chance.

I gulp in the scent of pine and the starlit air. I shake the splinters from my crutch, and push myself back on my feet. "Ever!" I don't know how clearly my voice makes it through the window. "We're not giving up. Stand back."

They nod and when they look up with a tearstained face, it only spurs me on more.

I've never seen Ever cry before. They were always the strong and stoic one, able to bear anything, no matter how hard. But now they're breaking, and it breaks me too. I want to be able to reach through the window and hold them, take what's hurting them and shield them from it.

So I won't accept this. I'm *not* accepting it.

"Finn, you need to go," Ever says again, their voice faint through the glass. Or perhaps it's because we're both tired and afraid.

"I'm not going anywhere."

"I need you to be safe. I can't lose you too."

"And I need us together."

They push their hand against the glass and then they back away, still within my sights, but where they'll be safe if I manage to break through.

I never told Ever how I felt, out of fear of rejection, fear of losing their friendship, fear of the two of us not being compatible. Out of *fear*. I forever thought, "I'll tell them tomorrow."

I still want that tomorrow, and all the tomorrows after.

"Ev, when we get out of here…" I angle my crutch again and slam it into the window. Once. Twice. Three times. Every time it connects, a dull shock echoes through my arms and shoulders, but the glass doesn't budge.

"Yes?"

"Let's do something fun, together."

"Something fun?" Ever asks softly.

"We can go to the observatory, or we can go ghost hunting in the Monte Vista. We can go to one of the farmers' markets or one of the summer festivals in the city. Even if it's only an afternoon."

I try my best not to ramble, and spectacularly fail. I glance around me for rocks or anything sharp enough to cut, to smash through the glass. Something that's harder than the rubber tip of my crutch. But without a good light source, it would take too much time to find.

I don't want to leave Ever on their own, without someone to look over their shoulder and make sure there's no one else in the cabin with them.

A small part of me wants to rush the window like in the movies. It wouldn't help. It would only make things worse. But I may not be thinking clearly right now.

The truth is, it terrifies me to stare into the empty void behind Ever. It's like looking in a mirror when you're home alone and you're *waiting* for someone to appear in the reflection behind you.

And it does feel like that's what we're waiting for. And if someone doesn't pop up inside, then they might somewhere behind me. I aggressively ignore any sounds around me. Rustling in the grove? Nah, not happening. The sound of birds overhead? Nature, nothing more. Calls and crushing leaves? Animals, surely.

There's only Ever. Ever is the only one who matters right now.

They don't respond to me, so I nudge, "Ev?"

Their head lowers. "But after the summer, you're still going to leave."

I try slamming the crutch against the window again. "Yeah. But that doesn't mean I won't always be here for you."

"Good. I want you to leave. I mean. That's not what I mean. I want you to go to college."

"But I also really want to take you out."

"On a *date*?" Ever's voice trips and breaks. "We only have so much time left."

I can't help it, I *laugh*. "Even if it's only for the summer and nothing more. It seems to me we'll never know how much time we have. Happiness for brief moments is worth it too."

But instead of leaning closer to me, they push away. "I don't know how I could handle that."

I'm going to try to break that glass, even if it takes me until the sun rises, even if I make myself a target by staying here instead of running.

This will not be where it ends.

TWENTY-FOUR

MADDY

don't know how I made it to the edge of the grove, but somehow I did. The very same spot where Ever and I talked…was it only a couple of hours ago? My once-upon-a-time favorite place.

I'm disconnected from the world, and not of my own volition.

In the dim light of the moon, I can see my feet amidst the undergrowth, but I don't feel like I'm walking on solid ground. I can move my hands in front of my eyes, but I might as well be a puppet on a string.

All that's left of us are the endless miles of mountain and the city on a distant horizon.

Something crashes through the trees, and I still, rooted in the ground. My hands stop flapping.

A branch snaps. A clean break through the night.

The leaves rustle on the other side of me.

I make myself smaller and slowly push my hands into my pockets, but the pills in them burn my hands like embers. They're tempting me, and I'm sure that's the point of it. I'm next on the list, aren't I? Liar. Thief. Addict.

Someone giggles. It drifts on the wind, not far from me.

I try to look everywhere at once, and see nothing. "Who's there?"

The laughter Ever and I heard might've been coyotes, but as far as I know, no animals *giggle*. When I settle again, a small wooden squirrel sits next to me.

I react immediately, without thinking. I send the figurine flying away from me, into the night.

I push my back against a tree, away from the cliff's edge that slices between the grove and the world.

"Stop it." I would squeeze my eyes shut if I thought it would make the world go away. "Stop it, stop it, stop it."

Near my feet, something moves. I push back more, folding all the way in on myself. And something slithers away.

Laughter.

Liar. Thief. Addict.

It's so tempting to swallow the pills and let the darkness take me.

Embrace oblivion. It's so tempting to stop running and accept there's no other way to let the pain end.

That night in January, when I'd asked Carter if he could find a way to help, he said, "Are you sure you need the pills?"

I had the prescription my doctor gave me, but by then, it didn't feel like enough. The maximum daily dose could barely mask the physical pain, and if I took them all quickly, she would ask questions. Or the pharmacist would.

There were ways to get more pills off the internet, but they were expensive, and I didn't have a clue if they were legitimate.

Once upon a time, I would've meticulously researched options, like I did with everything else. I would've tried to figure out how the drug worked and why, and how I could *understand* it. Like I did with sports. Or with people. At some point, though, that didn't matter anymore. Every time I closed my eyes, I saw the edges of my vision dissolve into flames. While I could mask the physical pain of my knee being torn and twisted, I still felt hurt all the time.

So why not give this a try and see what happened?

"I'm sure," I told Carter. "I do." We sat on the bleachers near the lacrosse field, though it was empty and the sky already darkening.

He hesitated.

"I promise I'll be careful," I lied, because I didn't know how to tell him the truth.

We sat there so quietly that a gaggle of maybe five or so middle schoolers didn't see us. They ran onto the field and chased after one another effortlessly. And right there and then, I hated them for it.

Carter nodded slowly. "I have to figure out a way to get more cash," he said, "but I can manage it."

I side-eyed him.

He shrugged. "Don't ask."

"I won't."

I expected him to relax at that, roll his shoulders back, stretch his legs. He didn't. He merely stared back over the field. "Look at how young and innocent they are."

"Sure, Old Man Carter."

"We were dating in middle school."

"We were terrible at it," I comment.

He laughs and shakes his head. "I wish we could've been better at it."

I didn't know what to say to that, and he didn't elaborate. After that day, I never asked about the money, and he never argued that I shouldn't take the pills, and it was as simple as that.

I wish he would've argued more. I wish I would've asked. But we were both messed up and messing up, and neither one of us was in a position to tell the other to stop it.

So no, I don't know what *Thief* means. I can guess. I could guess, back then. But I didn't want to know. In the light of all of that he did for me, all that he meant to me, why would I betray his trust? He was a good friend to me, and look where it got him.

Now, in the grove, I take a handful of pills out of my pocket once more and stare at them. They're so small, and at the same time, they're everything.

I didn't used to be like this. "Maddy before the accident" felt stronger. More sure of the world and her place in it. And somehow I lost all of that.

I truly needed the painkillers at first. I wouldn't have made it through those first weeks without them; the pain was too intense and all-consuming. If the pain had stayed on those levels, I still would've needed the pills to do what they are supposed to—kill it.

But no one—not the doctor, not my parents, not my sister, not me—took into account that life as I knew it was ripped apart by the accident. The pills didn't just kill the physical pain; they killed the emotional pain.

No one noticed.

How could they notice? I've grown very adept at lying.

And I *know* it's not my fault, not precisely.

Addiction doesn't work like that. Trauma doesn't work like that. Depression doesn't work like that. I know all about how human and neurotypical emotions are supposed to work.

Figure out the details, learn the language, learn the scripts.

The pills are warm to the touch now. If I keep holding on to them, they'll melt in my hand. Maybe that's the way to go?

I don't know how to get out of here alone.

Nothing would've been different, if Carter had said no that night in January. Except we wouldn't have grown so close.

I don't blame him for helping me; I could never.

I blame him for not being here. Because I really need a hand to hold.

Because I really want him to tell me it will all be okay. And I really want to tell him that I can survive this, that I can find a way.

The pills in my hand stick together. By this point, I usually swallow them. Often, I realize I don't have any water near, and I can't be bothered to get some and just swallow them dry. It's easy to grow skilled at swallowing pills.

I ball my fist around them.

The laughter has died away, but it doesn't make me feel better.

I want my best friend to be here.

But he's not. So I speak the words into the night instead. "Hey, C, remember that time at WyvernCon when we spotted those *Mask of Shadows* cosplayers, and we both immediately crushed on them?"

The words come out unbidden, soft, necessary.

"You on Sal and me on Maud. Neither of us knew if they would be into hanging out, and we were both worried they'd hate us for asking. We decided our best course of action was to admire them from afar, until Ever called us a bunch of bisexual disasters—which may or may not have been the case, but c'mon, it was rich coming from them. You walked up and ask Maud out for me, and the only thing I could do was ask Sal out for you, and we ended up on the most awkward double date in history. Later that night you said—"

I gulp in a fresh breath of air, a little light-headed.

"You said it's easier to do things that are scary when you're doing them for friends. It's easier to fight manticores when you're fighting them together. It's easier to run into a dungeon when you know there's someone waiting on the other side. And I know we were always far better at friends, but that was the night I understood what you meant when you said you wished we'd been better at dating."

I should never have picked charisma as my dump stat, he'd said, holding me and laughing so hard at how awkward the night was.

At least we picked our adventuring companions well.

I've started to squeeze the pills so hard, it's a miracle they haven't been crushed.

"I want you to be there at the other side, C. I need you to be here, so we're together, at the end of all things. And I don't know how to accept that you're not. Even if I make it down this mountain, I don't know how to accept that you won't be there, waiting for me. To make terrible decisions with me. To find a way for us both to heal. I don't know how to get out of here without you."

I sniff, and with my free hand, I aggressively wipe at my eyes. "If I somehow manage to walk away from this nightmare of a night, what do I do, then? I don't want to fail anymore. I don't want to be afraid anymore. I want the world to make sense again, or as much sense as it ever did. I want to feel like myself again, and I want you to be a part of that."

I take the fist with the pills and pound against my leg, harder and harder, until it's sure to leave bruises, because it's the only way to keep myself focused—and present.

It's so much easier to be brave in-game than it is to be brave out here.

And Carter doesn't reply. He can't. He never will again. Same for Liva.

This pain is so much. It's enough to make me want to stop. Give up. I don't know how to face more loss.

But it's also exactly why I don't want to. Because both Liva and Carter would be disappointed in me. Liva would scoff and tell me to be better than everyone who ever laughed at me, who ever told me I couldn't do something. Even if that includes myself. And Carter would hold my hand and storm into the fray for me—and with me.

I just need to take the first step, because it's all I can do right now.

One step.

Just one.

I unfurl my fist and stare at the pills. They stick together and to the palm of my hand and look so deeply, incredibly tempting.

I bite my tongue so hard, I taste blood.

Then I tip my hand over and let the pills scatter on the moss under my feet.

One step.

Just one.

I turn my back on the brightly lit city below, and all the emptiness it now holds, the parts of us it will miss, and I start back toward the cabin.

The only way through is together.

TWENTY-FIVE

EVER

C racks are starting to show. In the glass. In Finn. He is trembling, and it seems the only thing that keeps him standing is sheer willpower.

I hate that he doesn't leave, that he doesn't find his way to safety, but at the same time, I get it. I would've done the same for any of them. Especially for him.

Still, I can't help but look over his shoulder, because it's the only thing I can do. With every rustle of the wind, I expect to see something, and that only makes it harder. The terror itself might kill me.

When a shadow appears from the tree line, I yell and pound the glass.

Finn startles, and I point, though I don't know how much he can see. "Behind you!"

He immediately spins around, his back blocking my view.

I can't see what's happening. There's a rapid shift in his body language.

Shock.

Fear.

Then, relief. *Maddy.*

He steps away, and Maddy climbs onto the porch. She holds up her hands like she's afraid he might charge her if she doesn't, and briefly, I think that isn't such a bad idea. Then she says something and gestures to the crutch, and Finn steps aside, relieved.

She picks up the crutch and with renewed force starts slamming the glass, until both she is shaking and sweating, though the summer night is cool.

The cracks dance over the window like stars.

Then, miraculously, it shatters with a deafening roar.

Without pause, I tear off pieces of my tunic and wrap them around my hands, pushing sharp shards out. I throw Finn's second crutch out.

"*Ever.*" Finn reaches in, and his voice shakes as much as his hands. He doesn't seem to mind that the glass tears at him, but instead, reaches for me and I reach for him. He helps me through the window and then somehow, someway, we're in each other's arms. We're both scratched up and bleeding. And it feels so good to hold him, to breathe in the familiar scent, to feel his hair and his presence.

He holds me as though he can't be sure I'm really here.

I could cling to Finn and never ever let go.

"I'm sorry," Maddy starts, before we pull her in too, and she tenses but she doesn't disengage. The three of us hold one another and form our own shield against the world.

Of course, we can hardly keep it out forever.

"Are you okay?" I ask.

Her answer is a simple, muffled, "No."

"We have to keep moving. We have to get off this mountain." Finn disentangles and says what we're all thinking.

"Do you think that'll be enough to end it?" Maddy asks.

He shrugs. "Maybe. Probably not."

I grow cold again all over. "It has to be someone we know," I say, detailing the recording with Elle's voice. "I wouldn't have gone back for any other reason than the idea that someone might still be here. So everything about this...it's too personal. Everything is designed to hurt us."

Maddy's eyes go to the ground. "You don't believe it's either of us, do you?"

I stare at Maddy before I answer her question. I could have. I did. But what use is it to angle for other people's secrets when I've never shared my own? Their actions have proven they couldn't have been a part of it. "You wouldn't be here if it were you, now would you?"

She seems to shrink in on herself. "But *who*? I didn't think we'd have enemies."

"I didn't think so either, but maybe we do."

"Who, then?" Finn demands.

I open my mouth and close it again. *Zac* was nothing more than an educated guess. Aside from those of us here—and no longer here—he's the only one who knows our game well enough. He's the only one who might be angry enough about how things ended. "Let's move. We can figure it out once we're safe, or—"

"The moment they strike again," Finn supplies.

"Well, yeah. Are you okay to walk down the mountain?"

He winces. "It doesn't seem like I have much choice, do I?"

"Outside of the boulders, the road should be clear enough for both of us," Maddy says.

Finn nods. He licks his lips and glances at me. "Stay close to me?"

If it were up to me, I'd hold hands with both of them the entire way down, but I realize that's less than practical. "Always. We're here together. We'll go into the woods, and out of the woods, and down the mountain, and be home before sunrise."

He smiles at that.

The fresh air clears my head a little, makes it easier to think again, though the fear and anger don't wear off. It's brighter outside than it was in the cabin; the moon and stars give the world a dark blue hue.

Maddy leads us to the path because she knows the way best, and she has a memory for these things. She'd found a box of matches in the kitchen, and lights them occasionally to illuminate our path. It's not much, but it's more than nothing.

Still, we're miles away from civilization, and I can't help but feel we are well and truly adventurers now, in ways I'd never wanted to know. In games, I can narrate tension and loneliness, but I don't want to feel it. I can recreate grief, but I don't want to feel it weigh me down. Now it does. With every step away, I'm motivated by fear and pulled back by loyalty. Elle is waiting for me, and I *need* to get to her. But I don't want to leave Carter and Liva behind. That doesn't feel right. It doesn't feel real.

I might as well be in an alternate place, an alternate universe, an alternate story.

Maddy leads the way. We're circling around the cabin to reorient ourselves, because the pine grove is thick and there is no identifiable path here, when Maddy hisses.

"Stop."

She takes a step back and simultaneously lights a match. A thin wire peeks out from the undergrowth, at ankle height. "Want me to trip it?" she mutters.

"Please."

We all take a step back, and Maddy hooks her bread knife under the trip wire and brings it up. The wire breaks with an audible snap.

There's a beat.

A branch swings across the path like a morning star.

None of us quite know what to say. "I'm glad you saw that, Mad," I offer.

She shrugs. "Let's keep moving."

So we do, our eyes on the ground and our arms around one another.

There are no perception checks here, only luck and skill.

"I've think I've found the path," Finn whispers. He crouches down and rakes his fingers through the dirt and gravel. The trees seem to bend over him and watch while he tries to orient himself. There are so many shadows between the leaves and branches, there could very well be a dozen eyes watching us.

Maddy steps forward, matches in her hand, and starts walking in the direction Finn indicated. She moves slowly, checking for any more trip wires. When the path doesn't stop after another few steps, she gives us a thumbs-up. This will lead us to the parking spot we could no longer use, and from there, to the road.

I look over my shoulder every three steps, and so does everyone else. All three of us pretend not to notice how on edge we are. But Maddy's question keeps haunting me, bouncing around in the back of my mind.

Do I think going down the mountain will be enough to end it?

Frankly, if whoever targeted them in the cabin didn't get us there, we *haven't* seen the end of it yet. I don't plan on voicing that thought to the other two just yet, of course. I'm not that cruel; we all need a moment to pretend we're safe.

But Liva and Carter are both gone.

I was supposed to remain stuck in that cabin—to disappear too.

Maddy and Finn are left.

We're not done yet.

Still, we pass the imaginary boundary between Gonfalon and the real world, the cabin ground and the rest of the mountain, and something about that feels important. Like there is a world out there that still matters and is still waiting for us, even if it's a lifetime away.

We'll find a way home. We have miles to go yet, but it's a start.

"One step in front of the other," Finn whispers, probably as much to himself as to any of us. His crutches are a bit wonky after the punishment they got punching through glass. But they keep him upright enough.

"We'll be home soon," Maddy adds. "We'll sleep in our own beds tomorrow. My sister is waiting for me, and there's no one I would love to hate more right now. Your computer is there, Finn, with all the endless codes you've written and all the endless worlds you've built. Ever, your stories. It's all only a mountain away. We've walked this path before. We can do it again." By the end of her impromptu speech, her words are slurring with worry and exhaustion setting in, but I appreciate what she tried to do.

And it helped. To some degree, it helped.

Down this mountain, Elle is waiting for me, alone in our too-small shared bed. Dad is still sleeping. At four, he'll have to get up to go to his first job. Though our house is cold, the kitchen semi-dysfunctional, and often it's as dark as the cabin was, if I had to choose between them, I wouldn't trade my home for the world. It's not perfect, and honestly, the feeling probably won't last. Whether it's two days, two weeks, or two months from now, I'll go back to longing for functioning appliances, warmth when the nights get colder, fewer worries, and plenty of food in the fridge. It's not romantic to lack those things, though plenty of people with money are enthralled by the idea of poverty. But Elle is there, and that alone is worth immeasurably more than hardwood floors and carpets so thick you can sleep on them.

"I didn't anticipate the weekend would go like this. That the day would go like this." My voice is ragged and I pause to breathe between every few words.

Finn leans into me. "I don't think any of us did, but we're on our way home now."

"I wanted this to be good for you." Apparently, pain and exhaustion destroy my lack of self-control. But it's okay. I need him to know that. We're not down the mountain yet, and even if we were…I need him to know that.

"Anything you do is good for me."

"That makes no sense."

Finn laughs. Not audibly, but I can feel it in the way he breathes, in the way his chest rises and falls. "I don't think anything makes sense anymore."

"Good point."

We're silent for a while, though the pine grove around us isn't. Owls hoot, leaves rustle, and foxes yap. Weirdly, it's comforting. Actual silence would be too much to bear right now.

Step for step, we make our way through the woods and the foliage becomes less dense. The space between trees opens up into a barren landscape. Above us, the moon shines bright enough to turn humans into werewolves, and every blinking star is a gateway to a magic world.

I glance at Finn every other step. To make sure he's here. To make sure *I'm* here.

To finally figure out what I want to say to him—before it's too late again.

Because even while we make our way down the mountain, I want to do more than walk away from this nightmare. I want to walk toward something. I need to know there is good on the other side of this night.

THE CASTLE'S LONELINESS WAS CHARMING, AT FIRST, BEFORE YOU *discovered its secrets. Now you're simply too far from the magisterium to be at ease.*

After the first trap was triggered, all the doors around you seemed to be dangerous. Now, you check for traps as best you can, but your hands are shaking. It's so much easier to dismantle them when you're unscathed and convinced nothing will ever harm you. It's easiest to believe you're invincible while you still are.

But survival is your strongest skill. You decide the best way to dismantle traps is to force them, with crutches to help you keep a safe distance. You open doors, despite not knowing what lies beyond them, because you have to get through. You face the shadows to get to the light on the other side.

And you've done this before. You've scouted out locations, tracked your way through dark forests, survived. You plan to survive here.

More than that, you plan to live.

TWENTY-SIX

FINN

I glance sideways at Ever. I want to hold on to them and never let go. And I know what Damien would say: *What are you waiting for, you nerd?*

But before I can open my mouth to say anything, they speak up first. Their voice is so quiet, I have to strain to hear what they're saying.

"I thought I'd lost you."

Then, "I thought I'd lost *us*. Before we even had the chance to try to figure out what 'us' means. I don't want there to be so many unspoken words between us. I don't want there to be secrets between us. When we're home, when we're safe and we've made sense of it all…" They start. Swallow.

"We *will* make it out of here," I offer.

They shake their head. "Before you leave for college, rather…"

"Ever."

They stop talking.

"You don't have to try to say any of this right now. We'll have time."

"You don't know that."

"We'll make it. We'll claim it. We'll carve it out of the universe itself if we have to." Maybe if I can convince them, I can convince myself too.

They draw in a deep breath. "Don't let me be afraid."

I blink.

"I don't have the words you deserve. Not here. Not now. I don't know how to share the worst parts of me, because I never have. And maybe that's why I don't know how to share the better parts either, but I want to. Don't let my fear stop me from trying?" They glance at me and glance away again. And all I want to do is take them in my arms and never let go.

"Ev." I reach out and hold their hand. "We're walking down a haunted mountain in the dead of the night. There's *nothing* that can stop you."

We step out of the tree cover and onto the barren mountain slope. It looks so different at night. The sunflowers seem to be sleeping, though their yellow leaves still reflect the moonshine. They're slowly turning east, to where the sun will rise hours from now. Beyond it, the lava bed appears like a black hole on the side of the mountain. It's hard to tell where the edges are, and to me, it seems it devours all light.

Beyond both, Flagstaff. And north of it, Stardust. The small, suburban community we call home. Where I will happily tell Ever I want to spend the rest of the summer with them, even if it means sitting inside the bookshop when they work until the owners throw me out.

But first, the road stretches out before us. Blocked. Cracked. Broken. Almost three miles to go. It might as well be three marathons. As soon as we leave the tree line behind, I can see the shadows move alongside us. It's quieter here, and I hate it.

I want to cling to my determination, but shadows crawl up on me, like hands of ice along my spine.

While Ever and I pick up the pace again, Maddy falls back to join us. "Can you keep up? Are you okay?"

"I don't know," I admit. "You?"

"We may be the most unlikely people to make this trek in the dark," she says.

"Someone should tell the Konigs to—" *fix their road*, I want to say, but the words die in my throat. If we make it out of here in one piece, the Konigs will only be told one thing now, and it won't be anything about their road.

"I don't…oh." The words register with Maddy too. She pulls her eyes back to the road ahead, and a sense of distance washes over her. She pushes her hands deep into her pockets.

She's in pain, and so am I. With every step, lightning bolts of pain flash through my legs. My shoulders and hands are aching too. All my joints are revolting against me, ready to dislocate at any moment. I'm bursting in slow motion.

When Carter and I talked about the trip to and from the cabin, carrying me down seemed like the worst idea ever. I was wrong.

I try to keep my balance by leaning into my crutches and into Ever. They notice and stick as close to me as possible. I can feel them worry. I can feel them struggle with words. We're always too aware of each other.

But at the same time, Maddy is drifting, and we're still breaking.

"Help us," I whisper. "Don't let us be afraid either."

"I don't know how." Ever's breath shakes. But then they clear their throat, and like Maddy did earlier, they find a distraction. "If you were in Gonfalon, what would Feather do, Finn? If he were on the run from an enemy in Yester Tower? On his own, without his friends?"

I almost laugh, because I know what they're doing. I almost cry, because I know what they're doing. I almost *kiss* them, because I know what they're doing. Still, it takes me a moment to find my voice. "He'd try charging down the mountain first, and if that didn't work, he'd stick to the shadows." We're not the same, he and I. And thankfully, I still have some of my friends with me. "But after all this time and after all this training, he's still a city boy. He'd probably get eaten by wild boars before he reached the foot of the mountain."

They punch my arm, and it's a different kind of pain. One I don't mind so much. "That's a terrible plan and I forbid you following it."

"Okay."

"I'm serious," they say vehemently.

"Me too."

I know they're grinding their teeth. Feather's lack of self-preservation in-game has always been one of the things that annoyed Ever most. It's why I loved playing it up.

Ever sighs. "So what would Feather *really* do?"

They're slowly and successfully distracting me—and hopefully Maddy too. "He'd be a bit more careful. He'd try to remember what—" My throat tightens, but I push through. "What Corrin taught him about surviving. Depending on who he'd lost, on how events unfolded, he'd want revenge. Or he'd want to disappear into the secret side of Gonfalon. The side that Lente knows as well. One that doesn't play by council rules."

Maddy glances over her shoulder, her eyebrows almost up in her hairline. "How daring of you."

"I know my way around," I counter.

"What would Myrre do then, Mad?" Ever asks, their voice a bit softer, their breathing steadier.

Maddy shakes her head. "I don't know, honestly. Part of me wants to say she'd give up. I don't think she'd be able to manage on her own."

"You can't," Ever says with determination. "It's in the council rules that you can't give up. You're forbidden."

"I don't think that's how it works," she protests, but Ever is unbreakable.

"It is as long as I'm game master. For now, these are the rules, even if we leave this game behind on this mountain tonight. Giving up is not allowed."

Maddy doesn't answer, not immediately. She keeps walking as quickly as we all can handle, and the landscape around us keeps changing. From sunflowers to lava flows. From dark, to lighter, to dark. The path remains uneven, but our footing is a little steadier.

"Then Myrre would continue running," Maddy says eventually. "She'd run until she ran into someone who could help her survive everything that's still to come."

There's something to her voice that I can *almost* place, but not quite.

Ever flinches. "Oh, Maddy…"

I add up the pieces and everything grows cold. "Maddy and I are supposed to be the final victims, aren't we?"

Ever glances back in the direction of the cabin and with that, the spell has broken once more. "I think so. I mean…it would make sense."

Oh.

Maddy goes quiet. There's a faraway look in her eyes, and she takes a step back from me and Ever.

"Just you, I think, Finn."

"What do you mean?"

She hesitates.

I take a step toward her, but she tenses all over, so I keep my distance.

Her mouth works, but nothing comes out, like she's trying to explain to us what's happened, but she can't find the words.

Finally, she says, "It's just you. Trust me." Or: *Believe me.*

I'm not sure I can, but I'll try. "Do you know what's happening?"

"No! No, definitely not. I just…don't think they'll target me again."

Again. I want to ask more, and by the looks of it, Ever does too. Maddy sounds suspicious. I trust her, I do. But I can't shake that discomfort, nor the questions that are coalescing in the back of my mind. There's something there. I will figure out what it is.

But I set that aside for now. "If I'm supposed to be the final victim," I say instead, "then we should try to figure out what the plan is."

At that, all three of us fall silent. Clouds pass in front of the small sickle of moon and cast the world in more shadows. I keep looking at my feet, to ensure I'm sticking to the path. And the night folds itself in on us. The air smells of summer, a scorched, thick, flowery smell. The gravel crunches beneath our feet and the chilled mountain air crawls along my spine.

In the emptiness, no one can hide, but we're walking down a mountain in the dead of night, and we have no way to defend ourselves.

I feel vulnerable out in the open. I feel vulnerable on this path.

And that's exactly it. "The boulders," I say, aghast. "I could barely climb the boulders when we were all going up and there were *five* of us then. In the dark, on my own, it could kill me."

Ever frowns. "Yeah, I was thinking the same thing. As a trap, it makes the most sense and it's…" They fall silent and shudder.

"What you would do if you were GMing?" I finish. The words leave a sour taste in my mouth. "It's what I'd expect from any good game design too. Isn't that twisted?"

Ever shakes their head. "This is definitely not a conversation I ever thought we'd have. But in my experience, players never act as you'd expect in games, especially when you set up impossible challenges. Maybe it's the same here. Maddy and I are with you, and that will throw a wrench in the plan. We won't let you fall." They scratch their head. "I meant that figuratively, by the way, but it might also be true literally."

"Thanks, I guess." I keep my voice light. It's too difficult to wrap my head around everything otherwise.

Maddy doesn't get that memo, though. She nods solemnly. "We'll both be able to help you. To get past whatever trap there might be. We're in this together."

Mere hours ago, I didn't trust any of them not to let me fall, and Liva caught me. Now, Ever and Maddy are here, and I need to put my full faith in them. Frankly, this is all so intense that part of me wants to take off and run away for a darker part of the mountain, to hide and not have to deal with the emotions churning in my chest.

"We can also use it to our advantage, the fact that we know what's coming and that we're together," I say. "File this under things I never expected to say, but I'm so tired of *running* all the time. I'm tired of fleeing, and I'm tired of being afraid, and I'm tired of building walls around myself and not trusting others." I bite my lip and stare at Ever and Maddy with a kind of helplessness. "I trust you not to let me fall." I take another deep breath. "And I want this to be over. We need to find who's doing this, and we need to fight back. If we don't, we will never be free of it. If we only escape, we will always be looking over our shoulders."

Ever tilts their head, considering. "I want to know why all of this is happening. I want to know why us."

"I want to understand," Maddy puts in. "But I agree with Finn. We can't keep running. I mean, I assume we *could*, but I'd rather not be afraid of shadows either. I don't want to live life waiting for something or someone to jump at me. It's exhausting enough already dealing with how unpredictable all you neurotypicals are. Let's not throw mortal danger into the mix."

"That's the spirit." I reach out to pat her back, and this time she doesn't pull away. "Besides, we know their play now. At least to some extent. Probably. This is our only chance."

Ever pulls the tattered remains of their cloak closer and takes a step away from both of us, pondering, deciding. They keep their eyes firmly on the absolutely invisible horizon and the mountains that lie beyond us somewhere. They don't say a word, but a range of emotions passes over them. From uncertainty to the pure anger I saw from them back in the cabin, after they found the recording with Elle's voice. They breathe through it, though, their hands clenching and unclenching at their side. Their foot drawing some kind of design in the dirt. "I don't want these to be our only options," they eventually whisper.

"I don't think any of us do," I say gently. "But they are. Or at least, they're the only two I can see. Fleeing or fighting. I don't think there's a third alternative. Not without magic, in any case."

We keep doing that, somehow. We keep reaching—not for actual magic, but for our game, for the story between us. Because the truth is, if I'm just *Finn* here, I would've broken already. If this were just me and my friends, with no layers of protection or defenses, even imaginary ones, I don't think I would have gotten this far. For almost three years, we were *us* and we were inquisitors too, fighting for justice and one another.

When everything else felt impossible, having that alter ego was the crutch that kept me standing, the sword that kept me fighting, and the home that I could always return to.

I don't think I'm alone in that.

"Ever?"

After what feels like the better part of forever, they nod. "All right. I'm in. Let's make our stand."

TWENTY-SEVEN

EVER

O   ne condition, though," I say, and I look to the others in turn. "I don't want to harm anyone."

"Even if that someone might kill us?" Finn asks, but not with conviction.

"It doesn't mean we should do the same thing. That's not how this goes," I counter. "I'm not saying that nonviolence is the only solution. We should do what we have to do, and if that includes fighting for our lives, no one should hold back. I just think violence should be the last resort, not the starting place. This isn't who we are. This isn't who I want us to be. And more to the point, I want to see them brought to justice if we can."

"It's not like we have weapons," Maddy says. "Unless you count the bread knife, but I'd rather not use that either."

"Why did you take it?" Finn asks, with mild curiosity.

She laughs. "To fight off wild animals, I guess? It probably wouldn't be particularly helpful there. Point is, I agree with Ever. I want to catch our ghost. Or at the very least, I want to make sure they're neutralized and won't be able to harm us. Besides, if we can stop them and trap them, maybe they'll have a phone. We can use it to call for help."

"Fine," Finn says. "I want us to go home."

I nod. Me too. "Okay, then. What do we have to work with? We need to come up with a plan. They're ahead of us and have probably set up a trap near the boulders. Rocks fall, everyone dies. Something like that."

Maddy twirls the bread knife around, making me faintly uneasy, but she isn't even looking at it. "We have our cloaks," she says. "Or at least mine and yours. I don't think we want Finn to strip quite yet." He scowls at that. "Once upon a time, Selina, my cat, caught a massive raven and brought it into the house, alive and mostly unscathed. My parents weren't home and my sister was out playing somewhere, and I *freaked*. Selina chased it around the living room, ducking under the couch whenever it tried to attack her. I was on the verge of a full mental breakdown when Sav came back and helped me catch the bird. We threw blankets and towels over it, so it would be disoriented and not able to fly away. It worked then. It may work with humans too."

"Disorient them, overwhelm them, stop them." I tick the options off on my fingers. "That makes sense, but it can't be our whole plan."

Finn nods. "We'll need to lure our Big Bad Evil Person away from the boulders. They have the upper hand there, and it's dangerous territory. If something goes wrong while we try to overpower them, if the boulders start to move again, we'd all be in danger."

"I think there are two options there," Maddy says. "Lure them away, or sneak up on them."

"How do you intend to do that?" The moment I ask that question, I wish I hadn't.

"Easy," Finn says. "Me. I'll be the incentive. If I pretend to stumble on the boulders, they'll have to come to me. But if one of you tries to climb them, they'll know something is wrong. The one thing we have on them right now is they don't know we're all still together."

Oh, I *hate* this.

"I can try to run up to the Big Bad," Maddy adds. "I'm still good for short distances, I'm quite sure. Ever, you can flank them."

I hate this *so much*. I am responsible for this group, and I want to be able to protect them.

"No."

Finn grabs my hand and squeezes. "It's not your call, Ev. I can do this. I *want* to do this. And we have no other alternative, because all of us are hurt. And we can't keep going on like this."

"Agreed," Maddy says. "This is happening whether you like it or not. So we better figure out the second half of the plan."

I want to speak, but I don't have the words. Every time I try, my brain snags on a new thorn of fear, and I'm silent for what feels like an eternity. Long enough that it seems like the stars have changed positions, and bats fly overhead. "Right. I'll trail Finn as closely as I can. I'm still the nimblest of the three of us, so I'll be able to move around the boulders easiest. I'll be there to make sure nothing happens to Finn if our Big Bad attacks—or to help out Maddy so we can overpower them. Once we have…"

"We need to find a way to immobilize them," Finn says.

"Magic ward?" Maddy suggests, and I wince.

"How about this?" Finn unwraps the leather belt from around his waist. It's a few feet long, and though it's fairly narrow, it looks sturdy. "I don't have a rope on me, but this may be the best alternative option."

"I have the laces of my boots, but I think the belt is the better option." I can't believe how casually we're discussing all this. It's comforting to do something, but it's not a discussion we should ever have to have.

More worrisome still: I've yet to meet an RPG group who sticks to their plan.

But Finn is right. What other options are there? We might as well approach this scenario with the little we know about survival and surviving.

"We can use your crutches as weapons maybe," Maddy says to Finn. "I mean, if you're okay with it. If we need to knock them out or something."

He bites his lip. Without the long leather belt around his waist, the overcoat falls looser, but it still looks good on him. With Lonely Peak as his backdrop, and the cold blue moonlight illuminating his costume and features, he looks like a messy, wounded high elf stepped into the mortal plane. "I…don't know? If need be, of course. But it's complicated."

He stares down at his crutches. They're pretty torn up and damaged by our slamming them through a window, the crow skulls all torn off and shredded. A long cut runs up the metal on one side, tearing through the outer coat of matte black paint and showing the aluminum underneath. It's almost like a scar.

"I'm sorry we damaged them," she says softly.

Finn shrugs. "I did that. It was my suggestion. But to use them as clubs…I don't know. It's one thing to use them as a tool, and quite another to use them as weapons, you know? I'm not sure. My crutches are as much a part of me as my arms or my legs are. Besides, I need them. I'd rather you leave them with me, and I'll do what I can. Okay?"

"Of course." She hesitates, then holds the bread knife out to him. "Carry this, at least. In case you need to protect yourself."

Finn slips the knife into a coat pocket.

"It's okay," I say. "We'll have one another's backs. We'll all do what we can."

"We should try to get them as close to the cliff's edge as possible. I don't want to give them room to move around or escape. We don't know—well, we *do* know—how dangerous they are." Finn leans hard against his crutches. "If worse comes to worst, I'll do what I can."

"If it does, I'd rather they get away than any of us get harmed," I say.

"They'll keep coming after us," Maddy objects.

Finn glances in my direction. "Then we'll cross that bridge if we get there. We have to be safe, Maddy. All three of us. We can't forget ourselves. We have to survive."

She hesitates, then nods. And one step at a time, we walk to the inevitable blocked path. I look over at Maddy every step of the way, to make sure no part of her now dust-covered costume impedes her running. I look over at Finn, who's grown paler than usual and keeps biting his lip. He still avoids putting weight on his ankle, so I can't imagine he's looking forward to climbing, even if everything else wasn't part of the equation.

And it is.

Before we turn the last corner toward the blocked path, I reach out to both of them. "Are you absolutely sure?"

"Yes," Finn says immediately.

Maddy straightens her shoulders. "I'm absolutely sure."

I'm not. I hate this.

But I will do anything for the two of them.

Damien was wrong. My friends are hurting. It's my job to protect them. It's my job to keep them safe.

So I will.

YOU KNOW HOW TO DO THIS—LAY TRAPS, ENGAGE VILLAINS, WIN boss battles. You've fought against rogue mages before, and you stood tall against everything the magisterium threw at you. You've survived traps and alchemy attacks. You are strong. You are determined. And, most of all, you know how to fight for your friends.

It takes different forms, of course. Sometimes protecting your friends means a stealthy dagger and a well-placed arrow. Sometimes it's dismantling deathly traps with abandon, or bargaining for better chances against the odds. It's quiet companionship and loud laughter. And sometimes it is challenging words that cut with words that mend.

It's not giving up. It's standing together, not alone. It's facing whatever comes next. Because you believe in a cause, perhaps, but most of all, you believe in one another.

TWENTY-EIGHT

MADDY

T minus a few minutes until our last hurdle, our boss fight. It's not funny. It's not a game. But thinking of it in game terms is the only way to avoid being terrified out of my mind. Besides, if someone so clearly *wants* this to be a game, maybe the only way to win is to play by the same rules—or break them.

But despite our plans, despite our whispered conversations, with every twig that snaps, we all tense. Every time the wind picks up or the caw of birds echoes through the night sky, we huddle closer.

And every time we go over the plan again, I zone out a little more. I keep my eyes steady on the uneven ground in front of us, on the narrow path. The shadows around us move with us. I'd expect to see coyotes again, but the shadows that flank us are all two-legged. Maybe they only exist in my imagination. Maybe one of them is real. I keep waiting for Carter to catch up with us. Maybe we can keep running.

I miss being able to run.

"Maddy?"

I look up. I missed something Ever said, clearly. "Are you with us?"

"Yes. I'm sorry, just…thinking. Distracted."

There's that look again. The same look both Finn and Ever have worn over the course of the night. Not distrust, not *quite*, but something a lot like it. Furrowed brows. Hidden eyes. Their bodies slightly angled away from me. Curiosity. Hesitation. Trepidation.

There's only so much I can read, and still so much I don't understand.

"You are sure about this, right?" Ever asks for approximately the fifth time in the last few minutes. Our plan depends on trust, and it's getting harder and harder to keep up the mask of confidence.

So I finally drop it. "I've never been less sure about anything in my life. But yes."

Unexpectedly, they smile at that. "I know that feeling."

Huh. It's the first time they've alluded to the secrets they're keeping. They may hint at them, unknowingly, but they're usually so good at keeping to the background. "I wish you'd tell me what is wrong."

They open their mouth and close it again. "I always thought most of it is so obvious. And the rest…" They pull at a strand of hair and shake their head. "I'm not sure it matters."

"It does," I say softly.

"Maybe being scared isn't a bad thing," they say instead. "It means we'll be careful. It means we know this isn't going to be easy and we won't take any of this for granted. Because for all that we're approaching it as a game, it isn't. I wish it were, because if that were the case, we could press the reset button. Or take a break and reconvene and try again."

I don't know if Ever's words are supposed to make me feel better, but in a strange kind of way, they do. They make me feel more centered. "This isn't how I imagined my first time running again either. Missing it felt like life or death, and now…"

"Yeah." Ever lifts their hand and then drops it again, almost as if they wanted to reach out to me. I can't help but appreciate them for it. It's not that I don't like being touched at all, but I would rather it happens when I instigate it. When I know what to expect.

Finn paces ahead of us now. With every step, he winces, almost imperceptibly but not undetectable. Especially to someone who knows how to mask pain too.

He doesn't know how to mask his awkward glances in my direction, though.

I push my hands into the pockets that are still lined with dust from the handfuls of pills. Would Finn understand? Would Ever understand? They both have enough on their minds as it is. Now is not the right time to bring any of this up, and part of me thinks *never* is the right time to bring any of this up. I don't have the words for it. I don't know how.

I never found the words for it with Carter, no matter how much I wanted to confide in him. Or in Sav. I would completely freeze up, and all the words were too overwhelming, too impossible to say out loud. And every time, I could see the window of opportunity close. Eyes flicking to something else. Face turned away. A smile that I didn't want to disturb. So I never found the words, just the hunger and the need.

And now, the emptiness.

The only thing I have is this. As we near the closed-off section of the path, I fall into step with Finn. "I want to survive this," I blurt out, and it's as if the words are shards of glass in my throat, and at the same time they're too vague, not enough. But I don't turn away from him.

His eyes darken. "I know you do. We need to survive tonight, Maddy. But it doesn't stop there. Once we're home, you do not just need to keep surviving. You need to live."

He draws breath to say more, but this time, I firmly keep my eyes on the path again. "We're almost there."

The sky above us has lightened to a pastel midnight, but when we turn another corner and the boulders appear down the path, they're nothing more than shadows. And along the side of the path, all the way to where the boulders still topple over, a steep cliff.

It's almost symbolic. We weren't supposed to get off this mountain until a few days from now, until we finished our story. For some of us, it'd be our last hurrah before college, future, adulthood. And now we're stumbling toward it through shadows so hungry, we can hardly see ourselves. I'm not prepared.

Finn comes to a dead stop.

He's staring at the boulders. His shoulders hang low, and the overcoat he's wearing no longer looks like it's part of him. It's only a costume now and an ill-fitting one at that. It looks like all the color is disappearing from him. On regular days, Finn is fierce. Even when he isn't in costume, he wears enough pins to classify as armor and he's equal parts bad decisions and endless loyalty. Now, his crutches are the only things that keep him standing, and he's so pale, I half-expect his silver hair dye to drip from his hair.

Ever walks up to him, so close their shoulders touch. "Well then."

"Yeah."

Ever clears their throat, but keeps their voice low. "We have to find our positions. Maddy, we'll stick to the tree line, out of sight. We'll have to make sure that no matter what happens, we're both on the same side of the boulders as Finn, okay?" I nod and take in the path ahead of me. "It's a risk and we won't be able to shadow Finn exactly, but we'll stay close. It should be possible to get to you quickly." They look at Finn intently while they say that.

When Finn glances up, his mouth is set in a fierce line. He hands Ever the long leather belt. "It's the only way we can manage without walking into the trap. I'll be fine. I'll walk the path, ready for whatever this may bring."

I take the opera cloak off my shoulders and pull the fabric taut between my hands. "The moment I see the Big Bad Evil Person, I'll jump them."

Ever nods. "And we'll try to immobilize and tie them up."

"Or knock them out." Finn squeezes the grips of his crutches. "Let's do this."

"Game on."

We didn't decide on a way to say goodbye, because none of us considered we had to. But as we stand around awkwardly, before we part ways, I think the realization hits us all at the same time. This is it. This is where we make our stand. We don't know what'll happen from here.

All I can do is nod at two of the people closest to me, and disappear into the tree line, a sizable distance away from the path. I don't know what else to do.

I try to keep from snapping twigs or making too much noise as I creep closer to the boulders. At the same time, I listen for other movement, for anyone who might be hidden here. But for all that I've spent time on this mountain, and all the time on the lacrosse field, I'm not an outdoors person. The leaves rustle. Something flies against my face and I swat at it, before realizing that'll only make my position more obvious.

I duck down and try to creep again, and ignore the part where my knee is straight up screaming at me. Hands to the ground. Try not to mind the weird sensations of the undergrowth.

And creep.

Until I'm quite sure I'm in the right space, off the boulders that seem to have come down the mountain like a river of rocks. In my periphery, I can still see the faint shape of Ever as they scramble higher up the boulders. We're not quiet. We're not subtle. None of us are rogues in real life. But we'll have to—and we're going to—make do.

And I wait. It feels like it's hours, though it's probably more likely minutes. It seems as though the sky brightens, though it's far more likely my eyes have adjusted. My heart rate is a constant pounding, loud enough that I worry anyone could hear it.

I try to keep my breathing under control. Finally, Finn slams his crutches onto the path in front of him, the metallic clicks echoing around us, and starts walking.

At first, nothing.

The mountain remains as quiet and as empty as it was when we walked down.

But then.

A shadow unfurls from behind the trees, right next to the first boulder, a few yards away from me. It almost seems to glide in the direction of the path.

The moonlight catches it, and while I can't see a face, I can see the body language. Arrogant and comfortable, haughty and once kind.

It *is* someone we know, but it can't be. *It can't be.*

I can read the cold determination, and everything snaps into focus, and everything makes sense.

TWENTY-NINE

LIVA

Emotions are distractions, and the only way to grow strong is to break through your attachments," Father once told me. He'd given me a rabbit for my tenth birthday, and a year later he gave me a hunting knife and an assignment. "Don't be weak, Liva. To win, you have to make sacrifices. To win, you have to be willing to risk it all. To win, you have to show you're not afraid of anything."

And once you've reached that point, it's no longer a matter of people. It's a matter of value. And your own worth.

Father used to tell me a bedtime story. A story of his first hunt. It wasn't anything meaningful—a squirrel, perhaps, or a bird. The target changed every time he told the story. But he stayed on the mountain two days and two nights. He stayed in the same places that his forefathers colonized.

And he learned all about himself.

He showed me his scarred hands. He told me that we pay our price in blood because it reminds us to appreciate sacrifice. That every Konig before him has and that every Konig after me will too. It's what clinches our success.

He took me hunting on a regular basis after that. It was hardly ever about the circle of life for him—he didn't teach me to respect the mountain. It was the circle of power, of figuring out who exists as competition and who exists as prey. He taught me to take. He taught me to break.

I hated the sight of blood at first. And the smell of it was worse. It would coat my tongue for hours or days after. Those first nights, I had nightmares about empty eyes and matted fur.

But over time, I got better at it. I honed my skills. I learned to read my environment.

The mountain is hungry tonight, and so am I.

I mirror Finn through the trees, keeping pace with him, but staying out of sight.

A small part of me wishes I hadn't started this, wishes they were still my friends. But I quench that. I know better than to form attachments. I *should* know better than to form attachments. It'll only break me.

"You can't trust anyone." That's the lesson Mother taught me, the lesson, she said, we all should learn early. If given the power, we only end up hurting one another—and ourselves. We try to work together, but one of us missteps and everyone falls. We try to build bridges, but they're only as strong as the weakest link. And these connections we've forged, well…they can be the hand that saves us or the weight that drags us down.

Mother once told me that trusting the wrong people nearly ruined her, and she would do everything in her power to stop the same from happening to me. It took me too long to realize what she meant. It seemed so excessive, you know? She'd had a falling-out with her sister, accusing my aunt of treason. Mother said she'd "used her to get ahead in the world" and "stolen her opportunities." It wasn't until my friends threatened to do the same that I knew what she meant: people like them would always be tempted to do this to people like us.

I spent time with Finn, and it made him matter more, but somehow he expected more still.

I invested in Maddy's social standing, and she had the audacity to go from a sports star to a wreck.

I tolerated Carter, who got into my company and started stealing money. And my former best friend knew about it and let him do it.

And all the while, *I* got blamed for doing my best.

Then, despite it all, Dad offered to pay Carter's college tuition.

Finn got scholarships for his game development and saw a career ahead of him, through some kind of gender affirmative action, surely.

The people at school who heard about our game started seeing

Ever with new eyes—they got offered that internship—and Ever didn't even notice or care.

What did any of them do to deserve this?

Still, it's not that I don't wish them luck. I would've let it go if it had only happened once.

Probably. Most likely.

But it didn't. It kept happening over and over again. Finn and Ever found each other. Maddy and Carter. I got left behind.

And still, none of them seemed to realize they could only be successful in our game. After all, the game is the epitome of lying expertly. A place where all of them can be so much more than they could be in life. Too much truth would ruin it.

Frankly, that's a good life lesson too. We're all playing games. No matter how straightforward someone claims to be, *everyone* lies. And those of us who understand that? We know you can't just lose and start over.

We play to win.

I take a step closer to the road.

It does bother me that *Finn* doesn't seem to have broken. Not much, in any case. He has his scrapes and scars, but he moves with determination. He's calmer than I've seen all day, almost focused.

I don't mind that he has a purpose, but I'd like to know what it is.

I scan the environment. The patient mountain, with rocks that could still slip down in a heartbeat. The blocked path was a bit of good timing and exerting the right kind of pressure. I wanted to make life hard for him in all the ways that count.

It was so very easy to do just that. Cruel, too, perhaps, but the hunt never cares about cruelty. Only about power and results. This is my family's heritage: finding a way to advance despite the odds. Leaving those *lesser* behind.

Honestly, this was always something I had to do. I knew it the very moment Carter started to succeed at the company, the very moment he stole money and got away with it.

I whistle the tune of the music box, and Finn *tenses*. With a smile, I fall back into the trees a little. I went walking in these woods nights on end to get a feel for my surroundings. It's lovely now; I feel at home here.

Briefly, I planned for this to only be about Carter. He was the main threat after all, and the others could still be useful to me. My friends. Or, as Zac called them, my pet projects. I never said he was wrong about that.

I cared about keeping them close. I could've kept Maddy closer, but she was such a mess. I didn't want to burn my hands. There were matters of perception to think of, after all. She could've done more. She could've worked harder. I worked hard too, after all.

All of them—they could've not let their issues hold them back.

Finn hesitates now, and the cracks appear underneath the surface. I feel like a shark, smelling blood, and I can't help but smile.

A few more steps, friend. Keep walking.

To be fair, being seen with them never *was* just a matter of perception or pet projects. I did actually, really care about the game. It made me feel like I could be anyone I wanted to be. But whenever we found our way back to the real world again, I knew it would never be that easy. People like me, we don't have a choice. We have to be on top. It's the only option.

And when it all started to fall to pieces, I had to take back control.

The highest objective in the world is order, my father once told me. Order is imposed by those people whose duty it is to rein in chaos.

But occasionally, it's worth it to *create* chaos. And anger. And fear. It's pure and unfiltered. It strips everyone down to their core, and there is beauty in that.

It's curious what a little blood can do.

It's about the atmosphere too, of course. The right words. The subtlest whispers. Don't ever let it be said I do not have a flair for drama.

I chose them for a reason. I could've fulfilled my duty with anyone who wouldn't be missed, but there would be no value to that. It would not matter to me. And I want to give this rite of passage the respect it deserves. Not to enjoy it, but to appreciate it. To change my world for the better, and rid it of those who don't belong. Of the ones who hold me back.

Trust me, it'll be better this way.

If everything goes according to plan, once the dust settles, I'll be the sole survivor. The focus of the story. And sure, it's a bit radical, but it's also pragmatic. Two birds with one stone. It takes away the threat *and* it advances my own position, and in the end, isn't that all that matters?

It almost makes it better that Finn keeps glancing around, like he realizes I—or someone—might be here. That Finn is the last one.

Finn was my first friend. Before Maddy was there, he glommed onto me. Before Ever came around—and even after that—I was the one he told his secrets to. I met his mothers and I accepted them. I was the one he shared his games with, and I encouraged him to pursue them, even if I wasn't sure the gaming industry was such a great place to be. I was the one he went shopping with, though I always avoided his thrift stores and took him places with more class. I could've helped him become so much more than he is if he would've just let me.

I still *care* about him, and that is a problem.

I hear Father's voice in my head again. *Emotions are distractions, and the only way to grow strong is to break through your attachments.*

Finn stops and something rustles in the trees near him. Is there movement there?

I stop too and stare. There might be. It might also be a trick of the moonlight or an animal. Finn looks around, searching. Scared? He finds the same spot amidst the trees, and he *smiles.* He nods.

And he keeps walking toward the boulders that have so helpfully—with a bit of nudging, perhaps—become a deathtrap. Nature is quite impressive like that.

It looks like we're not alone here, though I don't see anyone else. But I've learned to read the environment and the body language of my prey. I borrowed a few studies from Maddy on body language, actually. I may not need it the way she does—I'm not broken the way she is—but it was helpful.

And quite frankly, it gives me a rush now. Like a boss fight at the end of a game, when you know you've done all you can to prepare and ready yourself, and you know only one of you will walk out alive.

Today, that'll be me.

This mountain is mine. I'm the hero of this story.

I wait until Finn's climbed his way up onto the boulders again, as awkwardly as he did when we first arrived here earlier today. I couldn't let him fall then. It would've ruined the game.

Besides, I'm not a bad person. I'm a pragmatist.

Liar.

Thief.

Addict.

Worthless.

"Finn…" I call out to him softly, and watch him tense once more. I reach for the hunting knife that's strapped to my leg and carefully unsheathe it. My hand throbs, and I welcome the pain. I don't plan to stab him—nothing so mundane—just to scare him and make him lose his balance.

Traitor.

"Who's there?" His voice trembles.

I hold my breath and let the silence draw out.

Again, "Who's there?"

There's so much fear in his voice. It's delicious.

"Finn…" I let my voice dance on the night air, as I start to circle around him for the best approach. The rocks are sharp and the cliffs are high, and I want to be careful not to slip.

"I know you're out there. Stop trying to scare me!" His voice catches and breaks.

I can't help it; I laugh.

And with that, I step into the moonlight.

THIRTY

EVER

Liva.

You're okay smashes against *No.*

This *hurts.* I'm frozen to the ground as she advances on Finn, a knife in her hand. She is only a shadow at first, and there's a distance between them, but some shadows have sharp teeth and sharper claws. Her free hand is carefully bandaged.

Finn has his back to her, his eyes focused on the boulders, to draw her out as far as he can, but he's already higher up them than either of us planned.

Unless he recognized her soft whisper, he doesn't know it's Liva yet.

Frantically, I try to catch Maddy's eye, to make sure she's on deck to stop Liva. She's as pale as I must be, but her gaze is trained on her former best friend. We move along the trees, using the darkness to our benefit, trying to catch up. She's holding her cape in both hands, but she has to find a way to get close without being noticed.

Liva's tread across the boulders is careful. Everything about her is tense and measured: the set of her shoulders, the clenching of her jaw. The way her eyes flick back and forward, and how they glow against the moonlit sky.

Does she know we're here? She must have an inkling.

How can it be *Liva*? Or maybe: Were we so oblivious?

It is a weird thing, observing her now. It's hard to consider her an enemy in the most rational sense of the word, because I'm convinced none of us feel it. Emotionally, she's still our friend. She's *alive. Of course* she is. I know we need to save ourselves, but I want to save her too. From herself, if need be.

What *happened* to her?

She walks closer to Finn still, and he must hear her, but he keeps his back to her.

A few steps away from me, partially covered behind a tree, a flash of movement. Maddy. Gravel crunches and the sound echoes through the night air.

Liva freezes. Her head snaps toward the sound. Her hands go to her belt, and she crouches into an almost defensive stance. As far as I'm aware, she hasn't done any martial arts, but she's certainly trained somewhere. She seems comfortable with these movements. She handles her knife with ease.

Finn comes to the most uncomfortable bit of the climb, and Liva has started to climb the boulders too. She gains quickly now, even if she keeps her pace steady and her eyes everywhere around her. She can't know for certain we're here, but she has her guard up.

I have to protect him.

"Liva!"

I dash out from the tree line toward the boulders, revealing my hiding spot. The single shout has a dramatic effect on Finn, who spins around and nearly falls over. It has a less dramatic effect on Liva, who simply turns.

There's a moment of realization that crashes over her. Of resignation. Then a smirk. A smile. And it's one I've seen a thousand times before. It's so familiar, but it was never yet so deadly. "So you managed to get out. How impressive."

I start walking toward her but slowly, like one would approach a wild animal. "You need to stop this, Liva."

"You were always smarter than any of us gave you credit for. You know that, right? You could've been the best of us." She takes a step back, to keep the distance between us. "With the right upbringing, the right people around you..."

Her words lash out at me. "You don't have a clue what you're talking about."

"You pieced it all together, didn't you? Clever Ever."

That's why the note was there, in her room. It wasn't to throw us off her trail, or not only that at least; ironically, it was the only truth she told. *Liar.* She lies. She always lied.

I haven't pieced the rest together yet. I don't want to.

I climb the boulders to approach her, and she backs away, keeping a careful distance between us. We circle around each other like predator versus prey, and I honestly wouldn't be able to say which is which. Perhaps we're all predators. Or perhaps we're all prey. If the latter's the case, we're fighting for our lives.

"We're your friends." I try to stay on the side of the path, keeping Liva cornered, with her back to the cliff's edge and away from Finn.

Liva laughs. "You should hear yourself. You don't believe that."

I don't. I do. "Lay off. Let us help you."

"I didn't want to hurt you. Not much at least. I didn't want to harm any of you. But you brought this on yourself. You've pushed me, and I have nowhere else to go."

"What is the matter with you?" I lean in, try to force her down from the rocks. We need to get her to the ground. We need to disarm her, push the cloak over her, and tie her up.

Liva's mouth splits open in a toothy grin. Her free hand twitches. "I am making things right."

The tension of the night flows between us, and with it, it seems time slows down and speeds up at intermittent intervals. She jumps down, slashes her knife at me. I'm too slow to step back, but she hasn't got the reach to wound me.

"I don't know what happened with Carter, but we want to be here for you," I shout. "Lay down your dagger, and we'll figure out where to go from here."

She may be right that I don't believe we're friends, but I do want to help her. It's the only way Finn, Maddy, and I have come so far.

The words seem to pass by Liva. If she hears them, she doesn't acknowledge them. Instead, she keeps glancing between Finn and me. An angry girl of my own age, who has the world and thinks it is against her.

Every time she looks at me, Finn takes a step down—and away—while to his side, Maddy takes a step closer. Her face is a mask of pain.

"I know it must've been an accident. But it doesn't have to be like this," I try again. When Liva looks at Finn, I glance past him at Maddy, who nods. Ready.

Five.

Four.

"An accident? I would've made it look like an accident. Victims of a haunted mountain," Liva says, with a singsong quality to her voice. She takes a step toward the boulders again, elegantly, like a danse macabre. "The night is dangerous terrain after all."

Three.

Two.

Then she smiles, and she shoves at the boulders, making the entire path into the deathtrap Finn so feared. And while Liva keeps her balance, Finn starts to slip.

"No!"

I dash forward, my steps loud and fragile, and everything around me happens in slow motion. The crackling of the path sounds like gunshots. Liva turns, her knife out.

One step behind me, Maddy leaps at her and throws her cloak.

It doesn't cover her, but it wraps itself around her face. And from then on, we both pounce.

Maddy dives in to try to wrestle the knife away, while I reach for Finn, who reaches for me. So close, *so close*.

I've found that even when you're falling, there are always hands that help you. People who understand and who make sure you can stand up straight before you have to walk again.

I grab onto Finn's hand. Or at least, I think I do. I miss, the first time. Thin air.

I try again. This time, I feel the comforting touch of Finn's fingers wrapped around me. He's trembling.

I am too, and I brace myself. "Hold on. *Please*, hold on."

I pull against the tumbling boulders.

Finn claws at my hand, and it's hard to keep the balance. But I am strong. Years of holding the world together and tensing myself against the judgment of others means I have quite a bit of upper body strength.

I pull Finn to a safe spot, while the boulders around us keep falling.

Rocks fall, everyone dies.

Shut up, brain.

To our left, Maddy is struggling to keep Liva down. She's stronger than she looks. Shaken but not defeated. They roll over and over, and the cloak that's halfway wrapped itself around Liva's head loosens. It still obscures her vision a little, but there are gaps enough that her eyes find mine.

She is nothing like the smiling, caring girl I once knew.

Finn scrambles to his feet, and without any of his early misgivings, though with trembling hands, he takes a crutch and slams it into the inside of her knee.

At the same moment the crutch lands against Liva's knee, she turns to Maddy, her dagger out. The blade runs down Maddy's forearm, leaving an angry red cut. But because Liva crumples, she cannot push through, and the blade slips from her grasp. It tumbles to the ground in the same slow manner that she does.

When her knees hit the rock, she cries out.

Maddy leaps to straighten the cloak. It arcs through the air, the sides of it billowing. It covers Liva, ever so slowly.

Immediately, I step in with the belt and try to wrap it around her shoulders, as tight as humanly possible.

Finn kicks the dagger away.

Both Maddy and I lie half on top of Liva, trying to keep her down until we can restrain her. But the belt struggles to cooperate—I wish we had a length of rope instead—and Liva keeps struggling. She tears at the fabric, tries to break through.

I brace myself.

One knee on her back, the other on the rocky ground. I lean over to secure the belt. And maybe my balance shifts. Maybe Maddy's grip isn't as steady as we thought it was either. But the moment I reach over, Liva twists and *turns.*

She lashes out at me—

And everything goes white.

When the world blinks into existence again, the first thing I'm aware of is searing hot pain.

I'm lying on the ground, and around me, people are screaming.

A second hunting knife sticks in my hand, almost straight through it.

I'm going to faint again.

Without thinking, I reach out and pull it—and realize a second too late it's the absolute worst thing I could do, because blood immediately gushes out. I'm not as savvy as any of the characters I play.

Just desperate.

I take a piece of tunic and push it into my hand, to stop the bleeding, and foolishly try to scramble to my feet. The pain is so intense, the whole world turns upside down, and I drop to my knees again, heaving.

In front of me, Maddy has managed to hold onto the belt around

Liva, and she's dragged back and forward by Liva's frantic movement. Maddy has no way to brace herself. She barely has anywhere to stand and hold her footing. She's pulled into a violent storm, closer and closer to the cliff.

The boulders have slowed to a halt again, but I don't know if that matters now.

Finn tries to push Liva down with his crutches, but she dances out of reach.

That was the flaw in our plan. We never thought we'd have to keep fighting.

Everything slows down and speeds up, slows down and speeds up, as if to form a heartbeat.

Liva flings Maddy to the side, and Maddy swings perilously close to the cliff's edge. She almost loses the ground beneath her and she screams.

"Maddy, let her go!" My voice carries.

Liva falls back again and tries to shake the belt off. She says something to Maddy that I can't make out, but Finn flinches. Liva's a whirlwind, a tornado, and she's willing to destruct everything around her to get free. And with the cloak still partially covering her face, it's hard to know how much of her direct surroundings she can see.

Meanwhile, Maddy clings to the belt like a lifeline. "I can't! I wrapped it around my hand!"

"Untie yourself!" Finn shouts in despair.

"I can't."

Liva flings all her weight to the side, and something *snaps*.

At first, I think it's the belt. Then Maddy *screams*.

And that's it.

When Liva rears up and tries to pull Maddy off balance again, Finn leaps toward her, the bread knife out. His knees twist and his ankles sprain, and he lets himself fall on top of Maddy.

With more determination than force, he pushes the bread knife against the leather belt and thanks to the constant strain of the two girls tied to each other, it cuts clean through.

The belt goes slack.

Liva's angry roar turns to a scream when she breaks free, but momentum keeps her stumbling backward, until the ground ceases to be.

Finn yells her name and reaches for her, but he's too far away.

She topples over, tears out of the cloak, not in slow motion but with determination. With the full force of gravity and inevitability.

I don't see her face when she falls. I don't want to see it. But I also can't look away, because once upon a time, only a few hours ago, she was one of my closest friends. And I don't know what changed. I don't know how she changed. Perhaps down the line, people will say there was something wrong with her, that there was a shadow inside of her.

Call it fear. Anger. Hatred.

But if that's true, there's a shadow inside of us all. The only difference is, she decided to feed hers, and we lit matches to feed the light.

WAS THERE A WAY TO WIN THIS? MAYBE LOSING IS THE SAME AS LOSS.

THIRTY-ONE
MADDY

S ilence.
        Pain.

Betrayal.

There's an actual piece of bone sticking out of my arm, and I'm starting to crack at the edges. We all are.

Ever reaches out with their good hand to support me to walk, but I'm all too aware of how uncomfortably close we are, well beyond my own personal boundaries. I shrug them off—and whimper.

The world floods in with the waning moon, the shadows a bright reminder of the past... I wish I could say days, or weeks, but it's only been hours. Strange how, when we climbed up this mountain, we thought the world looked so different.

Now, there's three of us left, and it feels like we've all gone to war in real life.

"It doesn't feel real, does it?" Ever says.

Finn shakes his head. He almost hangs in his crutches, pushing himself upright through layers of exhaustion. We pull ourselves together and push across the boulders, and I don't know how.

"I wish it wasn't," I say.

"Yeah."

I bite my lip until I taste the metal twang of blood. Then I'm crying. Big, heaving sobs, like my body doesn't care that my brain is still struggling to keep up; it needs a way to get rid of the excess anxiety. The pain from my arm finally floods me, and it threatens to knock me off my feet. Maybe I shouldn't have been so resolute in dumping all the painkillers, because right now, I wouldn't mind them. Still, it's probably a good thing. I need a clear head to get down the mountain. As clear as it gets through a haze of pain.

With every step, I lose my balance. With every step, pain courses through me. With every step, I lose another piece of me.

On somewhat stable ground, Ever kneels before me. They've taken a piece of their tunic and ripped it to shreds, and they've wrapped it tight around their hand. The cloth is bloody, and Ever's jaw is set. With Finn's assistance, they're using another part of the tunic to tie a makeshift sling. "Hey, shh, it's okay," they say. They pull the sling over my head and they motion toward my arm. "Can I help you put this on? C'mon, it'll be fine. Don't cry."

They say it with a hint of panic, and halfway through a sob, I start to laugh. "I thought I was the one who couldn't deal with emotions in this group."

Ever shakes their head. "You're not. I think we've all lost our footing a bit."

When I reach out my arm to them, Finn takes a careful hold of my elbow and wrist, almost as if he's pulling at the bone, and he guides my arm through the sling. "This may help."

The sling doesn't help. Which is to say, it keeps my arm in one place, but it doesn't stop the pain that cascades through me. "Did either of you see this coming? Because I didn't. Could we have done anything? What are we going to do once we make our way down? Do we think the police, our parents, *Carter's and Liva's* parents are just going to accept it when we tell them what happened? Why did this happen?" The pain is making me ramble.

Ever looks around them. Picks up a stick and discards it again. There are beads of sweat on their forehead, the only evidence of how much pain they must be in too. "I don't know."

"I think I do," Finn says. "*Liar. Thief.*"

Ever hesitates, then adds, "*Worthless.*"

Addict.

"I thought she cared about us." I wince when I remember Liva's exact words. The last thing she said to me before she fell.

I could have cared about you. If only you'd been better.

"I think she did. Once," Ever manages.

I don't know. I really don't. I don't know if you can truly care about people if you don't think of them as equals.

"All we can do is keep moving, make our way down, and face whatever the consequences of this night are," Finn says. "Are you okay to walk? We can try to splint your arm, if that makes it any better?"

He's barely holding on too. He flinches every time he bears weight on his ankle, which already took quite a beating from his earlier stunt. He's okay, and he's desperately not okay. There's a haunted look in his eyes. There's a renewed sense of resolve too, and the way he stares at me makes me uncomfortable. It always does, but right now it's worse. Perhaps because it's easier to see someone else's fault lines when you're breaking, and we're both vulnerable now.

"You're looking at me like I'm a puzzle to solve." I keep my voice light, but still it trembles.

"In my experience, most people are."

"Well, I'm not. I'm who I've always been. You know me. You shouldn't worry."

"I do know you. I also do worry." He looks away and shakes his head. When he turns his gaze back to me, it's as if he's made a decision. "And I don't think any of us is who we were anymore. Not me, in any case. But you're not either. You haven't been in a long time, and we never saw that. We never saw so many things. I know I already said this, but I'm sorry."

"What do you mean?"

He ignores Ever staring at him too. "Again, are you okay to walk?"

"As much as I ever am."

"Do you need anything for the pain?"

Oh.

I remember what I thought on the way up this mountain, so near this very same spot. That every single one of us in our group was lying. And we were, through our teeth. I still am.

With one of his crutches, Finn pushes at the dirt before him, like a shy boy scuffing his feet. Ever's grown completely silent. "I don't know if you need to hear this, but there's this thing I'm figuring out. Not being able to do everything on your own doesn't mean you're weak. It means you're as human as we all are, and we're stronger together. We survived because we were together. Asking for help isn't failure, it's strength. It means you trust yourself enough to be flawed and to learn. Because here's the secret: You don't have to be infallible. You don't have to know it all. No one is and no one does."

Oh.

Perhaps the pain makes me light-headed. Perhaps I'm tired of fighting. But I make a split-second decision.

"I'm not good with working through things." My voice takes on an almost automatic quality, telling him the exact same thing I've said to other people. Over and over. It's true enough to hide the lie underneath. "I'm fine. I'm doing better since the accident." I hold up my hand before he can respond to that. My lip trembles and I blink again. "Does that sound convincing to you?"

He breathes out hard and his shoulders drop. "No. It might've been if I hadn't seen you eye those pills so hungrily back in the cabin. But even then. You're hurting. We all are, but you look like you've lost yourself."

Ever glances at Finn. "What are you saying?" they ask.

He doesn't answer, but continues to talk to me. "I know how hard it is. I can mostly manage with the painkillers I have, with the support I have, and with the therapy I have. It's a careful balance. I know I'm lucky. I know for others, you'd want to do anything to stop the pain, whether it's physical or emotional, and without the right support system, it can be so difficult. Impossible, even."

"I don't think it was the physical pain that tipped the scales for me. I'm not good with working through things because everything is too much, too loud, too present. I don't know how you deal with it."

"I ignore what isn't relevant," Finn admits. "And maybe a bit more than that."

"And I *can't*." I look at Ever. "Finn's saying, in his guarded way, that if I need something for the pain, I should stay far away from these painkillers. It's not them, it's me. I can't be trusted with them. Not now. Not after everything. But probably not ever." I pull in a breath. "I'm going to want them, though, before the night is over. And before tomorrow is over. And probably every day after that for a long time. I'm going to want them even though I really don't."

"Do you still have any left?" Finn asks.

I shake my head. "I threw them out when I ran away. I found my pockets full of them and a note like we found for both Liva and Carter, so when I said she tried to stop me too…" I can't finish that thought. It's hard enough that I've shared this much.

The shocked silence that follows isn't particularly reassuring. Finn's gone completely white, and Ever opens and closes their mouth again. If they don't understand…if they can't deal with it…if they think less of me…

I trade the uneven ground for the scarred road once more and start walking, because it's the only thing I can think to do. I have to get away from the loaded silence, the unsteady breaths, the sympathetic glances, the crunching underneath their feet.

I can't actually move that fast, though, because I'm broken on all sides and the mountain is still dark. A bit brighter than it was, maybe, now that day is approaching, but not enough to light the way. We can only follow the road until we get to the next blockage before our cars.

"Mad." Ever and Finn both reach me at the same time. "Hold up."

Ever's still deep in thought, but Finn reaches out to me. I flinch.

"I think my therapist may have someone who can help you. I don't know what we'll find once we reach the foot of the mountain, so it might be a while before I'm back there, but I can ask. It's terrifying, I know. But we survived so far. We can figure it out."

Ever nods. "I'm sorry we didn't see that. I'm sorry you didn't feel like you could talk to us about it."

"I don't know what to say." Because I don't.

"Did you really think we'd leave you to fend for yourself? After I just said that whole thing about asking for help?" Finn's voice holds a note of teasing, but his expression is rueful.

I shrug, and then curse at my arm. "Yes."

I lie because it's safer. I lie because I'm used to people dismissing my perspective as special, different, not quite in touch with what is *actually* normal and how things *really* are. I'm not used to being taken seriously.

"Yeah, well." He scratches his head, and his eyes are dark to the point of being almost black. "I can't blame you. Anyway, the first time I went to therapy on my own was terrifying. I didn't know what to expect. I didn't know how to act. I could've used someone then."

I blink. This conversation is moving almost too fast for me to catch up. "Are you offering to go with me?"

"Do you want me to?" he asks. "You know I'm heading to college soon, but we can share the start of this, at least."

"If you still would like company once Finn is gone, I'll be here too," Ever adds.

The sheer force of relief knocks everything off balance, and when the universe realigns, the fragile pieces are a little stronger. "Yes. Please."

"Well, then, yes. I don't want you to have to do this alone. I want to help if I can. That's what friends are for, right?" Finn shrugs, self-consciously. "Figuring yourself out is never easy, and now less than ever. It may be a long road before you're there. And it may be a long road before I get there too."

"We're disasters, aren't we?"

Finn actually laughs at that. "Here's to the broken kids."

"Here's to the survivors." Ever weaves their fingers through his. And somehow, the idea that two of them will be here for me, in whatever way they can, makes the pain more bearable, but it also digs so much deeper. I didn't know it was possible to feel devastation and elation, grief and relief at once. I don't know how to either. I don't know how to contain all those emotions in my skin, my head, my heart.

I want to tear at my hair. I want to scream. I want my best friend here to hold me, to help me, to be.

All I can do is breathe.

THIRTY-TWO

FINN

We keep going. Our determination is bright enough to light up the night, but the silence grows deeper, and it reminds us of the empty spots around us. This walk isn't beautiful. The lava field is a black hole, the pine forest holds ghosts, and steep cliffs are too deadly. We only have one another—and the shadows of the people we have lost.

We keep going, because despair will catch up with us if we don't.

It turns out despair is fast on its feet.

"If we're sharing secrets anyway..." Ever draws in a breath. "I'm dropping out."

I turn so hard, I nearly lose my balance. "You what?"

Ever twirls the branch they picked up, and then they toss it off the cliff. "I'm not going back to school once you've graduated."

"Why? We only have a year to go, and I'll be there," Maddy says softly.

"We made college plans," I add. A pit opens up in my stomach. This is the last thing I should worry about now, but I do, because it's tangible, and everything else is too big and complicated to touch.

Ever grimaces. "*You* made plans," they say. "I have to drop out. Your plan wasn't going to work, anyway. I know how much this means to you, Finn, but…I don't see it happening." They sigh. "Even if I could afford it…I've failed half my classes. It doesn't matter."

Of course it matters. *Of course* it matters.

"How is that possible?" I ask. But before they answer, I know. It's a foolish question. Ever ran our games, they juggled everything their dad couldn't handle, they prioritized everything for Elle. Something had to give. We just hadn't noticed it. During our games, they didn't want to talk about it, and outside of it, they put on a brave face. We missed so much. "What will you do, then?"

"Work. I'll stay at the bookstore for as long as they'll have me, but I'll keep an eye open for other things. The comics store, perhaps, or the game store." They look down, dragging their foot through the dirt. "Or maybe I can find something that allows me more hours than any of those. They're the ideal options, but in reality, I'll settle for almost anything that allows me to earn enough money to help support my family. Up until a few hours ago, I thought I'd apply to work for Liva's father's company."

I hesitate, hovering from Maddy's side to Ever and back. "Will you at least try to get your GED?"

Ever places their good hand on my shoulder, and it's such a comforting gesture, it hurts. To my right, Maddy looks away.

"I don't know yet. Maybe someday, but for now I'm going to focus on doing what I can, which isn't school. Taking care of Elle is more important."

"I know. But." I don't have the right words to say more. I shouldn't judge them. So I clamp my mouth shut.

We slowly start to walk again, and I pace. I don't even notice how hard the ground is. Three steps forward. Wait. One step back. Three steps forward. Deep in thought.

The tension turns into physical discomfort, and Ever touches my shoulder. "But?"

The words stumble out. "I'm not saying your worth depends on going to college either. It doesn't. It would never, and I'm sorry if it sounded like that. You are not worthless. You deserve the universe. Truth is, I'd love you regardless of whether you never set a foot inside a school again or finish a PhD, but I want you to have the best chances in life."

"I'm alive," Ever says softly. They stare at me quizzically, and somehow their gaze centers me and pushes me off balance all at the same time. "That alone is a pretty good chance."

I launch a pebble off the path with my crutch. We can see it fly through the air and land in the grass, and it's the first thing that makes me realize the sky is brightening. "All our concerns sound so paltry now, don't they? In the face of actual death?"

Ever reaches out and slowly turns me to face them. "Do you know what Damien would say to that? Worries always sound paltry in the face of hatred. Failing a class sounds paltry in the face of a disaster. Breaking a leg, breaking a promise, breaking a heart all sound paltry in the face of a dying planet. It doesn't make any of them any less meaningful. Now…" They reach for my hand. "Can you please repeat what you said a moment ago?"

Maddy laughs softly.

What last thing? *Truth is, I'd love you regardless of whether you never set a foot inside a school again or finish a PhD, but I want you to have the best chances in life.*

I…

Oh. That.

I must blush or pale or perhaps a combination of both, because Ever winces. But before they can do or say anything, I take their hand and hold it. "Hey."

The corner of their mouth quirks. "Hey you."

We're all disasters, now more than ever. We're all falling apart. I don't know what happens next. I don't know how we can go home and explain to our families that two of our friends are dead. I don't know how we can explain to their families that they won't be coming back. I don't know anything, except this:

Both Ever and Damien were right. This world is a messed up and scary place. Life is too short and too hard not to embrace happiness and joy, courage and possibility, and sometimes fear and grief and sorrow too. We have to find our family. We are stronger when we stand against the darkness together, and if our brief moment of happiness is nothing more than a flare, it lights up the path for others too.

I'll keep repeating that. For Maddy. For myself. For everyone who needs to hear.

We lost our friends. I nearly lost Ever, and I never want to lose them again.

"So yeah," they say. "Let's do something fun together." A hint of panic flashes through them. "If you still want to... I'm sorry I made you wait. I was terrified. I didn't know what to expect. I didn't want to get my hopes up. Not after this night."

"I thought we didn't do despair," I say softly.

"Turns out I do," they admit.

"Me too." I grimace. "Yes. Please yes. Once everything that comes next is done, we deserve something good. We deserve something hopeful. I didn't think it was true anymore, but maybe we still have worlds to create together. Better ones."

"Wouldn't that be something?"

"It won't be easy," I say.

They nod. "I know. But that's okay. I know I said it would be complicated, but the truth is, I don't care about complicated, as long as it means we have a chance. I care about giving us a chance."

They pull me closer, and the cloak rustles.

"*Kiss* already," Maddy mutters.

I raise an eyebrow and let go of Ever's hand. I'm careful not to touch the wounded hand they hold cradled to their chest. Instead, I let my fingers follow their jawline while I look at them. They're smaller now than they were before. Less flamboyant, no flourish. The remains of the smudged and torn green cloak hang from one shoulder. Their thick, black hair has long since escaped its ponytail and there's blood and sand and sweat all over them.

"Were you going to tell me before I moved away?"

"I wasn't sure yet. I didn't want to…get in the way. I didn't want you to worry."

A thousand things go through my mind all at once. Anger. Disappointment. Love. Frustration. I can hardly blame them, when all that time, I did the exact same thing. We're both such fools.

I trace a mixture of mud and tears on their cheek.

We really should talk more, after tonight. This needs to be the start.

When I'm off to college, in some kind of future that is coming up quickly but feels so distant, we're going to have to figure something out. Long-distance relationships can work; we would've figured out our friendship like that too. And maybe friendships are considered easier and less fraught with expectations, but they're not any less work. We owe it to each other to try, one way or another.

Something soft and fast shoots past my legs, and I yelp. We both jump apart right in time to see a rabbit run across the path. It's light enough now that we can at least make out its shape, but right there and then it's as scary as any dragon.

"I *hate* the outdoors," Ever says with passion.

I can only agree, and I love how fierce they look, their eyes blazing.

I could kiss Ever, looking the way they do now.

Kiss already. Maddy's voice in the back of my mind, or perhaps she simply said it again.

And perhaps my intent is clear on my face, because when Ever looks back at me, the fierce annoyance has made way for vulnerable trust—and a desperate hunger.

I bring my hands up to their face again. I don't understand how I can count myself this lucky.

Hands along their jawline.

Eyes locking eyes.

The mountain smells of dew and early morning and the faint sulfur of lava. Ever smells of home.

I pull them close and wait for the almost imperceptible nod.

Then I press my lips to their forehead.

"I love you too much to steal that first kiss here," I whisper low enough that Maddy *probably* can't hear it. "So, not today. We still have tomorrow."

Three more rabbits cross our path as we make our way. Some kind of bird of prey calls loudly and sends all of us huddling closer together.

It seems the mountain isn't quite done with us yet, or at least wants to give us a memorable exit. As if we could forget any part of it.

We have one another, at least.

"Next time we go adventuring, let's skip the outdoors and stick to well-populated urban areas, please," Maddy says, her voice soft and worn. She's sweating, and she keeps clamping her arm closer to her chest and then realizing that only makes it worse. She sways. We take turns supporting her, but she's supporting Ever and me as much.

Ever tenses at those words. They stop dead in their tracks, and I have to swerve to avoid colliding with them. The sky around us has lit up to a pale blue, but Ever is paler. "I'm not sure I'll be able to play again. Not after all this."

"Do you think our game is responsible for this?" I ask.

"Don't you?" Ever hasn't quite turned to face us, and now, they look away entirely. They're all angles and tension. "I wouldn't blame either of you for thinking that."

"I don't even know how to blame Liva for this yet, no matter how much I want to," Maddy replies. She draws breath and then falls silent, Ever's question heavy between us. Do we blame the game? Does that make sense?

Eventually, Maddy finds the right words after all: "If it weren't for us, for our game, I wouldn't be here."

Ever flinches, but before they can say anything, she pushes on. "I don't mean everything with Liva or Carter. I mean surviving. Finding you. Finding ourselves. *I* wouldn't be here. Not without this place we built and without having you all by my side. Before, when nothing else was good enough, I had sports. After, at least I had Myrre. She kept me going. She kept me from falling too far. But she never turned me into a thief, simply because I play one. That's not how that works. I can't stealth properly, and believe me, I've tried.

"I honestly don't know if I want to play again. Not immediately. Or any time soon. Maybe not ever. But the world matters to me. The game matters to me. At the very least, if nothing else…the memories matter." Her face falls.

"What Maddy said," I agree softly. Gonfalon taught me to survive. Here. Tonight.

And it also taught me to survive in life. To find a place where I could be fully me, without anyone denying it. To start fights when necessary and not back down. To always keep asking questions. And to come back to the people who are your home, no matter how hard it sometimes is.

It's why I came back for it this weekend. And maybe that was the worst decision in my life—in many ways, it feels like it. But knowing that my friends were here, even if I'd had the choice, I wouldn't have wanted to be anywhere else.

"Gonfalon is still ours, Ev," I say. "It saved us. It'll always be a part of us and a part of our journey. Maybe we'll never play again, but I hope we do. I hope we play again, even if it's ten or fifteen years from now. Even if it's just us, sitting in an imaginary tavern, drinking imaginary mead, remembering the friends we lost and the friends who betrayed us. Remembering our shared adventures. I hope we do."

"And maybe we'll discover other worlds down the road, because who we are hasn't changed," Maddy adds. "Maybe we'll find others like us, because the two of us are going to be hanging out in Stardust for a while longer. But let's keep the door open."

Ever stares at both of us. For once, I can't read their emotions, but it seems like an impossible combination of hope and guilt. "Really? Are you sure?"

"I'm not sure about much of anything right now," I admit. "But I don't want to lose this. I don't want to lose you. We've lost too much already today. It turns out, the world we built doesn't have to be perfect. The people don't have to be perfect. It matters far more that they're here."

Maddy reaches for Ever. "You can trust us. This time, we're not lying."

I nod. And though I may not know how to go from here, I know *where* to go. Home. To my mothers. To Damien. With Ever, wherever we want. Wherever home is for us together, no matter how long. To the observatory, or ghost hunting in the Monte Vista, or hanging out somewhere in the city.

I told them I was still leaving after the summer, no matter what happens next, and that's true. I've got a taste for adventure. I want new worlds to discover and new worlds to invent. I don't feel safe here anymore, and that hasn't changed.

But I want to find a place or build a place where I do.

I'm here, I'm breathing, and somehow that matters. I don't know if we deserved to survive or whether we were just lucky, but we're here and I want to make the best of it.

THIRTY-THREE

EVER

We keep walking, because that's all we can do. Slower. In silence. In pain. We walk across a knife's edge ridge, arm in arm, together. We walk until the stars fade into the night and streaks of light blues and oranges crest through the sky from the east, though it feels like the shadows still cling to us. Until the lights from the city below blink into existence, like fireflies on the horizon.

It's so close and suddenly so far. It's as if time followed a different pattern at the foot of this mountain. Elle is home, hopefully asleep in our bed, and blissfully unaware. I don't want her world to be tarred by worry or fear yet. Dad must be awake by now, getting ready for work, and he won't be the only one.

In the city, life goes on as normal. It's a strange thought. Most likely, no one knows there was anything out of the ordinary. No one is aware yet that the city lost two people overnight, and some of them will probably never find out.

What was our center of the universe is irrelevant to other people.

I can't wrap my mind around that. I can't help but wonder what goes on around me that I've never noticed. I don't want to know everything, necessarily; I don't know if anyone is meant to know everything. But I'd like to know more.

In the bleak light of dawn, Flagstaff looks comfortingly familiar—and utterly foreign at the same time. Maybe that's why we create worlds, to make sense of this one.

The closer we get to the city, the more the exhaustion sinks in, the more that feeling of being out of place sinks in.

I reach out and touch Finn's hand, knuckles to knuckles. Soft enough for him to feel I'm there, not hard enough to impede him using his crutches. He steps a little closer, and we fall into step, our bodies molding around each other. Walking together with crutches can be a challenge—the first few months he accidentally tripped me more than a dozen times, and I tripped over my own feet twice as often. These days, we're so in tune, we both take them into account without consciously thinking about it.

I sneak a glance at Finn from the corner of my eye.

His long hair falls in strands across his face and he's pale. The fight took a lot out of him, and he's intensely focused on the treacherous gravel beneath our feet. As if he notices I'm watching, he leans into me for a shared heartbeat, as synchronized as our breathing and our walking.

"You know I'm sorry," I whisper.

"For what?" he whispers back.

"I don't know. Everything?"

He narrows his eyes. "You'd better not be feeling responsible."

"Have you met me?" I try and obviously fail to make light of it.

"*Ever.*"

I push both my hands into the deep pockets of my cloak and let the pain wash over me. I'm shaking all over. When I look up at Finn, his anger has flared. His jaw is set. His eyes are blazing. I try not to be on the receiving end of that look too often.

He shakes his head. "No. You don't get to do this. You don't get to feel responsible for something you could not do anything about. This is Liva's doing. These were the choices *she* made. You did everything you could to make everyone feel welcome. You aren't to blame." He grimaces. "None of us are."

That feels like an easy escape from my inner turmoil. I'm not sure I deserve that. I'm not sure I want that. Because the truth is that I made mistakes too. I may not be responsible, but that doesn't mean I'm not accountable. "But maybe we could've helped her. Maybe I could've helped her."

"Maybe we could have," Finn says. He moves his weight from one crutch to the other and winces. "Maybe we could have. We're both going to struggle with the fact that we'll never know. Maybe we failed her and Carter too. But if that's the case, we're to blame for not recognizing what she was going through. Nothing more."

"Isn't that enough?"

He pulls me close, and I know he feels me trembling. As quickly as it came, his anger fades again. "Oh, Ev. I don't want to be ignorant to my friends' pain. I would like to make sure it never happens again. But it's not a capital offense. I didn't know how much you were struggling, and you're as close to me as breathing. I didn't share everything either. The most we can do is try and be kind—to ourselves too. That's where we find our worth. That's how we stop from breaking."

"I know, I just…" I don't have words anymore. The relief from earlier, the connection with Finn, I've cycled through it all, and now I only have grief. Overwhelming, nauseating, all-encompassing grief. For Carter. For ourselves. Even, in a way, for Liva too. I don't know how to stop shaking. I don't know how to keep my eyes from burning and my head from pounding and the world from turning.

We're all so tired.

Finn drops his crutches and pulls me close, his own arms trembling but strong around me. His presence undoes me. He reaches through me and sees me at my core. He protects me even if he has to protect me from myself.

At the sound of the crutches hitting the ground, Maddy turns around, and when she sees the two of us, she immediately rushes back and we all cling to one another, like a scared and hurting huddle.

At least we're not alone. At least we can all hold on to one another.

At least we're here.

Finn pulls me closer. "I know I have no right to ask this of you, but…I would fight anyone who threatens to hurt you, including yourself. Please promise me you will still talk to Damien about that internship?"

I shake my head. "I doubt they want or need high school dropouts."

"They need brave voices."

I won't lie. "I'm scared."

"I promised I wouldn't let you be scared. You have so much talent, Ev. Elle wouldn't want you to sacrifice it all for her. And selfishly, I don't want to live in a world where I don't have *your* worlds to disappear to. They make our world a better place."

"I'm not a developer, though." It's one of the reasons why I haven't taken Damien up on his offer. One of many. "Or that into computer games."

"There are other options. He could help you with design too, or creative writing. He knows the con circuit. He could help you build contacts in the tabletop industry."

Maddy pipes up. "You are talented and dedicated and *loving*. You were always the best of us."

Finn squeezes my hand. "Besides, world-building makes you happy. You know you're allowed to be happy, right?"

I do, rationally. But at the same time, I don't.

I've always considered happiness a luxury. A bonus. Not something I should be focused on beyond scarce, hidden moments. "I don't know what is waiting for us at the foot of this mountain. I'm not sure I can handle more than we already have to face. I can't wrap my mind around it now."

"You don't have to. It doesn't have to be immediately. It doesn't have to be now. But sometime before I leave for college."

"I…"

"I know it's scary. Trust me, Maddy and I both do. All we ask is for you to try. Can you do that? For me, if not for yourself?"

To trust is such a radical decision.

With her good hand, Maddy brushes mine. "You *are* allowed to be happy. Please try."

"You are too," I whisper.

She breathes in sharply—and nods.

And for a while there, I stare at her—then at Finn. In the pale light of dawn, his hair seems to shimmer, but his eyes are still haunted.

We live on. We have tomorrow. We're still going to have to figure out what all of that means. But we owe it to ourselves and our friends to try. If we can face this together, we can face anything. Or, if nothing else, we can face the next step.

And some days, that's enough.

Maybe I was wrong. Maybe hope isn't a muscle you can train. Maybe life happens, and there is nothing more to it. But the truth is,

I don't want to believe that. I don't want to believe that life is nothing more than a pile of accidents and there's nothing I can do to influence it. I want to believe the world is malleable, if not for me, then at least for the people around me.

Because they deserve the whole universe.

I want them to be able to chase their happily-ever-afters. And I should extend that kindness to myself too.

When the darkness comes and the shadows gnaw and even the night has teeth, we fill those voids with love.

"How about—how about I try for both of us?"

"I'd like that."

"Okay."

"Okay?"

"Okay."

———

The path evens out. The city has disappeared behind the horizon. We're headed back into pine growth again, though sparser than the grove on the summit. Grass has taken over the gravel path. Our makeshift parking lot behind a last set of boulders is nearly in sight; we're maybe half a mile out which is all at once so close and so far. A narrow stream appears alongside the path, and Maddy drops to her knees next to it. Without any hesitation, she cups up a handful of water and splashes it into her blotched face. She shivers. She sobs. And I wish I could cry as easily as she can.

The water looks like a solid plan, though. Disentangling myself from Finn, I walk up next to Maddy and slowly lower myself.

I stick one hand in and let the water drip over my face. It feels heavenly, refreshing. I wish I could wash all the dirt and fear off me. Or the hot pain that's crawling up my other arm.

When I look up again, Finn folds himself onto the ground, cross-legged, crutches resting on his knees. He places his hands up to his wrists into the stream, and he closes his eyes.

Once we're all sitting, it feels impossible to get up again. The pale blue morning light is restful. The chirping of the birds is almost relaxing. We can take a short rest here, before we head into a new world. Recover some of our stamina. Shore up our defenses. Discuss strategy, even if that strategy is nothing more than how to get to the parking lot and alert the authorities from there.

"I hope we never come back here," Maddy says. Still she glances back at the road as though she's waiting for someone to follow us.

"I don't think I'll ever look at the mountains the same way again," Finn says.

His words may be meant jokingly, but at the same time, we're all broken and empty, sitting on the grass on the bank of a stream. Now that morning has arrived, the sky warms up rapidly, but the only thing I can do is shiver. "Me neither."

Maddy splashes the water. "What do we do from here?"

"We stick together," Finn says.

"What will we find back in Stardust?"

"I don't know. I don't know what to expect anymore."

"I'm so fracking tired of adventures and uncertainties," Maddy mutters. "You know what I told Carter once, after he tripped that arcane circle in Kilspindle Fort? I told him, let's retire and raise clockwork goats."

It's such an absurd comment and we're all so exhausted, that we're laughing until we're crying, and crying until we're laughing again, and the rising sun brightens the sky.

"I keep expecting Carter will catch up with us," Maddy says softly.

"Yeah."

I wipe at my eyes, though the tears keep coming, and I lie back in the grass. The movement leaves me with a spell of vertigo, and the uneven ground is an uncomfortable reminder of my hiding spot amid the trees. Before we fought Liva. Before we even knew it was her.

Under normal circumstances, we could stay here for hours. Play games. Get into fandom arguments. Eat endless cookies. No one thought to bring the bag from the living room, though, and honestly I'm not sure I'll ever be hungry again. I'm too restless to be hungry.

This isn't normal.

And we can't stay here. "Let's go home."

As I get up, I nearly lose my balance, unused to moving with only one side. Finn clambers to his feet. He reaches out for me and pulls me close. I rest my head against his shoulder.

"Can I lean on you?" I ask.

"Always."

He takes one of his crutches and hooks it on the leather straps that Liva once carefully fashioned across his back. The straps make the crutch look like a badass sword and Finn like a rogue knight. While Maddy brushes the dirt from her clothes, Finn wraps his arm around mine. "One step in front of the other."

His hand brushes mine and I hold on to it. I plan to never let go.

THE SUN RISES TO A NEW DAY, AND YOU LEAVE YESTER TOWER BEHIND. You leave the mountain behind. Your quest isn't done. In many ways, it's just starting. You don't have all the answers yet and you have a hundred more questions. You don't know what you'll face when you get home.

But the three of you are still here to face it.

You are relieved and mourning. You are alive, against the odds. You didn't expect to be here—none of you, none of us. But, you are. As the sun rises, Gonfalon glows in hues of deepest, bloodiest reds and orange. The early morning rays draw the night's chill from the air. The lantern lights blink out of existence and make way for daylight.

And you can't help but wonder if survival is a skill, or if it's nothing more than luck of the dice. Maybe you're an inquisitor, maybe you're an adventurer, because in being someone else, you can better learn to be yourself.

Maybe it's never been about winning, maybe it's about failing and getting up again.

Maybe survival is living on.

The dark shadows of the mountains behind you dissipate. You hear the song of birds and the buzz of cicadas.

And then you walk out from under the tree cover, and the sun's rays catch you. It's warm already and tender, like a cloak of woven starlight. You stand silent. You hold one another's hands and you listen to one another's breathing.

And you take the next step.

ACKNOWLEDGMENTS

When I was Maddy's age, I read every book on body language I could get my hands on. Human interaction didn't always make sense to me, and I hoped studying all those nonverbal aspects of communication would help me better understand people. Spoiler: it did and it didn't, because as it turns out, humans are complicated beings, and neurotypical humans in particular just…don't always make sense.

But (semi)understanding body language did give me a sense of security when social interactions around me were overwhelming and chaotic and I was still figuring out how and who to be.

I never saw something like it in books. I very rarely saw realistic neurodivergent characters in books. Being able to include that weird quirk of mine in a book with an autistic main character now would not have been possible without the tireless work of so many autistic writers reclaiming our narratives. To them—thank you.

And because figuring out how and who to be takes a lifetime: to my fellow trans and nonbinary writers who put pieces of themselves in books—thank you.

My spectacular agent, Jennifer Udden, is one of the cornerstones of my career. Thank you for being an advocate, a voice of reason, but especially for taking my ridiculous ideas and running with them, instead of running away screaming.

I had the good fortune to work with two editors on this book. Annette Pollert-Morgan, who encouraged me to write it, and Eliza Swift, who took it on, fell in love, and made me make it so much better (and probably changed the way I write books in the process). Thank you both.

Thank you to everyone at Sourcebooks for continuing to make my dreams come true: Dominique Raccah, Barb Briel, Todd Stocke, Steve Geck, Annie Berger, Sarah Kasman, Cassie Gutman, Christa Desir, Bret Kehoe, Nicole Hower, Kelly Lawler, Sarah Cardillo, Danielle McNaughton, Deve McLemore, Heather Moore, Valerie Pierce, Beth Oleniczak, Chris Bauerle, Chuck Deane, Sean Murray, Tim Golden, Bill Preston, Margaret Coffee, Sierra Stovall, Jennifer Sterkowitz, Kacie Blackburn, Tina Wilson, Christy Droege. You're all absolutely wonderful, and I am so lucky.

Thank you to my publishers around the world. I can't believe how much my books get to travel, and I spend way too much time petting my foreign editions. I'm infinitely grateful.

To my earlier readers, who told me what worked and especially what didn't. In particular, to those of you who untangled my many mistakes with endless patience and grace, *thank you*.

Writing would be a lonely business without a community, and I am so grateful for mine, both online and off-line. For endless chats, rants, generous criticism, cups of coffee/tea/other, cons, castles. Thank you.

Thank you to all my friends with whom I had the joy of sharing a gaming table, across countless systems and many years (and even the occasional Satanic Panic). I know I've said this before, but I would not be the writer I am today without you, and I certainly would not be the person I am today without you.

Thank you to my readers. To you, reading this right now. Chase your dreams. You never know where it'll lead you.

And to my Council of Wyrms, my found family, and my family. Thank you, always.